A FIRESTORM OF ECSTASY IN A DARK LABYRINTH OF INTRIGUE . . .

Pavel was lying on the bed in his underpants, looking for the diamond share quotations in the paper. But before he found them, Galina came out of the bathroom wrapped in a white bath towel.

Galina made a play of admiring the flowers on the table as his hands undid the bath towel. It fell away, and he had her neat damp breasts in his hands. She felt him hard against her.

"The flowers are beautiful!" she said, as his hand came off her left breast. She felt him taking off his underpants.

In the half-light of the curtained hotel room, he ran his hands all over her and felt the shivers run through her. He kissed her until they were both gasping. He gave no thought to diamonds or his job, let alone his first idea to use her. As he went into her, the sound of her gasp was all that meant anything. . . .

THREE POTATO, FOUR

Using a woman as a pawn can be the most dangerous game of all . . . .

THREE POTATO, FOUR

Wilfred Greatorex

POPULAR LIBRARY • NEW YORK

First published in Great Britain under the title *CROSSOVER*

THREE POTATO, FOUR

Published by Popular Library, a unit of CBS Publications, the Consumer Publishing Division of CBS Inc., by arrangement with Coward, McCann & Geoghegan, Inc.

ISBN: 0-445-04366-0

Printed in the United States of America

10 9 8 7 6 5 4 3 2 1

ONE

Pavel came up from the basement sauna and saw Brezhnev crossing the foyer towards him. Through the ring of apparatchiks and bodyguards he had a clear view of the rock face and the blotchy skin, and he could make out the hairs of Brezhnev's earlobes. He moved aside to let the VIP party pass to the lifts. He recognised some of the bodyguards—Lesechiko and Tulov and Kirilin—and he wondered if he looked as bulky as they did. The pistol under his left arm felt like a howitzer, and the package in its waterproof cover was sticking to his back.

He was suddenly sweating again despite the sauna. He saw Suslov bow slightly as Brezhnev lumbered past him, but there was no sign of Vader. Pavel stood still and lowered his head. Brezhnev walked on, the pig iron face impassive.

For a moment Pavel caught Kirilin's eyes on him and tried to curb his fear of the department's gorillas. He saw Brezhnev enter the lift past the Finnish Foreign Office man and the hotel manager. He was struck by the fact that Brezhnev's dark-grey suit was so much like his own, the three buttons of the jacket all done up.

The gorillas' jackets were all floppy and loose.

He was suddenly aware of someone standing behind him. He looked into Kirilin's dumb heavy's face. Kirilin plumped one cheek, then the other. The other gorillas were taking up stations in the foyer. It dawned on Pavel that he was on Kirilin's spot.

"I'm sorry," Pavel said, moving aside.

Kirilin grunted and stood where Pavel had been as though there were a special mark on the thick pale blue carpet. His deep brown eyes glistened with resentment. It was nothing new to Pavel: The gorillas knew that the bright boys took them for animals. Pavel felt an urge to give him a reassuring tap on the shoulder but thought better of it.

Suslov was near the news kiosk now. He looked like a professor with his alert face and steel grey hair and round shoulders. Pavel tried to catch his eye, but he was having none.

Pavel glanced over the racks of newspapers. It was like freedom of the press week. They were all there—the *Washington Post, Le Monde, Le Figaro,* the *Svenska Dagbladet,* and the rest of the heavies besides decadent Western glossy magazines. He plucked out a copy of *Die Welt* and skimmed through the front-page story about the European security conference. Then he spotted the headline on the *Times:* HEADS OF GOVERNMENT GATHER IN HELSINKI. He put back *Die Welt* and read: "The highlight today was the arrival of Mr. Brezhnev, the Soviet party leader, and his entourage by special train from Moscow. Drawn by two red engines, the immaculate green train was a schoolboy's delight. . . ."

He felt someone touch his arm. He expected Suslov, but it was Viktor Pohl from Special Service II. Pohl prodded a finger into the *Times.* His sun-browned face came out in a knowing smile. "Did you see the first thing President Ford did when he got here was to take a sauna and a beating with green birch branches?"

It was there all right datelined July 29.

"Who did the beating, I wonder?" Pohl whispered.

"It says here he did it himself," Pavel said coolly. He had no more time for Pohl than for the apes now stationed around the foyer like petrified wrestlers. He and

6

Pohl had got to Helsinki four days before, and Pohl had ignored him till now. It was typical of Pohl and his kind in Special Service II. They treated comrades in other departments like candidates for the reform wards in the Serbsky Institute of Forensic Psychiatry, and a number of people from Soviet embassies abroad had wound up there because of Pohl. Even ambassadors, never mind Aeroflot clerks and Tass correspondents, had shown sign of severe stress when Pohl showed up. He looked harmless enough now in a neat fawn lightweight suit which brought out his lithe, well-kept figure, and his grey eyes looked misleadingly sensitive.

"Ford is sucking up to the Finns or being masochistic," said Pohl, his smile showing gold-capped teeth.

"I'm doing neither and *I've* just had a sauna," Pavel said.

"I know," Pohl smiled. "I heard you were down there." He was pressing back the cuticles of his fingers.

Pavel's pale blue eyes were icy. It crossed his mind that Pohl knew something.

"You're still sweating," Pohl said.

Pavel nodded. "I should have stayed longer in the sauna. I want to get this off." He patted his middle, hoping this might explain why he was sweating. He was not much overweight for a man of thirty-eight, no more than a few pounds, and his muscles were still tight.

"Not enough work," Pohl murmured. He was still pressing back those cuticles. "Or perhaps you should marry again."

They hardly knew each other. Pavel had visions of Pohl going through his file.

"Are *you* still married?" Pavel said tartly.

Pohl took the dig with a smile. He put out his left hand to show the heavy gold ring on the third finger. He weighed up Pavel for a moment or two and then said, "I might see you over at the conference hall?"

7

It was unlikely, but Pavel nodded. Further visits to Finlandia House with its white marble and hordes of security men from thirty-five countries were not in the plan. Pohl would not know that, though you could never be sure with Special Service II.

Pavel watched him cross the foyer.

He shivered slightly, and his mouth was dry. Suslov was gazing idly into the window of the hotel boutique. The old fox wasn't for talking just yet. It had been like this the night before, with no sign of Vader and Suslov calling it a day with a slight tilt of the head. It was clear that Suslov himself was waiting for the go-ahead from higher up.

Pavel amused himself for a minute or two, trying to establish if Suslov's contract was in the foyer. None of the apes infesting the glary open-plan vastness were the sort you would find employed by Department A. Soon there would be even more of them when Brezhnev left once more for the Finlandia.

Suslov crossed to the news kiosk. He pulled out a copy of the New York *Times* and stood there reading it. The counter girl, a flaxen haired Finn in a thin red blouse, threw him a quick look. She didn't like the way the Russians treated her kiosk as a free library. Suslov got the message and put the paper back in the rack.

Pavel still had a warm spot for the now elderly operator who had done so much for him over the years. The last two years had been sticky, but that was a personal thing best forgotten. He still saw Suslov as a father figure. They had first met when Pavel was a recruit aged twenty-seven and Suslov a senior staff officer with Department A. Suslov had given a lecture on the work of his department, and Pavel had sought him out to ask about the chances of a job in Department A. Pavel had been streamed for the Surveillance Directorate, and the idea of spending his life just checking on people was enough to appal him. Suslov was noncommittal. Yet a month later Pavel was posted to Department A. He went to thank Suslov. "What for?" Suslov had said. His face was already wrinkled, though he could hardly have been fifty. "It was none of my doing."

"Thanks anyway."

That was nearly ten years ago.

Looking at Suslov now, Pavel felt sorry for him. He'd lost none of his guile, but his nerves were showing, and his general health was none too good. He was on pills for his blood pressure.

The foyer was filling up. More apes, some apparatchiks who would hope to catch Brezhnev's eye, and a few Finnish Special Branch officers. The Russians and the Finns seemed to be checking everything and each other.

"Go now, Pavel."

Pavel had been so busy with the big security show he'd not seen Suslov move. He turned sharply.

"Where's Vader?" he said.

"Just go now," Suslov said. "Stick to the programme."

There were beads of sweat on Suslov's forehead, and he ran his fingers over his neck. His pouched eyes were bright.

Gromyko had come in with his own retinue of apes. Pavel went round this herd of hair and brawn and saw Olga Malek among the VIP party. She noticed him and gave him a taut smile, and Pavel wondered what their affair meant to her now. It was more than two years since they had made love, and for six months it had been three times a week. He'd enjoyed her more than any other woman and felt a pang of regret now for having let it die. She had the body of a woman athlete with small, firm tits and strong thighs, and he never could see her as an economist with the Politburo. He threw a final look at her now, taking in the legs below the pale-blue skirt as she vanished beyond the scrum of security men.

He went out past the gorillas at the entrance and didn't have to bring out his KGB pass once.

The harbour was almost clear of boats. The *Moskva* was berthed in lonely splendour, all red and shiny, like some flagship of a proud new line. With Helsinki's hotels packed it was being used as a floating hotel by many of the Soviet delegation. It looked trusting and serene, but Pavel guessed there were frogmen about and that sonar was being used aboard.

It was just after five when he went into the Hotel Suomi. Byzov was buying drinks for Western newsmen and Kapitsa was laughing at some dirty joke told by a British Foreign Office man named Forrester-Hale. Pavel knew Forrester-Hale by now, as he knew the gangling pale-faced Suddick from the U.S. State Department who was sharing a quiet corner with Karpov. Suddick was worth a try, but to think of Forrester-Hale as another Philby was to assume Forrester-Hale had a brain, and this Pavel could never accept. He was no more than a pension-hunting Englishman, one of that new breed that were dragging Britain down more surely than any subversive group had ever managed before. He was a boring third-rater with nothing to offer but charm. The Foreign Office must be even more rotten with nepotism than the KGB, Pavel thought. How else could a bloody half-wit like Forrester-Hale be part of a British delegation to the greatest diplomatic conference since the Congress of Vienna?

Pavel tried to avoid Forrester-Hale's eyes. He'd wasted two hours in his company on Monday night. He moved behind Forrester-Hale and was almost lost among the Western newsmen when Forrester-Hale turned suddenly and put an arm across his shoulder.

"My friend," Forrester-Hale said. "Do join us, and what will you have?"

Pavel cursed his luck. "I'm on the wagon," he lied. "So a Bloody Mary without vodka."

"Dear chap, you can't be serious."

"If you don't mind," Pavel insisted, "I had a heavy session last night." He'd actually been in bed by ten, but this was no night for touching liquor.

"If you insist." Forrester-Hale flailed a long arm over the head of a dumpy West German newsman who was between him and the bar and used his height—he was all of six feet four—to get the barman's attention. He ordered the drink and introduced Pavel to the rest as Maisky, the name Pavel had used on Monday night.

"This chap's from Basket Two," said Forrester-Hale with a smoker's laugh.

Pavel saw Kapitsa's face go tight.

"For my dough Basket Two's the best of the lot," said a square-set American with a *Viva Zapata* moustache. "I would give a year's pay to see Basket Two working."

"Steady on," said Forrester-Hale glibly. "We *are* professionals. We mustn't become too involved."

"I know," said a French newsman, his eyes dancing. "You're on Basket One and it makes you feel superior."

"Do you know, I am indeed," said Forrester-Hale heartily, stretching out that crane of an arm over the small German to take Pavel's tomato juice. "I've worked on it, I almost say man and boy, for two years in Geneva and here, and it's the best thing that's happened in this world for ages."

A hand grabbed his shoulder. He turned to face Andrew Coley, a middle-aged Foreign Officer expert in East-West confrontation with an impeccable record all the way from Yalta. "We all know"—he smiled sternly—"that you secured peace, security, justice and cooperation all off your own bat."

"His own basket surely?" quipped Suddick.

The word was a cliché already.

It had been invented by diplomats in the détente buildup in place of the old "heads of agreement" phrase

11

and possibly to avoid using the word "package" which had an American ring to it.

"Basket Two?" Pavel had said when Suslov first briefed him in the office at 2 Dzerzhinsky Square. Suslov said it was the section of the détente agreement concerned with trade and science.

Pavel went away and did his homework.

Now he knew all there was to know about the contents of Basket Two. It was a good cover. He still hated the use of the word "basket," though. It made it seem that peace and détente could be got like groceries at Gum.

Forrester-Hale was tossing the word around as if he'd personally coined it. He had an actor's style and waved his hands a lot, and Pavel could hardly take his eyes off the heavy signet ring on the little finger of his left hand. Maybe it *was* a badge of membership of the British queers' club as some had claimed in Dzerzhinsky Square. *They* should talk, thought Pavel. There was a joke going the rounds in the KGB, where jokes were scarce, about a new Department Z to combat homosexuality in Department A.

Pavel sipped his tomato juice and studied the group at the bar. Most of them could be neuters in love with diplomacy and news leaks and expense fiddles and tax-free perks. He lost interest as Forrester-Hale led a chorus of small talk, and his eyes wandered to the door. If Vader didn't show in ten minutes, it meant another day's delay.

Forrester-Hale simpered on and the State Department man Suddick was calling a round of drinks when Pavel saw Vader come in. Lightly built with a sharp face and thick black hair and eyebrows, he made his way to the far end of the bar, and Pavel could see the scar which ran from his hairline to his chin. Once during their six weeks stay in Siberia, Vader had told how he copped the scar when he belly-landed a Mig fighter near Volgograd. He wouldn't go into detail.

12

He looked much older, Pavel thought. He could be fifty, but he was only thirty-six, two years younger than Pavel. He was half Jewish on his mother's side. This had given him problems in recent years, but Suslov found him, as he once put it to Pavel, "the most talented young staff officer we've got." It was an exaggeration, of course—meant to spur Pavel out of a lazy spell.

Pavel caught Vader's eye. No hint of recognition passed between them.

It was possible that the other three Russians at the bar would know Vader by sight and that Forrester-Hale or Suddick or some other Westerner might also have met him. He'd been working on Basket Two for some time, in Geneva before Helsinki, as one of the Soviet commodity experts. It was a perfect cover. He had three years' experience with Directorate T handling trade with the West while also keeping an eye on Soviet missions abroad. Nobody knew him—or if anyone did, he didn't let on.

Only Karpov of the Russians in the bar would know that both Pavel and Vader were with the Basket Two team, and he was too long in the tooth to make an issue of the distance they kept between themselves now. Vader drained his lager, slid off the barstool, and went to the lavatory. Pavel glanced at his watch and waited. Another minute would give Vader enough time.

Less than half a minute went by, and Forrester-Hale—it would have to be him—excused himself from the group and made for the lavatory. Pavel grabbed his arm.

"May I return the compliment?" Pavel asked.

"That's awfully kind. Large vodka and T if you don't mind." He began to make for the lavatory again.

"You're right about Basket Two," Pavel said.

It was enough to lead Forrester-Hale into a brief rerun of his thesis, and he would have gone on for an hour if he hadn't been dying for a piss. Nobody else went to the lavatory. Pavel reckoned that Vader must be clear now, so he ordered the drinks while Forrester-Hale was in full flow on the subject of Russian oil for the West. Forrester-Hale frowned, but the hiatus gave him a chance to satisfy his pressing need. When he came back, Pavel pointed to the vodka and tonic on the bar counter and went into the lavatory himself. The first cubicle was engaged. Pavel let himself into the next cubicle, locking the pine door. He stood on the seat and prised himself up to the recessed window. He lifted the catch and pushed the window open. The courtyard below was deserted. Some unopened crates of beer were in stacks between the window and the door to the hotel kitchens. The window recess gave no room to turn. So Pavel eased himself out head first, pressing his feet and legs tight against the sides of the recess to control his descent. He was dangling from the window from the waist when he heard a movement beyond the beer crates.

He froze.

Hanging like a bat, he peered through the gaps between the crates and made out a figure in white. The gaps were narrow, and it was some time before Pavel saw that it was a chef having a secret smoke.

Pavel tried to get back, but he was too far out, and he was getting cramps in his legs. He tried pushing with his hands against the whitewashed wall. He felt the sear of pain as the friction ripped his left hand between the thumb and wrist, and he saw the red stain on the whitewash. He went still now, screwing up his eyes to see the smoking chef through the gap in the crates.

The chef was moving to and fro, pacing a line of no more than eight feet or so, and Pavel stayed flat against the wall, his hands tight against it, his legs wedged against the window recess. And then he heard someone try the lavatory door behind him, and the sound of another door being opened. There were only three cubicles in there. One had been locked by Vader and another by him. The

14

third was now in use. Its occupant had only to peer under or over the partition to find an empty locked cubicle. And Pavel wouldn't put that sort of behaviour past some of those who were in the bar, especially those with rings on their little fingers.

He was still suspended like a bat, hardly daring to breathe.

The chef was moving to and fro, appearing in Pavel's line of vision through first one gap in the crates, then another. Pavel tried to make out how much of the cigarette was left, but the glimpses were too brief. He could hear a lavatory being flushed. His calf muscles were hurting like hell, and his right leg was beginning to lose its power. His left hand was stinging, and he was having to put more pressure on his right hand which he moved more directly under him. He peered through the gaps in the crates. The chef was still pacing as though in an open-air cell. And Pavel saw now that the chef was just as dependent on the stacks of crates as he was.

He dropped to the yard.

He winced with pain as his left hand hit the concrete. He rolled over once like a gymnast and went rigid, listening, trying to find an eyeline to the chef between the crates.

Then he saw the chef moving towards the kitchen wall. Pavel crept to the beer crates and put his face against them. The chef was standing over a drain squeezing the last urgent drags out of the cigarette. He took a climactic draw and dropped the fag end down the drain, then he went back in the kitchen.

Pavel found the Volvo in the third bay of the staff car park. He already had the ignition key. As he drove west out of Helsinki Square, he had a good view of the Russian delegation leaving their hotel. He spotted Pohl and remembered Suslov's warning that Special Service II knew nothing of the task and that he and Vader would be strictly on their own.

He felt his chest go tight.

Vader was leaning against a rock in the cave at Porkkala when Pavel got there. He was edgy and depressed. He lit a cigarette, turning into the rock face to smother the lighter's flare.

"Were you followed?" His eyes were bright from the moonglow off the calm fiord.

Pavel nodded.

Vader's nostrils quivered like a rabbit's, and his hand shook as he furtively cupped his cigarette. It was a warm night for the Baltic, clammy and calm—and silent as the North Pole. Vader's eyes were like opals set in pearl. His jet black hair merged into the rock.

"The Finnish police stopped me, that's all."

"That's all?"

"They followed me for a bit, then lost interest."

It had been touch-and-go coming out of the city. The security conference had brought the Finnish police out in force, all eighteen hundred of them backed up by eight hundred special troops. They were looking closely at anything that moved. Pavel's false papers showing him to be a Swedish marine engineer had worked.

"You're certain?"

Pavel nodded.

Vader was twitchy. "I still don't see why we couldn't have gone out by air."

"It was gone into," Pavel said.

"Or so we were told."

"Oh, come on," Pavel said. "The ports and airfields are crawling with Finnish security men."

"So why here? Why not some other time and place?"

Pavel weighed Vader up. He was a bad case of nerves. His mouth was working, and his eyes were full of alarm.

16

"Come off it, Oleg," Pavel said. "It's a natural takeoff point."

Vader cupped a hand over his cigarette and took a deep drag. "You're leaving no one behind, Pavel."

It wasn't true, but that was no business of Vader's.

"Have one of these," Pavel said, offering a tube of dextrose pills and taking one himself.

"I have my own," Vader said stiffly.

They could hear the gentle sound of water lapping against the rocks. Pavel began to pull his wet suit from the bag someone had put in the Volvo.

Vader glared at Pavel in the half-light of the cove. "You're leaving no one behind and that accounts for it."

"What do you want?" Pavel asked. "You want me to say it will all turn out fine?" He shook out the wet suit.

Vader's eyes were small dark glows. "I have a wife and three kids."

"I have a wife," Pavel said.

"You don't even know if she's alive or dead."

There was a long silence as Pavel began to strip off.

"Mine was a close family." Vader was taut and angry.

Pavel just took off his trousers and pants and began to pull on the wet suit.

"You're not leaving a family behind." Vader's voice was rising.

Pavel said coldly, "Do you think they'd send me out if I had no relatives?"

"I'm half Jewish," Vader said, scuffing the sand with his foot.

"That's why you were chosen," Pavel said irritably. "One of the chosen people."

Vader stubbed the butt of his cigarette against the rock face. "That's funny?"

"Sorry," Pavel said. "But you were getting on my tits."

Pavel was hauling the wet suit over his thighs, and it was a tight fit. Vader watched him struggle.

17

Pavel looked up and said, "Isn't it time you were getting into yours?"

"I'm still thinking of my wife and kids," Vader said, leaning against the rock face. "They're partly Jewish."

Pavel paused.

"Suslov said they'd be looked after. I was there when he told you."

"And who will they be looked after by?" Vader's eyes were afire in the light from the moon.

Pavel drew in his breath and tugged the wet suit over his navel. It was some time before he said, "You'll be looking after them, Vader, when you get back."

"If I get back," Vader said. "If—"

He unzipped his holdall and dragged out his wet suit. Pavel was nearly ready now, pressing his arms down the clinging rubber of his wet suit and thinking of Olga Malek with nothing on but her pants. Vader had begun to strip.

At least the Baltic was calm and the night warm.

It was twelve minutes past seven. The three brief flashes came right on cue. Pavel nodded his good wishes, and Vader shuffled forward a few paces in his wet suit across the shingle. Then he turned back, shaking his head. He was running his hand against his wet suit just above the right thigh. "It's no good," he said. "I'll have to change."

"Don't be stupid," Pavel said angrily. He saw that Vader had bitten his lip so much he'd drawn blood.

"I'll be all right in a minute or two," Vader said.

They faced each other in a shaft of moonlight. Pavel's face was full of disgust, and his deepset eyes blazed. "You know the schedule," he said.

"I have to change!" Vader hissed. "I'm not ready. You'll have to go first."

"The schedule said you first!"

Vader moved to bring his right side into the shaft of

moonlight so that Pavel could see the rip in the wet suit. "It must have torn when I was pulling it on."

There was a spare wet suit in Pavel's car. It would take some minutes for Vader to change, so Pavel agreed to the switch. He crossed the shingle carrying his frogman's flippers and turned to see Vader watching him, as though petrified among the rocks. Only then did Vader start for the car. Pavel felt sure Vader had torn the wet suit on purpose—or cut it. He pulled on the flippers and took to the water. When he was in up to the waist, he turned again. There was no sign of Vader.

He felt the shock of the Baltic water. The strap which held the package to his back was too tight, and he could feel the pistol pressing in his abdomen. He moved with a lazy crawl stroke, letting the flippers do the work and causing hardly a ripple. He felt like turning back to urge Vader not to be a bloody fool. He paused in the water and looked back, but all he could see was the stark outline of the rocks and the deserted shingle glinting in the moonlight. He pressed on.

He had been swimming for almost half an hour when he made out the cabin cruiser in the lee of the sheer cliff face. As he swam closer, he saw it was a twin diesel. It carried no marks of identity—no flag, no number—and its name had been covered with a plastic sheet. The only sound was the irregular plop of ripples of water against the hull. He saw the ladder that hung from the port side and kept away from it, unsure and afraid. He kept his distance and began to circle the boat at a range of twenty yards or so.

"Soviet One?" The voice was friendly and low-key.

Pavel peered through the gloom. He could see nobody.

"Soviet One?" the voice repeated.

Again Pavel strained to see the owner of the voice. He was treading water.

"Are you all right, Soviet One?"

19

Pavel could make out the figure of a man leaning out from port side. He put a hand against the bulge caused by the pistol and began to swim towards the boat.

He made a grab for the ladder and just held on for a while, spitting out water and breathing hard. He felt a powerful hand come under his armpit and almost lift him up the ladder. He saw a thick forearm matted with blond hair and gazed up into the big, open face of a giant in a thick roll-collar pullover. The man had wide-set blue eyes and a mop of flaxen hair with long forelocks that ran wild down the right side of his face. He hoisted Pavel aboard and began to frisk him almost before Pavel's feet had touched the deck. A few feet away was a wiry man with high cheekbones. He wore a zip-up storm jacket and a rakish navy-blue yachting cap perched high and at a sharp angle on hair as blond as the giant's.

He was nursing an M10 automatic rifle.

The giant's hands found the bulges caused by the pistol and the package inside Pavel's wet suit. He felt at the pistol pressing out its shape against the suit.

"Pistol," he said to the other man. He spoke in Danish. He indicated that Pavel should strip off the wet suit. The other man looked on cradling the M10.

Pavel began to strip off. His heart was thumping, and he was only just starting to breathe naturally, and his legs were aching.

As soon as the pistol was exposed, the big man took it. "You speak English?" he asked.

Pavel nodded.

"I take this just for now—okay?"

Again Pavel nodded.

From Suslov's briefing he guessed the big man was Jens Olefsen. The other would be Kaxel Olefsen, his half brother. They were well known to the KGB. And by repute to Pavel.

Jens was a salmon fisherman, some ten years older

20

than Kaxel, who at twenty-one had commanded a Danish navy motor torpedo boat on the Baltic patrol.

Pavel grimaced as the wet suit nearly took off the skin above his hips. Jens dipped a bucket in the sea and poured sea water into the suit to loosen it. It came away more easily, and Jens helped pull it down. He took the package and passed it to Kaxel. It was a large brown envelope folded twice. Kaxel slit it open to disclose a file of papers and a smaller envelope. He felt at this and held it against his right ear, rattling the contents.

"Personal things," Pavel said.

Kaxel shrugged. He put the small envelope back inside the large one and held out the package with a small smile playing on his lips.

Pavel was naked and limp and feeling the cold. Jens pointed to the cabin below the cockpit platform. They went down and Jens brought out a pair of heavy-duty jeans and some thick socks and pullovers and gym shoes.

"Your friend will be with us in twenty minutes?" Jens said, watching him put on a navy-blue pullover with a high roll collar.

"I doubt it," Pavel said.

He saw Kaxel watching from the doorway.

"Twenty minutes exactly we were told."

Jens was pouring brandy into a paper cup.

"His wet suit was torn," Pavel said. He was still cautious. It would be the end for Vader if his last-minute loss of nerve got back to Dzerzhinsky Square. "He might still make it."

"We will not stay more than half an hour," Kaxel said.

He was peering down from the cockpit platform, the M10 still under his arm. His face was in shadow, but Pavel knew from the voice that Kaxel was still on his guard.

Jens gave Pavel the cup of brandy. He had none himself. Neither did Kaxel. Pavel gulped it down and felt an instant glow of warmth.

The brothers were looking at him as if they wanted to hear more.

"I'm not Soviet One," Pavel said. "I'm Soviet Two. I came first because he had to get another wet suit."

He moved out into the cockpit area with Jens following. He took another swig of brandy. He could see Kaxel's lithe face now, the keen eyes, calm and unyielding—and full of doubt. "He didn't change his mind—your friend?"

"No," said Pavel, "I told you. His suit was damaged." One careless statement now could mean a death sentence for Vader.

Kaxel said nothing for a few moments. He watched Pavel finish off the brandy while Jens amused himself with the Russian-made pistol. "We'll give him half an hour, no more," he said finally. He looked sharp and alert as a sea eagle.

Jens suddenly lost interest in the pistol. He stuck it between his belt and his slacks and reached out to a skip of tomatoes and picked two out. He tossed one to Pavel and put the other in his mouth—whole. It was an enormous tomato, and Pavel half expected him to choke. Instead, he laughed at Pavel's reaction. Kaxel didn't laugh. His eyes were still searching the black waters.

They must be little different now, Pavel thought, from what they were when they won their places on the KGB's assassination list. It all began one summer night when a Danish trawler picked up an exhausted Russian defector from a small boat which had run out of gasoline. Two nights later Jens and a third brother called Niels were trawling for salmon deep inside territorial waters in the north Baltic when a KGB ship came right at them. In spite of Jens' warning signals, the ship smashed into them, leaving a big hole in the stern of their trawler. It then careered through their nets. The trawler's crew sealed the hole. But Niels was unable to help. His skull was fractured in the collision, and they couldn't stop the bleeding. Niels was treated in Sweden and wound up in a mental home at Aarhus.

Jens saw the incident as an indiscriminate act of revenge—indiscriminate because it wasn't his and Niels' trawler which had made that pickup. And Jens was not the only one who saw it this way, or the only one who loved good-natured Niels. Kaxel also loved Niels. The half brother was as unforgiving as the brother. Since then they had set out to settle a score. They had picked up more Russian and East German defectors in the Baltic in four years than all the ships of the combined navies of NATO.

It had gone through Pavel's mind from time to time that he and Vader might be no more than bait in some big-game fishing by Department V to hook the Pimpernel Danes. In that case it would be a real *mokrie dela*—with the half brothers as food for the salmon Jens used to catch.

Pavel watched Jens eat another whole tomato, green tuft and all.

Kaxel was up on the cockpit platform, ready for anything, still nursing that M10.

Vader sat in the cove with a bottle of vodka in one hand and a half-smoked cigarette in the other. Wearing the spare wet suit, he glanced at his waterproof watch. There was still time; he could swim faster than they knew. The color had gone from his face, and he couldn't keep his eyes off the sea. His mind was blank one moment and alive the next. He took another swig of vodka and felt it burn him inside.

The moon was bouncing light off the calm black sea. He listened to the water lapping into the rocks and sifting the shingle. The only other sound was a high-flying jet he couldn't see.

He clasped his hands tight and made the knuckles crack. His eyes felt sore, and he burped twice. He made to toss the bottle away but took another swig. He stood up and ran his hands up and down his wet suit as if trying to find another rip, keeping the neck of the vodka bottle between his thumb and forefinger. The suit was intact. He gazed at the bottle for a long moment, then at the sea, then at the path that led back across the island, and finally at his watch. He couldn't make out the time.

He began to make for the sea. He was still carrying the bottle when he went into the water, gasping for breath at the cold shock. As the water came up to his neck, he took a final gulp of vodka, then placed the empty bottle on the surface of the sea and saw it gently bob away.

A cloud cleared the moon, and by the extra light he tried to check the time. The watch face was spinning.

He lifted his feet off the bottom and began to swim. He wore no flippers, and he was doing the breast stroke. It seemed his vision began to clear, and he swam more strongly but not straight. He stayed close to the western shoreline in the lee of the cliffs that ran out all the way to the promontory. Another half kilometre and he would be round it with less than a kilometre left. He was feeling better by the minute. Even a slight cramp in his left foot couldn't shake his morale. He was humming quietly to himself, an old folk song his brother taught him in Kiev.

From somewhere behind him he could hear the sound of car engines. He trod water and turned. Above the cove lights were flashing—car lamps, hand torches. Vader felt the adrenaline race. His throat went tight. He coughed, and the sound was like an explosion. Once more he was swimming, hard now, a touch desperately, and his lungs were suddenly crying out for air.

24

TWO

Suslov leapt out of the Saab and scrambled down the path to the cove, slipping, sliding, and sending showers of small stones into the shingle below. Pohl and two apes from the *mokrie dela* squad came down behind him. Suslov and Pohl had pistols, and the other two automatic rifles.

"Pavel?"

Suslov crept round the rock face. He had the pistol at the aim.

"Pavel?" Suslov's voice echoed round the cove. "Pavel? Vader?"

Pohl went in behind Suslov. One of the hit men moved out on the shingle and flung himself into a prone position with his rifle aimed at the heart of the dark cove.

"Pavel," Suslov called. "You'd better come out."

The moon came on full power again.

They saw the discarded wet suit in the shingle near the cove opening. Pohl was emboldened to switch on his hand torch. The beam found two heaps of clothes and footprints in the sand and disturbances in the shingle—and the litter of fag ends left by Vader near the rock seat where he'd fought himself. On the shoreline one of the hit men found the empty vodka bottle. It meant nothing, and he let it lie.

Suslov glanced at his watch and smiled. "Come with me," he ordered one of the hit men.

"I think we'd better call in," Pohl said sharply.

"Call in?"

"They'll expect to be informed."

"What can *they* do?" The tone was scathing. "Give the kiss of life if we find these two?"

Suslov didn't want the *mokrie dela* mob swarming all over the place like rats and ruining everything. It had taken patience and daring to get this far. He knew what he wanted out of this night. He knew it so precisely he marvelled at his own sophistication.

"The last thing they want in Helsinki is a scare," he said quietly. "Don't forget why we are all here, Pohl. Remember we have a security conference on. And remember also this is Finland."

They moved quickly now. Suslov drove the Saab very fast over the grit road which was not made for more than second-gear driving. The hit man, too big to fit into the front passenger seat, sprawled over the back seats, nursing the Armalite and peering down at the moonlit bay four hundred feet below. It was a sheer drop, yet his eyes held no fear. He wound down the window and sniffed deeply, drawing the sea air into his lungs.

They were close to the promontory edge, where the road ended in a patch of gorse, when Suslov pulled up. He switched off the headlights and moved out nimbly for a man in his sixties. He was already over the cliff edge when the hit man forced himself out of the Saab. Suslov scrambled down the face, skidding on the damp gorse and dislodging rocks that went hurtling over the big drop. He could hear the hit man grunting and cursing as he came down and a shower of rubble cascaded past Suslov. The hit man could not know that the route was familiar to Suslov.

It was Suslov's third time down.

The path had a primitive buffer—a vast boulder right at the tip fifty metres over the water and with a view encompassing the bay. Suslov slid into the boulder, taking

26

the impact with his outstretched left leg. The hit man sledged in now, grunting in pain. He had both hands in the air, the left holding the Armalite, the right bleeding from a nasty friction burn. The seat of his trousers was ripped, and there were deep friction burns on his backside.

Suslov peered down at the bay. It was as still as a pond as far out into the Gulf of Finland as the moonlight showed. Somewhere round the promontory lurked the Olefsens' boat. Suslov feared he might be minutes too late and that any moment he would hear the sound of the boat's diesels. The silence was complete.

It was another three or four minutes before he heard the cough. And then another. Suslov lay full length by the side of the boulder, scanning the waters below. He heard another cough, and then a series of coughs, and still he could see no swimmer below.

The big hit man was kneeling on the edge of the cliff next to Suslov. His backside was bare and raw, and he kept it clear of his heels. There was another cough and a faint splash of water.

Suslov flicked his fingers. "The torch," he said.

The hit man fumbled in his jacket pocket and brought out a hand torch. Suslov waited for the next cough, then flashed the torch. The beam picked out the swimmer.

Vader closed his eyes against the glare and put his head lower in the water and then dived under, holding his breath and feeling the ache in his chest. He surfaced into darkness. Then the beam got him again. The pain in his chest was sharp now, and he was gasping for air and the cramp in his left foot was excruciating. He wanted to scream, but his lungs didn't have the resources. He swam on.

Suslov held out his right hand and indicated that he wanted the Armalite. The hit man passed it to him and took the torch.

"Now tell him to go back," Suslov said.

The hit man shouted an order to Vader to turn back. If he does, Suslov thought, I'll still kill him.

But the swimmer kept going.

Vader took another lungful of air and submerged. His chest was about to burst. He had a pain around the heart. His head was throbbing. He'd lost all sense of direction. When he surfaced, he saw the torch's beam picking out a circle of water just ahead. He tried to submerge, but he had neither the wind nor the will.

He floated. He turned his face away from the source of the beam, hoping his black hair and the black wet suit would merge with the water. He desperately wanted to cough and stifled it. He paddled gently with hands and feet trying not to leave ripples or splashes.

But the ripples showed.

The beam glided over the flat sea. It passed beyond the swimmer for a few metres. Then it came back and stayed on him. He was hardly moving, and the moonlight and torchlight were making confusing shadows on the water's surface. It made him a difficult target, for he was almost one with the sea.

But Suslov got him with the first burst from the Armalite. The bullets tore into Vader's body, and he could hear the rush of air as his stomach was punctured. He tasted salt water and coughed and spat. He was screaming now, using up the air he had left. Suslov hit him with a second burst. Vader's convulsions were like those of a harpooned fish. He was still threshing. But not for long. In the torch beam Suslov and the hit man saw the red stain merging with the sea. The swimmer was face down.

Images of his daughter Katerina at the age of nineteen raced through Suslov's mind. He felt a great sense of relief. He got up and handed the Armalite back to the hit man and ran his fingers across his eyes. So far, so good.

They heard the shooting aboard the cabin cruiser. Kaxel panned the bay through binoculars. Pavel thought they would get away in a hurry. But Kaxel waited for a while, leaning against the bulkhead as he chewed a matchstick. He idly cocked the M10, and Jens came up from the cabin with an identical weapon.

Kaxel gunned the twin diesels into life, and the cruiser—its name was *Pelikan*—idled round the promontory.

It was Jens who first saw the torch beam way up on the cliff as Suslov and the hit man sought footings. He had the two shadowy figures in his M10 sights. He braced himself against the bulkhead, his left elbow on the edge of *Pelikan*'s cabin roof.

"Leave it," Kaxel said.

He put *Pelikan* on full throttle. The torch beam went out.

Pelikan's engines soared, and she was soon cutting through the water at over thirty knots. Kaxel put on the searchlight, and Jens moved behind it as *Pelikan* curved round, spewing a high wake in the moonlight. Jens was scanning the bay with the searchlight beam.

As *Pelikan* skimmed through the calm sea, the hit man on the cliff edge lined her up in his Armalite sights. Suslov stood behind him. The hit man was on one knee with his grazed backside just clear of his left heel. It didn't need much of a push. But Suslov finished it off with his left foot and the hit man fell, screaming, into the sea.

Nobody aboard *Pelikan* heard the scream under the roar of the diesels or saw the hit man drop from the cliff. Jens had got the searchlight on Vader. The wet suit had inflated to make Vader like some bloated black turtle. As *Pelikan* made a racing turn round the corpse, Pavel could see that part of Vader's face had been shot away. But it was Vader all right. There was no mistaking the two green stars on the wet suit. It was official issue.

Kaxel brought *Pelikan* round in one final circuit. It was going through Pavel's mind that they should retrieve the package he knew was strapped under Vader's wet suit. He called to Kaxel to slow down, but the Dane paid no heed. His attention was on a motorboat which had rounded the promontory and was heading straight for them.

Kaxel put *Pelikan* on full power. She surged through the water on a collision course. Jens knelt against the bulkhead, his right knee on the deck and his left leg braced against the cockpit platform. He took up a secure aiming position and got the motorboat in his sights as Kaxel threw *Pelikan* into a racing turn. The motorboat was now being left to starboard. Pavel gripped the bulkhead to keep his balance. He could see a man in the motorboat pointing an automatic rifle and a smaller man with a loudspeaker. Nothing could be heard but the surge of *Pelikan*'s twin diesels and the hiss of spray and the bangs below as *Pelikan*'s hull humped through the waves left by the motorboat.

Pavel ducked as he heard a burst of automatic rifle fire. He saw Jens brace himself and fire. A short burst that missed, and then a sustained one. The explosion seemed to rock the bay and a wide plume of flame, all oranges and reds, shot skywards.

Kaxel put *Pelikan* on a southwest course into the Gulf of Finland. None of them spoke. Pavel and Jens went up to join Kaxel, whose face was set. He was still chewing that matchstick. He was not the sort who would hang about to pick up survivors.

Pavel threw a glance at the receding bay. There was no sign of the motorboat. Smoke drifted up against the moon over the cliff top. Pavel wondered who could have been aboard the motorboat. And then he thought of Vader. And it struck him how easily it could have been him floating back there in the dark bay.

It was two hours later when Suslov went into the Helsinki mortuary to identify the body brought in by coastguardsmen. The grotesque lump was hardly recognisable as a human being, let alone a particular man.

Suslov looked down at the half head protruding from the bloated black wet suit. He started in shock. He'd expected to see Pavel, but Pavel was blond, not dark. The raven black eyebrow on the intact side of the head and the gold eyetooth exposed in the lopsided death grimace left him in no doubt it was Vader. Suslov blanched. He ran nervous fingers through his silver-grey hair.

"You feeling all right, Suslov?" It was Kursky who had noted Suslov's shock, Kursky from Special Section II.

Suslov tried to cover up. "It's just that he worked under me for a long time."

Kursky just gazed at him coldly. They get sentimental with age, he thought.

Two charred bodies were brought in now and put on the slabs. Kursky identified them as Pohl and a hit man from the *mokrie dela* mob who had been almost cut in two by bullets. A third man was known to have been aboard the motorboat, and the coastguardsmen were still out searching the bay for his body.

Suslov slit open Vader's wet suit, cut away the strap round the corpse's waist, and took the package. Nobody questioned his right to do this, though Kursky was curious.

The next morning Suslov sat facing three men in the Soviet embassy in Helsinki. In the chair was Filatov, a senior Ministry of Foreign Affairs official. One of the others was Kursky. Filatov read through some papers in a blue folder. His ascetic's face and the way he read over the top of his half lenses made him look like a judge.

"Well, just explain why this has happened," he said without looking up from the folder.

"I think you know this task was planned five years ago," said Suslov. His face was wary but tired. He had been unable to sleep after the shock of seeing Vader slabbed out there, and not Pavel.

"Before détente," Filatov murmured. He kept on reading.

"During the cold war," said Suslov.

"Go on," Filatov said. He lifted his head now and peered at Suslov through the lenses.

"Pavel and Vader were the two men trained for it."

"And they knew it was cancelled," Kursky put in. His eyes and tone were full of reproof.

"It was put on ice," Suslov said. "It was still on the six-month list."

Filatov looked puzzled.

"Some projects are ongoing," Suslov said. "Some are cancelled. Some we review every six months."

"Are you telling us this was never cancelled?"

Suslov nodded.

"I think it's time we were told what else is on the six-month list," Filatov said. He was flipping his bottom lip with his middle finger. "Pavel and Vader weren't authorised? Is that what you're saying?"

Suslov felt himself go hot. "They weren't authorised, Comrade Filatov."

"What was their motive?"

Suslov shrugged and shook his head.

"You knew them," Kursky said tartly.

"No better than I know you, Comrade Kursky."

"You do realise the gravity of all this?" It was Filatov again, and he was pinning Suslov with his eyes.

"Absolutely."

Filatov stretched back in the leather-padded chair. "I mean here we are in the midst of the greatest security conference Europe has known . . . a momentous coup for our country . . . and the Disinformation Department turns it into a slippery pigsty. If this were to get out, Suslov, it would give our imperialist enemies, the hawks of the West, just the ammunition they want." His nostrils flared.

Three hours later Suslov went under escort to Helsinki Airport. He was put aboard an Ilyushin 92 for Moscow. His hands were shaking, and he had a bad headache coming on. He took a couple of aspirin and closed his eyes. He thought he would be able to talk his way out of it, and his low state was less due to what he would have to face than to the Pavel-Vader cockup.

As the Ilyushin took off, Brezhnev was just arriving at the Kalstagatoppa Hotel in Helsinki for a reception given by the Finnish government for the thirty-five world leaders at the summit. Among the diplomats present a story was doing the rounds that three Russian delegates had been killed in a fishing accident while drunk. Brezhnev's face was stiff and pale, and his eyes were drained. He left after only twenty minutes, confounding etiquette and leaving the rest to speculate behind their hands. It was being said that he was ill or exhausted. A Russian official spokesman said he had left to attend to paperwork.

Filatov, who was also there, could think of another reason.

THREE

Calder was watching the test match on television when the phone rang.

He waited for Galina to take it.

He had his feet up and he was feeling good after a day in the garden. He shifted his suntanned body irritably as the phone kept ringing.

"Galina," he called. "Take the bloody thing, will you?"

He knew she was upstairs and thought she would take the call in the bedroom.

The phone rang on. "Bloody hell," he muttered. He lifted his aching legs off the coffee table and went over to the phone. He took it off the hook without announcing himself. It was one of his tricks that could turn close friends white with frustration.

"Who's that speaking?"

It was Amberley using his commanding officer voice.

"It wasn't anyone speaking," Calder said.

"Shay, I do wish you'd not be so uncouth," Amberley said. "It's not clever."

"It's different," said Calder. "What can we do for you?"

"I'm coming round, if that's all right?"

"It's actually bloody inconvenient." It was just like Amberley to ruin a pleasant half hour.

"I trust you've been making the most of the sun?" The tone was one of rebuke.

"I've been doing my bit for the grow-your-own-food campaign."

"But you're not on leave, old chap." It was exactly what Calder had expected him to say. "I'll be with you in a few minutes. Don't let Galina put on anything special."

Arrogant sod, thought Calder.

He could hear the shower running upstairs.

He went up and peered through the steam. The bathroom walls ran with condensation, and water seeped out where the plastic curtain met the tiles.

"Didn't you hear the phone?" he called.

"I can't hear you," Galina shouted, and there was the sound of her blowing spray from her mouth.

"You heard the phone all right."

"Can't hear you."

He smiled and tried to tug the curtain aside, but she held it on the other side. "You'd best come out," he said. "Romeo's on his way over."

Her young round face came out now between the curtain and the pink tiles. Her long auburn hair clung to her shoulders. "What did you say?"

"I thought that would fetch you."

She pulled a face and put her tongue out at him and went back behind the curtain. The vacuum effect of the shower drew the wet plastic to her, and Calder could make out the shape of her thigh. Suddenly he threw his arms against the curtain, pulling it round her like some plastic cocoon.

"Shay!" she cried. "No, please! No, Shay!"

He started to laugh and pressed the curtain tight over her breasts.

"Shay, no! Stop it! I'm getting cross!"

It only turned him on more. He wrapped her more tightly in the curtain, holding the ends over her bottom.

"Now for cold," he said, and she saw his other hand stray to the taps.

35

"No, Shay! Please! You mustn't! No!" She began to beat at the plastic with her elbows.

"You heard me then!"

For some moments he held her as she tried to wriggle and escape. Then he let her go and put his head round the curtain. She flapped her hands, sending the spray into his face, screwing up her face in mock anger.

"I still say you heard that bloody phone."

"Yes." She nodded firmly. "I heard it." The water was running off her high cheekbones and splashing off her nipples. Her body was flushed from the hot water, and globules of water glistened in her pubic hair. He put a hand out and touched her.

"Stop it!" she said, knocking his hand away.

Calder grinned and drew back. She thought he'd gone. She peered out and saw him peeling off his shorts.

"I'll show you." Calder laughed. "You lousy rotten Russian women's libber."

"You look sweaty and vile," she said, going back behind the curtain.

He got in behind her and put his arms round her, one over her small breasts, the other across her soft belly, and drew her tight against him.

"Let me turn round," she said, blowing out spray.

As she twisted against him, he saw her green eyes were moist but not from the shower. He began to lift her.

It was just after seven when Amberley got to the two-bedroom terrace house in Swiss Cottage.

Calder gave him a large scotch and said, "Just remember this hospitality when next you go slow over signing my fiddle sheet."

"What a way to greet Colin," Galina said. She was wearing a see-through slate-coloured blouse and no bra, and it was upsetting Amberley, who didn't know where to appear to look, he was so taken with her nipples, dark and firm under the silk.

Lascivious old sod, Calder thought. He blamed Galina, though. She knew the effect she had on Amberley.

"Good job I'm used to him." Amberley smirked, feasting on her again.

"Anyway," she said, "I'll see you before you go, Colin."

She started out.

"I don't mind your hearing," Amberley said. He didn't want her to go just yet, and he felt cheated that he couldn't just look at those breasts without pretending to see other things.

"It's always secret between you two." She smiled.

"Oh, I don't know," Amberley said. "We certainly didn't keep you in the dark last time."

"Lübeck," Calder said. "Everybody and his Auntie Mary knew about that crappy job."

She winced and then smiled. "I'm going. I don't like words like that."

She went out, and Amberley never took his eyes off her. The back view was just as stimulating when she walked.

"It can't be that much of a job if you'd discuss it in front of Galina," Calder said.

Amberley crossed the small living room and stood looking out of the open french windows at the pocket handkerchief of garden. "Your petunias are quite splendid," he said.

"It's the nearest I'll get to becoming a botanist," Calder said, chewing a stuffed olive.

"Lots of time, Calder. I mean you're only thirty-five and hardly dedicated to your present profession."

It was clear why Amberley gave him such dreary jobs. Two years ago it looked as if Calder would be sent back to a routine Foreign Office desk. Only Meade had saved him then——Christ knew why, except that Meade wasn't exactly enthusiastic about Amberley and seemed to like having a player like Calder in among the gentlemen of the section. Even Meade had been tried to the limit over Galina. As for Amberley, his mouth had set prim and narrow and he had put on his bishop's voice. "Good Lord, Calder, we could hardly permit you to marry a Russian!"

"I'm not going to marry her," Calder had said. "We're going to shack up and see how it goes."

That made Amberley sit up.

"You can do that either," he said piously. "Just remember your commitments and your oath to your queen."

He felt strongly about it. Calder after all was a Russian specialist in the East Europe section. His job was to turn or recruit Russians or help them to defect, not to marry them or, what was worse, shack up with the blighters.

Calder had sat picking his fingernails, bloody-minded as hell.

"The girl's quite obviously KGB," Amberley had said.

"She's an interpreter," Calder said icily.

"Haven't you learned *anything*? Good God, we sent you to keep an eye on that Russian athletics team, not to carry on with its interpreter." His eyes blazed behind the horn rims.

"Carry on?" Calder said in a voice thick with scorn.

"If you must have an affair in the interests of——"

"*My* interests only," Calder said. "Not yours. Not the section's. Not even the flaming queen's."

Amberley had snatched the red telephone.

"You needn't ask them to sack me," Calder said. "There's my resignation." He tossed an envelope on the red-topped desk.

"You can't damn well resign either."

Calder was neither fired nor allowed to resign. He was

38

frozen out for some months on full salary. He was treated like a security risk, notably by Amberley, but it didn't bother him much. He spent that summer in bed with Galina. They got up only to eat cheese and pickle sandwiches and borscht and caviare they got from a delicatessen near Baker Street. Sometimes they would spend half a day exploring Selfridges and Harrods and the Oxford Street branch of Marks and Spencer.

"In those places," Calder told Meade, "she's like Cinderella in Aladdin's cave."

"Stop mixing your pantomimes." Meade had chuckled, holding out his hand.

For some reason unknown, all was forgiven and Calder was back in the fold. He'd not been given any job since that stretched him, though, and he had no doubt that what Amberley had come about now was another nothing task. He suspected that Amberley came only for a horny old man's glimpse of Galina.

"Any regrets?" The question was casual, and Amberley held out his empty glass for a refill.

"Regrets?"

"About Galina?"

Christ Almighty, Calder thought, he doesn't want a rundown on our sex life? It wasn't so long ago that Amberley had asked if Calder would let Galina have the child if she got pregnant. Calder had just outstared him then. He did the same now.

"I was merely being solicitous," Amberley said.

"You were being fucking nosy."

Amberley sat down, running his fingers through his thinning grey-brown hair. The heavy gold ring on his little finger looked enormous. Not for the first time, Calder wondered what it stood for.

Amberley dipped into his inside pocket and brought out an airline ticket.

Calder took it. "Stockholm?"

"I thought I'd drive you to Heathrow."

"Galina can get me there," Calder said, nothing that the SAS flight was due to take off just after ten.

"I'd rather I took you," Amberley said firmly.

"What is it?" Calder said. "Overnight? Long weekend? I've no doubt it's a load of nothing, whatever it is."

"You should manage," Amberley said mysteriously.

Twenty minutes later Calder went out with the black zip case Galina had packed. Amberley let them kiss good-bye without looking and, when Calder joined him at the front door, turned and called to Galina, "I'll give you dinner when I get back."

"No thanks, Colin. You're very kind."

Kind? Calder thought. That's the last word I'd find for the bastard.

"Ladies' prerogative." Amberley shrugged.

They were halfway to Heathrow along the M4 when Amberley first stopped talking about Galina.

"You could be back by tomorrow unless you choose to savour the joys of permissive Sweden," he said. "Let me know if you decide to stay on a bit."

The night was still trembling with heat. Calder was in a pale-blue linen shirt open to the waist and could have been taken for a tourist. Amberley still wore his Whitehall uniform of light-grey flannel suit, striped blue shirt, and white collar. He was ill at ease, and Calder reckoned it was the sight of Galina's tits through the see-through.

"If I stay on," Calder said suddenly, wanting to taunt Amberley, "promise me one thing."

"I'll approve reasonable expenses and no more." He was at his pious best again.

"If you manage to get Galina out to dinner, don't take her to one of those parade grounds you call posh restaurants. She's dotty about fish-and-chips or Chinese nosh. Stepney's a great place for both. It'll only cost you a couple of quid."

40

"With no limit on salt and vinegar," Amberley sniped back.

"Smother and drown 'em in a copy of the *Times*."

The thought made Amberley want to vomit. He wondered if standards had fallen quite so far in recruiting for other UK institutions. Calder should have been employed in some car plant in the Midlands.

They were almost at the Heathrow spur of the M4 when Amberley came to the point. "Our embassy in Stockholm has an embarrassing guest," he said, running his hand through his hair as though to suggest impatience. The ring glittered as it was struck by the lights from a car behind.

"What's up with him then?"

"What's *up* with him, Calder, is that he's a delegate from the Soviet détente delegation in Helsinki."

Calder chuckled. "That's cheeky," he said.

Amberley said sternly, "He's political TNT at this moment, Calder. With leaders of thirty-five countries there trying to sort things out he's a live bomb, diplomatically speaking."

"Most of that lot do well to be in Finland," Calder murmured.

"I'm sorry?"

"They could do with a few saunas to sweat out the poison."

Amberley threw him a hard look. "The day after tomorrow they'll be signing the security agreement. Our masters don't want to upset things, all the goodwill, the—"

"Bollocks," Calder said, twiddling his thumbs.

"So you'll see that this chap's put right back on the Soviet gravy train."

"First stop Siberia?"

"After Moscow, I should think."

Calder sucked at a slight cavity he'd just noticed in a

back tooth where part of a filling had broken away. "I don't get it. You've got half the section in Helsinki. You've got Lander and Price-Jones and McInnes and Tinkler and other lesser nits out there." His voice was a touch bitter. He'd wanted Helsinki in the first place. But Amberley had said the assignment was too important.

Amberley waited until he was off the M4 before he replied. "It's crucial that the less that becomes known in Helsinki of this affair the better."

"So you call in your second team?"

"You used the word, Calder," Amberley smirked. "You really will have to do something about this chip on your shoulder."

Calder studied him for a while. "So I'm to deliver the poor sod back to the Russians?"

"You're to do what's best," Amberley purred. "As long as you keep him away from the United Kingdom."

"Bloody charming," Calder · said, weighing him up. "Will you join me in a chorus of 'Land of Hope and Glory'?"

Amberley was glad to see the back of Calder. He found his style and accent deplorable. He also had it in mind to call Galina and renew his offer of dinner. He might even say that Calder had suggested he should take her out for fish-and-chips in Stepney. The thought of the smell filling the car put him off. She might just say yes to them. All the way back into London he was tempted to call her. He couldn't face another turndown, and neither could he risk fish-and-chips in the East End.

He drove home via Shepherd's Bush.

He called at the pet shop near the Green and roused the proprietor, Sid Cooper, from his flat over the dingy shop. Sid drew back the four bolts on the door. He showed no surprise at seeing Amberley and led the way into the shop which smelt of sawdust and urine. The walls

42

were full to the ceiling with caged birds flapping in a multicoloured display of excitement but unable really to fly. There were whining puppies and mewing kittens and an assortment of squeaking rodents. A couple of snakes that looked dead from heatstroke curled behind glass and a guinea pig, the last of a batch, tore around its sawdust prison in frantic misery. A sales sign read BARGAINS.

"This weather's the death of this trade," Sid grumbled, dipping a small net into a tank full of tropical fish. "My write-off rate's something horrid."

He got a Siamese fighting fish almost in the net. "Come on, you little bugger," he said.

A Labrador puppy tried to nuzzle Amberley. He put out a tenuous hand but then turned away.

Sid netted the Siamese fighter—a striking red-and-purple male with fins like fancy curtains and wild, staring eyes.

He put it into a heated can. "I'm a bit low on Siamese fighters these days," he said.

"Thank you," said Amberley, paying in cash.

He was back in his second-floor flat near Marble Arch less than half an hour later. Mrs. Dryden had left him a cold turkey salad under sealed transparent plastic in the refrigerator, but he had no appetite.

He poured the Siamese fighting fish into a small heated tank next to a larger tank full of swordtails and black mollies and angels. There was one male Siamese fighting fish among them, red and purple like the one he'd just bought, but slightly smaller. He poured himself a scotch, then netted the Siamese from the large tank and put it in with the other. He polished his glasses and put his face almost right up against the tank as the two Siamese males closed and circled and then ripped into each other in a violent splash of red and purple. His left hand was clenched against his mouth, and his face muscles were twitching. His eyes were glazed. It was the larger fish that died.

Pavel was shaving with a cutthroat razor when he heard the knock. It was the first time anyone had called except on the internal phone since he had arrived at the British embassy in the Skarpogatan. The staff had been correct but cool. He missed the warmth of the Olefsen brothers, who had put him ashore in Stockholm with an embrace from Jens and a firm handshake from Kaxel before they made off, leaving a high curving wake behind *Pelikan*.

The lanky Swede in immigration was used to all kinds of asylum-seeking long-distance runners from East and West. He'd coped with freedom-chasing Balts and GI deserters, hippies after heaven-on-earth and drug-hazed dropouts. But he'd never had to face a Soviet diplomat on the run.

He let Pavel into Sweden after four hours of questioning by a stream of men from the Interior Ministry. They found the package and sniffed at it, not really suspecting drugs but checking all the same. One of them slit open the small envelope and sniffed at it. He let two others sniff and peer at the contents. They looked puzzled.

"They're not drugs or explosives," Pavel said quietly.

"No," said the senior of the ministry men, shaking the envelope and raking over the dull stone chips with a finger. "I can see that." He took out one of the stones and rolled it round the palm of his hand. The others peered at the irregular chunk of opaque rock, pale grey and chipped at the edges. It was roughly the size of a sugar cube.

Pavel grinned. He let them puzzle the thing out for a bit. Then he said, "They're rough diamonds."

More ministry men came over, and the lanky immigration officer and a customs officer. They delved among the stones and kept throwing long looks at Pavel, whose wide smile had them thinking he was pulling their legs. There was nothing in the rules against people bringing bits of rock into Sweden, even uncut diamonds, even if the owner was a refugee. The senior ministry man put the envelope back in the package with the papers and handed the lot back to Pavel.

"I suppose the British have been told?" Pavel asked.

The lanky IO nodded.

Nobody bothered about the papers. An hour later Pavel was in the embassy in the Skarpogatan. He was interrogated for a while by a sallow first secretary named Drayton, who had thick grey eyebrows and a habit of raising them even when not showing surprise. Pavel found it confusing. Drayton had gone on for a while, trying to tell Pavel he might be doing the wrong thing. Wasn't he letting the side down? The Russian side? It was hardly honourable to defect during a détente conference, surely? But Drayton had also been kind. He'd personally brought a change of clothes for Pavel in the third-floor suite they gave him. And that cutthroat razor was Drayton's.

Crossing the room now, Pavel felt sure it would be Drayton again. He opened the door. His face was white with shaving soap. He had the razor in his hand.

"Hello," Calder said in Russian. "Could we have a talk?"

"Come in."

Calder saw the cutthroat and pulled a face. "I thought you'd got round to electric shavers in Russia?"

"It's British." Pavel grinned. "One of the antique exports that are knocking your trade figures."

Calder thought, I've got a right one here.

"Help yourself to a drink," Pavel said. On the sideboard were bottles of scotch and vodka, sodas and tonics.

Calder began to pour a vodka. He could see Pavel through the open bathroom door, the well-muscled body with the embryo paunch, the young man's face with the high cheekbones. "If you'd like to pour me one—scotch and soda, please."

"Where did you pick up your English?" Calder said. Pavel had an accent, but he sounded as if he'd spent years in the States or possibly West Germany, where they speak English with an American twang.

"In Moscow."

"Where in Moscow?" Calder was pouring Pavel a scotch.

"The university, then special training."

"Drayton tells me you were in the Ministry of Foreign Trade?"

"That's right," said Pavel, rinsing his face under the tap.

He came into the bedroom, wiping his face and smiling. "Where did you pick up *your* English? The north of England?"

"Manchester," said Calder. He glanced at the stack of clothes on the bed.

Pavel sipped the scotch and laughed. "They intend I should be properly dressed while in the embassy."

There was a blazer and suede shoes among the clothes, two pale-blue shirts with white collars, and three bow ties. "I can see your outfitter was Drayton."

"He's very kind," said Pavel. "Cheers."

They held up their glasses.

Calder cast his eyes over the room with its watercolour reproductions of owls and herons and other British birds. He saw the chess set laid out. Another of Drayton's bright ideas to make Pavel cosy. "I'll take you on when we've had a chat," Calder said.

"I don't play," Pavel said with a grin. "It's a game for old ladies."

"And Russian masters."

"I'm not one of those," Pavel said with some feeling.

There was a long pause as Pavel began to sift through the clothes. He chose a smaller pair of underpants than the ones he had on. Calder sat on the chintz-covered sofa while he changed.

46

"You were taking a bit of a chance, weren't you?" Calder said.

"Leaving the delegation at Helsinki?"

Calder nodded.

"It would have been more dangerous direct from Moscow."

Pavel tried on a pair of pale-blue serge slacks that were too big round the waist.

"All the same," Calder said, watching him, "it's a helluva place and time to pick. In the middle of a mutual security conference."

"I thought it rather appropriate," said Pavel. He found a pair of wide-bottomed pinstriped slacks and was pulling them on over the mauve underpants.

"I hear you have relatives back there?" The thought was gnawing at Calder that Pavel would not easily be put off.

Pavel nodded. He went over to the dressing table and looked at himself in those appalling slacks.

"All the more reason why you should think again."

"Too late for that," Pavel said, crossing to the bed and sifting through the shirts. He didn't like the look of the slacks on him, but they'd do to be going on with.

"I still don't see why you're crossing over," Calder said. "All you seem to have told Drayton is that you're fed up with Russia."

"Don't you get fed up with your country sometimes?"

"Yes—but I don't run away."

"But you'd like to?"

"Often."

Pavel grinned. "All it takes is an act of will."

Calder couldn't help smiling. Pavel was so bloody cool he could have been on a package tour. "I mean nobody's after you for anything? You've not been selling secrets or anything like that?"

Pavel shook his head.

47

"You've not been bashing the commissar's daughter?"

Pavel threw him a sharp look. "What do you mean by that?"

"I thought your English was good, but I'm not so sure."

"I'm in no trouble with the commissar or his daughter. And I've no secrets for sale." He paused. "That is, unless I have to buy sanctuary in the United Kingdom."

Calder was hooked by that final remark. But he said, "How the hell do you think the UK can take you in, in the middle of a bloody détente meeting?"

Pavel took a swig of scotch. "Your prime minister was telling the conference about the need for free movement of people."

"He's a politician," Calder rasped, as if it explained all. "They're all bloody window dressers really." He paused, watching Pavel slip on one of those Foreign Office blue shirts with white collars the pansies wore. "We'll give you a one-way ticket back to Helsinki. You could always say you got lost on a fishing trip."

Pavel was shaking his head. "I could do nothing of the kind," he said, buttoning up the shirt. He went into detail now about his escape, Vader's death, and the blowing up of the motor boat.

Calder frowned. "What made you both want asylum in the UK?"

"We didn't," Pavel said. "Vader was aiming for Israel."

"He was Jewish?"

"Half Jewish."

Pavel chose a short wide tie in navy blue. As he put it on, he said, "I have no intention of going back to Helsinki and certainly not to Moscow."

"You might have to."

"I don't think so," he said, knotting the tie. "I'm sure the Americans would take a more liberal line."

48

Cunning sod, Calder thought. He said, "You must have upset *somebody?*"

"I'm actually a privileged citizen," Pavel said, with a quick smile. He was having trouble with the tie.

"I've known Heroes of the Soviet Union run out of welcome outside their own country."

"You seem to know a lot about Russia."

Calder nodded. "Quite a bit."

"How about that?" Pavel said, showing off his shirt and tie like some male model.

"You'll get by," Calder said. "But I still don't know why you want to become British."

"I don't," Pavel shot back. "I want asylum."

"Well, that's something," Calder said. "You do realise we're on our way to becoming the poorest nation on earth."

Pavel pulled on the blazer. It had a Royal Air Force squadron crest on the top pocket. It made Calder's day. He burst out laughing.

For a second Pavel didn't catch on.

"All you need is a flaming moustache," Calder said, "and they'd have you flying Spitfires."

Pavel got it.

He began to laugh, quietly at first, then almost uncontrollably.

"You're a rum case," Calder said after a moment or two. "How long is it since your mate was shot to bits in the Gulf of Finland?"

Pavel stopped laughing. He weighed up Calder for a bit, then crossed to the bedside cabinet and brought out the old seaman's pullover Jens had given him. He unfolded it to find the package. He drew out the small envelope. There was a rap on the door.

Calder glanced quickly at Pavel, who said, "Come in."

It was Drayton, sombre in a navy blue suit, his face anaemic between the long sideburns. He flipped a pink file against his thumb and gazed at Calder. "Would you mind stepping out a moment?"

In the corridor Drayton opened the file to disclose a memo. It read:

> Date: Sat Aug 2
> Time: 1923 hours
> Source: Soviet Em-
> bassy
> Received by:
> J. D. M. Foley
>
> Kulakov called to inquire if we know anything of the whereabouts of a Soviet diplomat named Pavel, who has been reported missing from their delegation in Helsinki.
>
> Message ends

"What do we tell them?" said Drayton. He didn't quite know how to treat Calder. And he disapproved of Calder's dress sense. He found something deeply sordid about diplomats who wore open-necked shirts and cotton slacks and moccasins. Those moccasins were inexcusable.

"*Tell* them?" Calder spat out the words. "Do you have to tell 'em anything?"

"We have to live with them here," Drayton said primly. "And the *détente* thing is in full swing just across the water."

"Fuck détente," Calder snapped. "Just express mild shock and say the FO is doing a check as a friendly power."

"One can hardly say that," Drayton protested.

"Then let's keep our trap shut," Calder said.

He went back into the bedroom, leaving Drayton high and dry on the third-floor landing.

The night was humid, and Pavel had thrown the windows open. He was drinking scotch and playing patience.

"At least you play one old ladies' game," Calder said.

"I've not played since I was about nine."

"How about poker?"

"Sure," said Pavel, gathering the cards.

Calder sat down facing him across the oak coffee table. He took the cards and began to shuffle.

"Why do so many Englishmen wear rings on their little fingers?"

Calder looked up. "*I* don't."

"Drayton does. And a lot more."

"Don't tell me it bothers you as well?"

"As well?"

"It bothers *me*."

Pavel chuckled, throwing his head back and showing his strong even teeth. One of the eyeteeth was metalcapped.

"In Moscow"—Pavel laughed—"we sometimes have bets when one of your new Foreign Office men is due whether he'll have a ring on his little finger."

"You've likely heard of one explanation." Calder had begun to deal.

Pavel was still laughing.

"Well, don't tell me you don't have poufs in *your* Foreign Affairs Ministry?"

Pavel nodded. He was solemn all of a sudden. "We put rings in their noses," he said.

Calder tried to keep a straight face but couldn't. He dealt the cards. "I don't know why I'm playing you at poker," he said. "I mean you're broke."

Pavel's ice-blue eyes came alight.

"I could outbid you ten thousand times over," he said.

They studied each other across the table.

"How many scotches have you had?" Calder said.

Pavel pushed the small brown envelope across the table. "Open it."

Laying his cards face down, Calder took the envelope

51

and studied its contents. He saw the stones, grey-green and opaque and ranging in size from that of a small ball bearing to a dull cube half the size of a matchbox.

He poured them into his right palm. His heart was thumping, and he felt the blood rush up his chest. "All right," he said as if casually, gazing at Pavel, "don't tell me they're diamonds?"

"And good ones." Pavel's eyes took him on.

"Pull the other one." He took the biggest stone and held it up between thumb and forefinger against the light.

Pavel said, "You can't check a diamond in that light. You should be facing north in daylight."

Calder threw him a guarded look. His fingers were trembling slightly. "You'll tell me next it's worth a fortune."

Pavel nodded. "It's a special."

Calder's gaze moved between the stone and Pavel.

"Any stone over fourteen point seven carats is a special. That one's a twenty-three carat octahedron of nearly perfect proportion. It's also clean."

"Clean?"

"Diamonds have flaws deep inside them that show up like bubbles or black flares."

"Come off it," Calder said, sensing a challenge he'd not faced in years. "You can't see inside this bugger. It's opaque."

"I've seen inside it," Pavel said. "We have a machine. It's a bit like an X ray."

Calder was lost. He put the stone on the table and picked up the cards and said, "Fine, I'll accept it as your stake on the first game."

Pavel put the big stone back among the rest and pushed out a pea-sized rough. "You'll accept *that*," he said.

"What's it worth?"

"In dollars or roubles?"

"I'm glad you didn't say sterling." Calder smiled. "Or beads."

"Beads?"

"Never mind."

Pavel sized him up. "Between three and four hundred pounds."

"What, this?" Calder twiddled the pea-sized stone between his fingers. It was almost spherical and rough and grey.

"Three hundred." Pavel nodded.

"And this?" He flicked the big one.

Pavel shrugged. "It will depend on the cutter. It should make two brilliants of roughly equal weight."

"What does that mean?"

"It should make half a million."

"Roubles?"

"Dollars."

Pavel took the stone and pushed the pea-sized second-rater into the centre of the table. "Where's your three hundred pounds to cover it?"

Calder would have had to mortgage his house or sell his car to raise three hundred.

Pavel smiled. "There's no point in staking your shirt. It would never fit me."

Calder's cards were disastrous anyway. He flung them on the table.

"Next question," said Calder, feeling diminished. "If they really are diamonds, how do you come by them?"

Pavel tossed his cards and leaned back. "I worked in our diamond mines in Siberia."

He looked so bloody relaxed it was beginning to aggravate Calder.

"You were sent to Siberia?" Calder said. He'd given up smoking a year ago, but he fancied a cigarette now.

"Not as punishment," Pavel said. He looked serious. "I took a degree in economics and went into the Ministry of

Trade and then—Siberia." He had got up, crossed to the window, and was leaning against the central heating unit under the window.

"I don't think you'd better sit there," said Calder.

He crossed to the window as Pavel moved away. He looked down on the gardens of the Skarpogatan. He had no idea if the Soviet embassy was in the area or even if the Russians would feel any compulsion to knock off Pavel. But he had no intention of letting them kill Pavel just when the job was beginning to look interesting. Calder drew the lined cotton curtains with their wild-birds motif and sat on the sofa. "You were telling me about Siberia."

"I was trained in mine administration and sorting."

"Sorting?"

"Checking the rough, grading it for size and shape and colour."

"And you helped yourself?"

"Compensated." Pavel smiled.

"For my time in Siberia. And the lost years."

Calder raised his eyebrows.

"The years without freedom."

"It's still theft," Calder said, feeling there was much more behind Pavel's defection. "The UK's no haven for criminals."

"What you mean is that you have orders to keep me out?"

Calder just studied him over the vodka glass.

"It would be politically convenient to send me back even though I'm a refugee from an oppressive state. Your people find me an embarrassment just now."

Calder nodded. "We have shits on our side as well."

"You have orders to turn me back?"

"You're certainly not coming to Britain," Calder said harshly.

"In that case," Pavel said, spreading himself in the

54

chair and placing a leg over one of the arms, "I'll offer myself to the Americans."

"Whenever you like."

Pavel reached out and took the pack of cards and began to shuffle them. "One game first, eh?"

He pushed one of the diamonds temptingly into the middle of the coffee table and shifted himself until he was leaning right over the table in a posture of confidentiality. "I'll stake that against whatever you've got in your wallet."

"What's that worth?" Calder said, curbing an urge to fondle it.

Pavel picked it up and held it between thumb and forefinger, turning it under the light with his middle finger. It was one of the bigger stones, thick and roughly triangular. "Maybe ten thousand dollars," he said, tossing it and catching it and then placing it on the table again.

"I've only got about fifty pounds on me," Calder said.

"That's fine," Pavel said. "Why not try your luck?"

Calder stifled a nervous laugh. "You'll never buy your way into Britain, you know."

A pained look came over Pavel's lean face. It didn't go with the mischievous glint in the ice-blue eyes.

"I think you should know one thing," he said. "I'm not just a trade official. I'm with the KGB."

Pavel dealt the cards.

Calder picked up his hand. It crossed his mind now that he would have to ask for more scotch to be sent up to see them through the night.

FOUR

It was midafternoon the next day, just about the time Brezhnev was signing the Helsinki agreement, when Pavel reached Heathrow with Calder in an SAS Boeing 727.

As Pavel prepared to move out, Calder grabbed his arm. Two rows back across the aisle a short, thickset man in an open-necked white shirt was zipping up his cabin case. Several times during the flight from Stockholm Calder had caught the man watching them. And Calder had tried the old ruse of pretending to mistake him for someone he knew in the hope of drawing him into conversation. He didn't get very far, but he did succeed in establishing the man was Russian.

The Russian was not known to Pavel. But Calder had a hunch he was after Pavel, and Calder was right. Lenkov had been sent direct from Moscow to Stockholm with a brief to recover Pavel or kill him.

Calder hadn't let him get near Pavel all through the flight. When Pavel went to the lavatory, Calder turned in his seat and never took his eyes off Lenkov until Pavel was back. Calder was now paying the price of his close watch. He'd wanted to go to the lavatory himself for some time. And he was in great discomfort now.

Calder met Lenkov's gaze and challenged him to leave first. The cabin was almost clear of passengers. Lenkov held on for a few seconds and then moved out.

Amberley ran a hand through his hair as he studied the passengers from the Stockholm flight. The temperature

56

was in the low nineties, and a corn on his right foot was giving him hell. If Calder had only followed orders, there would have been no need for him to go out to the airport, and his foot wouldn't be hurting now.

"I don't suppose your chap could be wearing an open-necked sports shirt with patch pockets." Jayston, the head of immigration, who towered above Amberley, chuckled. He'd spotted Calder and Pavel over the heads of the advancing passengers.

"I'd not be surprised," Amberley. "He could well have emblems stitched on saying 'Pot for Peace' if I know him."

Jayston chuckled again. He let his sharp eyes rove over the passengers, his immigration officer's antennae busy. Presently he fixed on Lenkov. He took in the loping slow walk, as though the man were trying to let people go past him. Jayston was always curious about the tail of an immigration queue, and besides, Lenkov had shifty eyes. As Lenkov went by, Jayston turned and with a quick movement of the hand pointed him out to an IO some thirty yards farther along the enclosed pier. He would get special attention.

Calder came up with Pavel. There were no handshakes, no introductions. The four moved on towards the private door used by the immigration men. Amberley saw that Calder was walking stiffly. "Have you been hurt?" he asked matter-of-factly.

"Hurt?"

"I thought you were walking badly."

"I'm dying for a piss," Calder said huffily. "And he's the reason." He indicated Lenkov, who was rolling slowly ahead of them on those short, thick legs. "I think someone should ask him a few questions."

Jayston smiled but said nothing. He led them through the private door into a newly painted long corridor. "Your place is third on the right," he told Calder.

Jayston left Amberley with Pavel while he spoke to two of his men near the passage leading to the immigration hall. Pavel put his case on the floor and pushed his hands in the breeches-style pockets of the slacks Drayton had given him. He looked too sure of himself for Amberley's liking. "I do hope you're not going to undo all the good work achieved in Helsinki." He sniffed.

Pavel kicked his case aside to let an IO pass. "I don't see why." Pavel smiled. "They've still got two hundred and fifty million of us left in Russia."

"But you're not a peasant, Mr. Pavel."

"We're all peasants."

"I'm sure you don't believe that."

They went on like this till Calder came back. Calder was slightly puzzled. Looking at Amberley, he said, "You've not come on your own?"

Amberley nodded.

"So who's taking him over?" Calder indicated Pavel.

"He's yours, Calder." Amberley smirked. "After all, you brought him."

Calder had expected one of Amberley's more favoured Russian specialists to take over, and he had been looking forward to a bit more layabout living in the heat wave with Galina.

"I thought you'd leap at the chance." Amberley sneered. "Considering the importance you attach to Mr. Pavel."

Pavel grinned and leaned against the wall with his hands in his pockets.

Calder was trying to figure out what people like Kemp, Arundel, Ridgeway, and Temple-Jones were up to. No doubt they were busy on super nonjobs with expense accounts built in like the mob sent to Helsinki.

"I know what you're thinking," Amberley said sourly. "Don't say it because I've heard it all."

Pavel was enjoying the squabble. It crossed his mind

they might be putting it all on for his benefit, but he saw no reason why they should.

Amberley threw him a cold smile and told Calder, "If Mr. Pavel really is one of the comrades from Dzerzhinsky Square, you might make a name for yourself, Calder."

Snide bastard, Calder thought. When he had sent the coded telex from Stockholm to say Pavel was claiming to be a KGB officer, Amberley had telexed back, "Take your time and make sure." It was a play-safe reply typical of Amberley. The embassy security man, Slater, then warned Calder that the Russians were staking out the embassy. Calder made his mind up on the spot to take Pavel to Britain right away.

Jayston came back now and led them through to his outer office. A young IO brought in four coffees. Amberley took Calder aside and whispered, "You still presumably aren't sure that Pavel's really one of their spooks?"

"There wasn't time to be sure," Calder snapped. "And the comrades were ganging up."

"I suggest you get him down to the warren as fast as you can. Is there anything else I should know?" There was something about the setup that gave him the scent of trouble.

Calder shook his head. He wanted to be sure those bits of rock really were diamonds before sticking his neck out.

Jayston caught Calder's eye and said, "We've got something you should see." Laughlines creased his face. He led Calder into the private office, leaving Amberley with Pavel. Duty rosters smothered one wall, along with airline schedules. There were Home Office manuals on the big mahogany partner's desk, a copy of *Who's Who*, and two dictionaries covering Arabic and Russian. On a small pine table near the window was a black-framed TV monitor giving a picture of the Terminal 2 concourse.

Jayston pressed the intercom. "Andrew, let's have another look at our chummies, please."

"Yes, sir."

The picture began to change as the unseen camera roved the concourse, finally settling on the area near Gate 7 and zooming in on two men in lightweight suits, one grey, the other fawn. They stood near a bank kiosk, studying the passengers coming out through Gate 7.

"One of them's from the Soviet embassy for sure," Jayston said. "We're not certain about the other."

"They're both from the embassy," Calder said.

The information pleased Jayston, and he made a quick note on his desk pad. "I must say the chappy on the right looks capable of plucking wings off butterflies."

"And then kicking 'em in the teeth," Calder said coolly.

Jayston laughed. "I suppose you don't know his name?"

"Ismailov," Calder replied.

The hidden TV camera was now searching the concourse again.

"There's a third one," Jayston said. "We seem to have mislaid him temporarily."

The picture changed yet again, cutting to the exit to the multistorey car park. In the centre of the shot stood a tall man of about thirty in a pale-green golfer's jacket.

"Know *him?*" Jayston asked.

Calder nodded. "His name's Gorsky."

Calder and Pavel didn't leave via the concourse. Jayston took them out air side among the small yellow service vans and fuel trucks. One of the car pool drivers, who had once driven tanks with BAOR, stood by the open door of a dark-green Austin.

As Calder was getting in, Amberley took his sleeve and said, "Would you like me to tell Galina you're back?"

"I'll do it myself, thanks."

Calder's eye was caught by an airline worker in bright-yellow overalls who was showing interest in the special departure. Calder didn't spot a tractor driver who seemed to be checking the warning light on the roof of his yellow van. What the driver was trying to do was to impress images of Calder, Pavel, and Amberley on his mind. He knew Jayston. And he could see that Calder and Pavel were the vital ones. He caught a glimpse of both of them in the back seat of the Austin as it went past. He walked slowly back to the crew room. If he'd called his contact in the terminal building right away, it is just possible the Russians could have got on the Austin's tail. But, true to form, he took his tea break first. So by the time the Russians heard of Pavel's discreet departure the Austin was doing ninety miles an hour on the M4—travelling west.

The driver kept glancing through his mirror at Pavel. He was used to chauffeuring Russians in conditions of secrecy. Nobody ever told him who they were, and he'd have liked to know.

Calder closed his eyes and twiddled his thumbs over his stomach.

Pavel ran his tongue around his dry mouth. The black coffee had left its aftertaste, and he didn't like it. He settled back and saw that Calder had opened one eye and was sizing him up.

Amberley was fixing himself a filet bourguignon when Calder phoned. He undid his plastic apron, threw it on top of the fridge, and wiped his hands on the wall towel, then took the call in the living room.

"I hate to ruin your Saturday night," Calder said. "But where do I get hold of Pinky Drabble?"

Amberley's face went taut. "What do you want *him* for?"

"Should I explain on an open line?" Calder taunted.

"No, but I should like to know." Amberley sat on the Georgian library steps with their red and gold leather inlays. He was gripping one of the brass caps. Why did he let Calder annoy him so much?

"I'll send a despatch rider." Calder couldn't resist the remark.

"That won't be necessary. When do you require him there?"

"Preferably now."

Amberley found Drabble's ex-directory number in his contact book. The phone rang out for some time before Drabble's voice came on drowsily. Amberley apologized for getting him out of bed.

"I wasn't in bed," Drabble said. "I was having a nap while watching a TV thriller."

Drabble was not pleased to be called out on a Saturday night but was with Amberley within the hour.

"It must be serious," he gasped, flopping his bulk into the sofa and running a fleshy hand over his freckled bald head.

"I don't know about serious. I do believe it's important."

Drabble grunted in disbelief.

"I think you've been to the warren before?"

Drabble nodded. "Three or four times over the years."

"I suppose you'd like a gin and tonic?"

"It's our Sabbath remember," Drabble said. "But with ice, please."

It had been some time since Drabble had been called on at all. He was now a diamond dealer with the sort of free-lance business nobody asked questions about, but he'd spent most of his working life in Africa, first as a diamond buyer in Sierra Leone, then as a wheeler-dealer doing intelligence work for the British in South-West Africa and Tanzania.

"Can I know yet what this job's about?" he said as Amberley poured his drink.

"You'll be told when you get there," said Amberley. He couldn't very well admit he didn't know himself.

The entry phone buzzed. It was the car pool driver, and Amberley asked him to wait in the hall downstairs. Ten minutes later Drabble was on his way.

Amberley reset the cushions which Drabble had flattened. It was dark outside, and he could see the inviting glow of amber light from Marble Arch. He was glad to see the back of Drabble, but he felt lost. He went over to the phone and thought of calling Galina. It took him some moments before he began to dial. He sat watching the tropical fish as the engaged signal blared out.

He went over to the fish tank and sat on the edge of a chair, studying the fish as though in a trance. Then he went and called Galina again.

The line was still busy.

He paced the room for a while. Then he pulled on his jacket, took out his wallet, and removed his club credit cards, his driving licence and cover note—everything bar the money. He had about forty pounds in fivers.

He went out and took a taxi to Knightsbridge. He went the rest of the way—about half a mile—on foot. He sauntered past the house twice before he rang the bell. The door was opened by a man in his late twenties who was wearing a bow tie and smoking jacket in royal-blue velvet. He wore a gold bracelet on his wrist and three rings on his finger.

"Oh, good evening, sir." He smiled.

Amberley went inside.

"If you'd like to take Number Four, sir?"

The young man indicated the thickly carpeted stairs. All the decor seemed to be in royal blue, and there was a cascade of cut flowers on the hallstand. Amberley went up past the fake Renaissance erotica on the staircase walls. Room 4 was a few yards along the landing to the right. He had a slight head cold, but he found the smell of roses very strong.

He went into Room 4, a narrow bedroom no more than six feet wide and twelve in length, heavy with the perfume of roses. There was a single divan bed with a royal-blue cover, a small chest of drawers on which stood a tray with unopened bottles of scotch, gin and Vermouth, and a small chintz-covered armchair facing a wall mirror.

Amberley took off his jacket and loosened his tie and opened the top buttons of his shirt.

The only light came from a discreet bedside lamp with a royal-blue shade. He eased himself into the chair, leaned across and switched off the light, and peered at the dark mirror. Suddenly it came alive as the light in the bedroom beyond was switched on.

A young couple came in past a huge bed, and the man stood behind the girl as she came right up to the mirror as though it was a dressing table. The man was very powerful and the young girl slender. Amberley stared unblinking at the mirror. His hands began to tremble.

It was nearly midnight when Calder heard the sound of a car on the steep gravel drive. He went to the window and saw two of the RAF Special Police corporals going up to the official Austin as Pinky Drabble's huge backside came out from the nearside back door. Calder reckoned there must be two hundred and ninety pounds of him. The corporals held onto their Alsatians' leads.

Drabble had to show his official pass for the second time—he'd shown it at the main gate guardroom of the warren—and he hated formalities. Too many people didn't have enough to do these days.

"Pavel." Calder beckoned Pavel to join him at the window.

They watched as the Austin driver brought out Drabble's zip-up holdall which was full to bursting. He

64

ut it on the gravel while Drabble put away his pass. One
of the Alsatians sniffed around the holdall and was about
to cock a leg when Drabble drew its handler's attention to
it. The handler tugged the dog away.

"Pity." Pavel grinned.

Calder went into the hall, an oak-panelled monument
to some free-spending lush of the 1930s. Its wide staircase opened right and left to wide galleries where once
tapestries had hung. Over the main doors was a coat of
arms in red, blue and gold with a scrolled motto in Latin
which Calder translated as "Judge Us By Our Labours."
Not much labour had gone on there for years now since
the mansion had been taken over by the civil service.

The night was very humid and sweat was running off
Drabble's bald head and his shirt was soaked black under
the armpits.

"Nice to see you, Pinky," Calder said, holding out a
hand.

"If I don't get this wet shirt off," Pinky said, "I'll very
likely get pneumonia."

The duty officer, a Special Air Services captain, came
from the duty room and said, "Leave the case, sir. I'll get
someone to bring it up to your room."

"Come and have a drink first," Calder said.

"Make it quick then," Drabble said. "I don't want
pneumonia. I can't afford it."

They went into the drawing room with its chandelier
and an Adam-style fireplace blocked with an ugly print
screen. Calder introduced Pavel and said, "Like to show
Pinky those souvenirs?"

Pavel held in his stomach and unzipped his slacks and
Drabble wondered what the hell he was going to be
shown. His triple chin wobbled, and he frowned. Then the
Russian undid the band round his waist and brought out
the pouch. He tossed it on the baize-covered card table.

Drabble held back for a moment, his large dark eyes heavy with caution.

"Please," said Pavel, indicating the pouch.

Drabble threw a quick look at Calder, who was coming across with his gin and tonic. He then opened the pouch. He peered into it and then poured the stones out on the baize. Calder had been playing poker with Pavel who now pushed the cards aside.

Drabble ran his fingers through the stones. He gazed firmly at Pavel as though to warn that nobody had better try to take him for a fool. Pavel grinned and dug his hands into the pockets of his slacks. Drabble picked out the very big stone, the special. He weighed it roughly in the palm of his left hand, using his right to push his glasses over his bald head. He then fumbled in a side pocket of the bulging jacket which he'd carried in over his arm and dumped on a chair and brought out a brass loupe. He flicked it open to expose the magnifier. He put the glass tight against his left eye, drew the table lamp closer, and peered at the stone under the light. He grunted three times and didn't even notice that Calder put his gin and tonic by his elbow. He held the stone expertly between thumb and forefinger, using the middle finger to turn the stone. He was in another world.

The only sound was Pavel sipping his scotch and, from outside, the bark of an Alsatian.

"So what is it?"

"Eh?" Drabble turned a look of sharp reproof on Calder. "What do you mean, what is it?"

"Is it a diamond?"

"Of course it's a bloody diamond."

He fingered through the stones.

"They're all bloody diamonds," he said. He shot a sharp look at Pavel. "Mostly mined in Russia, I'd say."

"*All* mined in Russia." Pavel smiled.

66

"How can you tell that?" It was Calder, baffled.

"The shapes," Pavel said.

"They're mostly maccles for one thing," said Drabble as if that explained all.

His fingers dwelt lovingly on the diamonds. He let them run off his fingertips and then gathered some of them up again, using his fingers like the jaws of a crane.

"What are they worth?" It was Calder again.

"I wondered when you'd come to that," Drabble said.

He went into the hall, unzipped his case, took out a heavy woollen dressing gown, and unwrapped a small wooden box from it. He opened it on the baize-topped table to reveal a set of small diamond dealer's scales. He weighed the special.

"I can tell you what it weighs," Pavel said, with an innocent's glance at the ceiling. "It weighs twenty-four point seven carats."

"Twenty-four point eight five," said Drabble firmly.

"Value?" Calder asked.

"You on a percentage or what?" Drabble asked irritably.

Pavel burst out laughing, showing his fine teeth.

"I'd just like to know, that's all," said Calder, trying to keep a straight face himself. For Drabble was peering at the special under the loupe again and evidently going through that range of emotions from greed and envy to sheer total suspicion the situation was bound to produce.

"I couldn't put a figure on it till it's cut," Drabble said. He'd forgotten all about the risk of getting pneumonia. "But I've no doubt it would buy a few pensions equal even to those our top civil servants are helping themselves to nowadays."

One of the things Calder always liked about Drabble was his detestation of their Whitehall masters and the temples of greed masquerading as public service institutions. "We've taught the Africans how to be corrupt," he once told Calder. "But the poor sods haven't learnt to be corrupt with integrity all over their faces like our lot."

Calder touched the special with his forefinger. "You couldn't give us a very rough figure?"

"It could make two brilliants when cut," Drabble said. "One very large, the other biggish. Both probably exceptional." He palmed it again. "Say two hundred thousand quid."

"And the rest? Are they *all* diamonds?"

"Give me a bloody chance," said Drabble, taking his first sip of gin and tonic. The sweat had dried on him, and he began to shiver. "I must get into a hot bath. Do you think they'd send me a Horlicks up?"

"I should think that's possible." Calder smirked.

Pavel began to scoop up the diamonds. Drabble put out a podgy hand. He took the special in one final affectionate embrace as though he were bidding it good night. He then dropped it into Pavel's open palm, and it went back in the pouch.

Drabble put on his jacket with the worn and floppy side pockets heavy with what seemed the debris of a busy life. He turned a solemn look on Calder and said, "Would you mind reminding them I don't have bacon for breakfast or pork chops for lunch?"

He held out a hand to Pavel. "Nice to meet you, Mr.—"

"Pavel," said the Russian.

"We'll talk in the morning, eh?"

Pavel nodded.

"Only I mustn't catch pneumonia, you understand."

Pavel smothered a laugh.

In the hall Drabble's face set in a pout, his bottom lip spreading up almost to the tip of his nose. "I don't know where he got them, Calder. But he shouldn't be wander-ng around with a fortune like that. He'll get his throat cut."

"What, here?" Calder laughed.

"The civil service is today's Mafia, Calder." He went over to the duty officer to enquire about his room.

Pavel was looking out through the salmon-coloured curtains when Calder came back. All he could see was the ribbon of the gravel drive under the moon stretching out to the blackness of the woods below. There was the sound of an Alsatian's bark.

Calder said, "You're quite safe. Not even a midget Russian could creep in here."

"One hand of poker and then bed." Pavel yawned.

"Never mind the poker," Calder said sharply. "I still want to know how you really came by that lot."

"Tomorrow," Pavel said lazily.

"Now," Calder insisted. He had an idea that Pavel was not so far gone as he was making out and that in some way he was pacing himself as if geared to a strict programme.

"I'm too tired now," said Pavel, fixing Calder with his left eye. The other was closed.

"One word from me," Calder said, "and you'll be thrown back to those bloody wolves."

Pavel had both eyes closed now. He was almost flat in the chair, his legs stretched out. "I can still go to the Americans."

"The Yanks don't even know you're here," Calder said testily. "And there's no reason why we should tell them."

Pavel smiled, his eyes still closed. He dragged a cushion under his head. "Anyway you want to know about my work in the KGB."

"You could have dreamt that up."

"Like I dreamt up the tale about those pieces of glass being diamonds?"

Calder stood with his back to the fireplace where nothing had burned for years. If Pavel were really tired, now was as good a time as any to press a few questions.

"So let's talk about the KGB," Calder said.

A dog was barking outside.

Pavel had started to snore.

FIVE

Lenkov's contact lenses were bothering him. He put some gentle pressure on the left eyelid and then read the decoded signal First Secretary Mazarev had passed to him over the desk.

"That's no different from the orders I was given on leaving Moscow," he said.

He offered the signal to Galkin, chief KGB resident in the Soviet embassy in Kensington Palace Gardens.

"I've already seen it," Galkin said stiffly. He resented Lenkov's arrival even more than the contents of the signal: *"Pavel will be retrieved and brought back to face interrogation and disciplinary action. Only if this is impossible will terminal action be taken."*

Galkin lit a cheroot from Mazarev's desk lighter. Lenkov leaned across with an English cigarette between his lips, and Galkin gave him a light. What was troubling Galkin was that Lenkov's threshold of impossibility was a lot lower than his own. A lean and sharp intellectual who'd been with Planning and Analysis before joining the Third Department of the First Chief Directorate, Galkin got the shivers at the very thought of the *mokrie dela* mob moving in to help. The sight of blood made him want to vomit.

"I don't see how we *can* retrieve him," Lenkov said calmly, the dark eyes blinking.

"We still must try," Galkin said.

"Before Pavel's presence becomes too widely known,"

added Mazarev. "Before he has a chance to damage all that's been done in Helsinki."

Galkin studied the first secretary. He was the archetypal Soviet diplomat, blank-faced and stony-eyed and very professional. And Galkin wasn't at all sure whose side he would come down on, his or Lenkov's. It also struck him that Mazarev and Lenkov might not know as much as he did of the background to Pavel's arrival in Britain. For despite all his fear of the *mokrie dela* mob, represented by Lenkov, and his revulsion for their methods, Galkin was still a hawk. "We must be careful," he said neatly. "We must not offend the British by a blatant attempt on the life of Pavel while he's in their hands."

"Why?" It was Lenkov.

"Galkin is right," said Mazarev. "This is a time of détente. We must persuade Pavel back."

"Or take terminal action," Lenkov insisted. "That's what the signal says."

"We might just have to discredit him," said Mazarev.

"*Discredit* him?" Lenkov was appalled at such moderacy.

It meant something else to Galkin. It meant that Mazarev knew more about Pavel's role than Galkin had suspected.

"It will not be easy," said Mazarev. "But we do have our means."

"By suggesting he's insane?" Lenkov sneered.

"Possibly." Even Mazarev knew the word sounded empty.

"I doubt," said Galkin, drawing on his cheroot, "if the authorities here are quite so amenable as our comrades in the Serbsky Institute."

"I concur," said Lenkov.

Galkin thought it worthwhile to suck up to the *mokrie dela* man for the moment.

"Meanwhile," said Mazarev tartly, "we don't even know where he is."

Lenkov glared at him and began to rub his left eyelid, very gently considering his powerful fingers. "I'm surprised," he said, turning to Galkin. "We surely don't let our comrades just disappear. Especially in a small country like this."

He'd had enough of that lens in his left eye. He leaned forward, screwed up his face, and took it out. Even Galkin shuddered.

The pigeons had Trafalgar Square to themselves as Amberley drove into Whitehall. He found seven o'clock on a Sunday morning in central London to his liking. Whitehall was deserted except for the odd eccentric, and he wondered if things were as quiet in Washington and Red Square, Moscow. He turned right into Downing Street and then into the Foreign Office quadrangle.

The car park was almost empty, so he pulled in near the main doors next to Meade's silver Mercedes coupé. It went through his mind that Meade must have a private income to afford such a car, though the steep rises in civil servants' pay put it just within income reach at his level. Amberley peeped nosily into the Mercedes. There were copies of *Time,* the *Sunday Telegraph* and the *Observer* on the front passenger seat, and squash rackets and an anorak and a book on sailing in the back.

Meade watched Amberley looking into his car. He was in Sir Harwood Caine's office on the first floor of the Foreign and Commonwealth Office. He turned back into the high room with its dreary nineteenth-century oil paintings and that mighty old teak desk with its photograph of the Caine family at Buckingham Palace when Harwood got his KCMG.

Caine entered, aglow with eau de cologne, and pushed back his unruly forelock. He didn't hide his annoyance at being called from his Sussex home at such an ungodly hour.

"I do hope your chap won't be late," he said, primping his cheeks with his finger ends.

"He should be with us any moment," Meade said. With his broken nose and stocky frame he could have been taken for just another paratroop commander. But his degrees from a variety of universities in countries where he had been stationed implied a quite different personality.

As Caine subsided into his deep chair, Meade said, "I do hope we are not lightly going to send this Russian back to some awful death or worse."

Caine picked a piece of breakfast bacon out of one of his back teeth. "You of all people shouldn't indulge in hysterics, Meade. We are neither journalists nor members of the National Theatre. If our masters consider this chap is a threat to the aims of the Helsinki summit, then so be it."

"I'm not clear whether that means you would have him sent back or not?" Meade's bright grey eyes were defiant.

"It wasn't my intention to make that clear," Caine said, swallowing the bit of bacon. "I mean we don't yet know the quality of his defection, do we?"

"The quality?"

"*Why* he's come over?"

"He does claim to be an officer of the KGB."

"Any peasant with the equivalent of our O-levels could get away with that." His mouth was tight set.

"Not with the lad we sent out," Meade said coldly.

Caine leaned back in the black leather chair with his hands clasped behind his head. "Do remember, Meade, this is no time to indulge in ideals that run counter to détente."

There was a knock on the door. Amberley came in tentatively.

74

"Good morning," Caine said frostily. "Though it can hardly be that at half past seven on a Sunday."

"I would also prefer not to be here," Amberley said.

"Golf?"

"Church." Amberley threw them a pious smile. "I should be reading the lesson this morning."

"There may still be time," said Caine with a glance at his thirty-year-old wristwatch.

There was a long silence.

Meade began, "The deputy under secretary would like to know where we stand with our Russian friend?"

"He claims to be a KGB officer," said Amberley.

"I damn well know that."

"I doubt if you also know he came in with a quantity of diamonds," Meade said quietly.

It would not have been more effective had he said that Pavel had brought an atomic bomb. "Diamonds?" Caine rasped. "Where does a chap get diamonds in the Soviet Union?"

"They do have mines, sir," Amberley said. "In Siberia."

"You mean he's stolen them?"

"He says he's entitled to them," Meade said.

"I could trot over to the Soviet Union with the crown jewels and say I was entitled to them. I shouldn't expect to be believed. We must not appear to be offering sanctuary to a common criminal. It seems to me the sooner we give him back to his odious masters, the better."

Amberley nodded, but Meade's face hardened. "That's official policy?" Meade asked sharply.

"Let me remind you again, Meade. We're in a period of détente."

"What you're saying is that we should unload him and send him back to God knows what as a matter of political expediency?" Meade's eyes blazed.

Caine's forelock strayed over his right eye. "I don't

75

fully understand your concern for a common thief, even though he is Russian."

"He's not any old Russian."

"If he *is* a KBG officer, I agree."

"Until I'm sure he's not, we'll keep him as long as he might be useful to us."

"Be it on your own head, Meade," Caine said. "But our masters may well have something to say about it tomorrow."

He got up and went out.

"Time we went," Meade said.

"How soon can I expect a decision?" Pavel swished a dead branch to clear a way through the rhododendrons.

"I doubt if the Home Office even know you're here yet," Calder said.

They came through the bushes to the head of the steep meadow that led down to the warren's main gates. Two SPs were out with their Alsatians and a pair of magpies were dive-bombing a tree where greenfinches were trying to feed from nut cages hung out by some bird lover.

"If this hadn't been the English weekend, you might well be on your way back to Moscow right now."

"So my timing was good." Pavel smiled.

They could hear the sound of church bells now and two shots rang out from the woods below.

"What are they shooting?" Pavel asked.

"Russians." Calder grinned. Then he said, "Rabbits very likely, maybe squirrels, some little furry bastard that can't shoot back."

"I like that," Pavel said.

They could have been weekend house guests out for a stroll before sherry time. Both were wearing open-necked shirts and cotton slacks, and Pavel had on the blazer Drayton had let him have in Stockholm.

"I would like a decision today," Pavel said.

"Not possible," Calder said. "You don't realise that the British civil service needs to yawn its way through Sunday, clocking up another day on the road to its pensions."

"All the same," Pavel insisted. "I must hear today."

"What's the hurry?"

"I wish to sell my diamonds." His voice was matter-of-fact.

"You could do that anytime."

Pavel shook his head. "I'd like to dispose of them not later than tomorrow."

"I don't see why."

"No, you don't," Pavel said, tossing the stick away.

"Anyway," Calder said, weighing him up, "you've not come clean about the KGB yet."

"I've told you I'll talk when I'm sure I can stay in Britain."

Calder shook his head. "They'll never do a deal, Pavel. I mean if you've pinched those diamonds, it would be like giving sanctuary to an American bank robber."

"Not at all the same thing," Pavel said. "Not even if the bank robber were also with the CIA and willing to talk to you."

Calder looked puzzled.

"The diamonds are my compensation for loss of freedom over many years. And for other offences by the state against people near to me."

"What other offences?"

"Personal," said Pavel.

His eyes were glacial.

More shots tore the bland morning. "I'd not mind getting that bastard myself," Calder said, looking towards the source of the shooting.

"You sound bloodthirsty," Pavel was smiling. It was one of those sudden switches of mood Calder was getting used to.

"I'm against blood sports."

77

"So what are you doing in this job?"

"I'm just a bloody interpreter," Calder said, straight-faced.

"If you have me sent back, you'd be no better than the shooter down there."

Their eyes met for a moment.

"Come on," Calder said, "let's get back for breakfast."

He was expecting to hear from Amberley about the FO meeting with Sir Harwood Caine. He also wanted to call Galina. He'd phoned her in the early hours, after Pavel had gone to bed, and she'd been cool and remote, upset that he had taken so long to speak to her since his return. He had hung up in a temper.

As they made back for the house now, Pavel said, "It's important that I sell my diamonds soon. Perhaps your friend Pinky will help me?"

"I shouldn't do it through that sharp sod." Calder laughed. "He'll turn it into a right rip-off."

"He seems to know the diamond market here."

"He also knows a mug when he sees one," Calder said. "Besides, they'd never let him mix commerce with this job." He studied Pavel closely as they went up the drive leading to the front terrace with its stone parapets and carved lions' heads at the head of the steps. "And they'd never let you sell 'em till they've agreed you can stay. And they'll not agree to that till you've come out with something tasty about the KGB. And maybe not even then."

They were halfway up the steps when Pavel reached inside his blazer and drew out two papers. One was stained and curling at the edges. The other was crisp and new. He handed the well-worn one to Calder.

Calder threw him a guarded look. He was in a sceptical mood, but he felt the rush of adrenaline as he began to read. The paper was—or was made out to be—an internal KGB memo sent to the Controller, First Chief Directorate, from Department A. Department A had always fascinated Calder from a distance. It was known to him as the Disinformation Department.

"You won't require me to translate," Pavel said calmly.

"No," Calder said. "I can read it quite well, thanks."

The memo ran:

After meetings with Yukatulmaz and the Ministry of Foreign Trade, it was decided:

1. It will be feasible to swamp the world market with our gem diamonds. Our annual production of 2,700,000 carats far exceeds the world supply which is controlled by the diamond monopoly operated from London.

2. The effect will be to disrupt the diamond industry of the West and to discredit the bourgeois classes in the United States, Britain, West Germany, and Japan in particular, where gem diamonds are a major means of tax evasion.

3. South Africa's trade will suffer severely. The capital value of the mining industry will collapse. Its military capability would then have to be cut back.

4. Israel's exports will suffer. Diamonds are its largest export item. Our allies in the Arab world will benefit.

5. The United States will have problems. The diamond monopoly is illegal there. The United States will find it difficult to offer help to its capitalist allies in Britain, Israel, and South Africa.

Under the subheading "Methods" there followed two and a half pages of detailed plans. Calder's heart was racing. He was sure the document was authentic.

"How do you come by it?" he said, his face blank with fake unbelief.

"I'm a KGB officer." Pavel didn't even blink.

79

"And who the hell is Yukatulmaz?"

"It's the diamond trust that plans the industry."

A young officer came past and Calder let him get out of hearing and said, "What about Russia's diamond exports? Wouldn't they suffer, too?"

Pavel nodded. "The market we're really into is industrials."

"But you still export gems?"

"In limited quantities," Pavel said.

Calder's probing eyes were still on him.

"There's nothing for nothing," Pavel said. "Everything has its price. Most of our people think this one's a good buy."

"Even the apparatchiks who run Yukatulmaz?"

"They're first of all citizens of the Soviet Union."

"I still don't see where you fit in?"

They were leaning against the parapet. They waited a few seconds to let a Special Police corporal go into the house with an armful of Sunday papers.

Pavel said, "Have you heard of Mir?"

"It's the Russian word for peace."

Pavel nodded. "It's also the name we gave our biggest diamond mine in Siberia. I worked there for nine months."

"You seem pretty versatile," Calder said. "I suppose you weren't a weekend cosmonaut?"

"I had this flair for languages. I studied English, and they recruited me into the KGB straight from university. I was first a Komsomol organiser, and then I was attached to *sluzhba*. I don't know if you know of the *sluzhba*. . . ."

"I've heard of them," Calder said sharply.

"I'm not proud of that bit."

The sun was strong in a vivid blue sky. Pavel shaded his eyes against the glare.

"Come on," Calder said. "We'll get you some eggs and bacon."

A busty WRAC sergeant with mousy hair came in for their orders. "Will the other gentleman be joining you?" she asked Calder, adjusting the knives and forks.

"I doubt it," said Calder. He'd rather Drabble stayed away for the next half hour or so. "Bacon and eggs for our guest."

"One egg or two?" She clasped her hands over her stomach.

"Could I have three?" said Pavel. "And what's your name?"

She raised her pencilled eyebrows. "Sergeant Skeene." She smiled. She had excellent teeth and an excruciating lipstick on. She indicated they should help themselves to cornflakes from the trolley, and then she swayed out. Pavel watched her all the way.

"You look as if you're missing it," Calder said.

"I can't go long without it." Pavel smiled. "In Siberia we never stopped. It was the best way to keep warm." He could have taken the sergeant to bed there and then without problem.

"You ate well in Siberia?" Calder asked, pouring cream on his cereal.

"Like lords." Pavel grinned.

The smile switched off just as quickly. "The food and sex compensated for the climate and the job."

Pavel then went into detail about his work at the Mir mine in the basin of the Vilyui River, and among the mineworkers at Mirny, the town built to house them. "I kept dossiers on them," he said, tucking into the eggs and bacon Sergeant Skeene had lovingly placed in front of him. "It was a hateful job."

"But you did it."

To Calder he seemed no less a trimmer than so many

81

of the specimens in snooping jobs in Whitehall. But probably he had a better excuse than they could rake up.

"It was a job."

"You were a snooper?"

"I was graded Trainee Controller." He studied Calder over the table. "I was trained by the KGB to snoop, you by the Foreign Office to do much the same."

Calder sensed he was probing. "Sinecures both," he said. "Only I wasn't trained. I just crawled out of the swamp."

"You didn't learn Russian in a swamp."

Calder ate another forkful of scrambled egg. He'd been taught Russian in the army during his national service after showing a knack for modern languages at Manchester Grammar School. But he said, "I picked it up listening to Moscow Radio."

Pavel smiled and got on with his bacon and eggs.

"What were you supposed to do?" Calder asked. "Root out anyone who called the Russian leaders shits?"

Pavel's gaze was hard. "I was also supposed to catch economic criminals."

"Like miners helping themselves to the odd diamond?"

"Like them," said Pavel. His face gave nothing away. Calder couldn't make out if he was sorry or indifferent.

"They must have been strong characters," Calder said.

"Eh?"

"Well, you didn't beat 'em, you joined 'em. The only difference being you never went down the mine for the loot."

"Nobody goes down the mine at Mir." Pavel smiled for the first time in minutes. "It's more like your opencave coal workings. It's about six hundred by four hundred metres at the rim and a thousand metres deep." He leaned back and wiped his mouth with a napkin. He said, as if just making up his mind, "I'd like to contact the American embassy."

Calder said nothing.

Pavel got up, rubbing his stomach. "They make decisions faster than the British."

"We don't have their phone number," Calder stalled. "And you've given me nothing about the KGB yet."

"Enough to be going on with," Pavel said, crossing to the window. "Until your Home Office confirms I can stay."

Calder watched him closely. He still had this feeling that Pavel was programmed.

Drabble came in now. "Did you tell them no bacon?" he asked Calder, who nodded. Only then did Drabble say good morning, adding, "I slept badly. Owls and things."

"We'll have you back in the smoke as soon as possible," Calder said. "But first I want to know about those diamonds."

"He still thinks they're glass," Pavel quipped to Drabble.

"I'd not mind having a few splinters," Drabble said. He sat down and helped himself to wheat germ.

Pavel leaned with his backside against the radiator under the window. "He's also sceptical about our mines in Siberia."

"You mean between the Lena River and the Yenisei?"

Pavel smiled.

"If I were twenty years younger, I'd have a crack at a place like that—if the Commies didn't grab what I brought out."

"What's up with you, Pinky?" Calder smiled. "You're rich anyway."

"Oh sure," Drabble grumbled with his mouth full of wheat germ. "Call me Rothschild."

Calder got up, patting Drabble on the shoulder, and went out with Pavel.

In the hall Calder took the KGB papers out of his inside pocket. "One thing, Pavel," he said. "The bloody thing's dated 1970."

"Before détente." Pavel grinned.

"Right."

Pavel now gave Calder the other paper. It took him only a few seconds to read it.

Ten minutes later he had his foot down hard on the road to London.

SIX

It was the first time Calder had been inside 10 Downing Street. He was struck by the sheer ordinary style of the place. The dreary corridors had been turned by generations of civil servants into a typical haven for bureaucrats.

"Perhaps you could tell us a little more about the chap?" suggested Humphrey Girton, MVO in a voice both measured and upper-crust that was meant to keep Calder in his place. Calder had been glancing out over the Horse Guards. He turned now to face the under secretary, bland behind an immense Gothic desk, his elbows resting on a blue-based blotter, his hands pressed against his mouth as if in prayer.

Calder felt his hackles rise. "There's no more to tell."

"Come now," said Girton, fidgeting in his high-backed swivel chair. "We should know if he is really a KGB chap and whether this document is genuine." He indicated the 1970 papers.

"Then it's a forensic expert you need, not me."

Amberley let out an embarrassed cough, and Meade tapped Calder's leg with his right foot under the desk. "All he's asking, Calder, is whether you consider Pavel genuine."

"How should I know?"

Calder was feeling the pace. It was nearly seven and he'd been given the runaround since his dash from the west country. He had reported to Amberley, who had driven them to see Meade, who had contacted Sir Harwood Caine, who was busy playing croquet in Sussex and had referred them to Girton of the Cabinet Office. Meade and Amberley had gone over the whole story with Calder while Girton made his way from Hampshire, where he had been dragged from a charity cricket match. He'd insisted on first having his strawberries and cream and made a point of it when they went into his office at Number 10.

"I can hardly call the PM on the basis of one defector's wild claims and one piece of paper."

"That's your decision." Calder shrugged.

Amberley winced.

"Besides," Girton said, slapping the paper with the back of his smooth hand, "the damn thing's years old."

Calder had waited for that. He'd held back the other paper. He tossed it across the desk in a way Amberley took as lacking in respect, uncouth even. There was a long silence as Girton went through it twice. He pursed his lips, which were quite small.

He said gravely, "You were quite right to raise this matter, Calder. I do wish we could be sure that he and the papers are genuine."

Calling prime ministers from what they might be up to on a Sunday evening was a serious, not to say dodgy, venture. Careers had been ruined for less. Calder knew what was going on in the undersecretary's cautious mind. "Why not nip down and talk to him yourself?"

"That's enough, Calder," snapped Amberley, twisting the ring on his little finger.

Girton put on a wintry smile. "I was not trying to diminish your professionalism, Calder. But we only have this chap's word for it that his comrade and those others lost their lives near Helsinki."

"No," said Meade, snapping his clasped hands. "We

now have confirmation that three men died in the Gulf of Finland in circumstances that tally with Pavel's story."

Girton fingered his grey tie. Even after a Sunday-evening dash from a cricket match he had the look of a middle-aged model from Savile Row. "In that case I must make the contents of these documents known to the PM right away."

Girton put out a hand to the red phone. His eyes bade the others good day.

They were back in the Foreign Office car park when Amberley said curtly, "You hardly served us well today, Calder." He'd been bottling it up. His face was sombre as a disgusted parson's. "I think someone else might take over Pavel now."

"As you like." Calder shrugged. "I don't mind." He didn't, either. He'd much rather be back in Swiss Cottage with Galina. And he'd not even called her to say he was back in London.

Meade had begun to unlock his Mercedes. "I want no change, Amberley. I want Calder to see this through. I personally believe our man *was* with the KGB . . . *is* with it . . . and Calder's quite capable of putting him through the drying machine." He threw Calder a wink on Amberley's blind side. His face was tough with that broken nose and strong chin, but his grey eyes sparkled inside the laughter lines.

He got into the car and wound down the window. "Don't leave him alone, Calder. I think we're on to a gem."

"No pun intended," Calder said, boosted by Meade's support.

"None." Meade laughed.

Amberley touched his glasses closer against his eyes. "I'm not sure we'll not be accused of alarmism by going to Number Ten."

"Stop agonising, Colin," Meade said, leaning out of the

car. "What we've just left is worse than a bomb. Until we sort this out, a lot of normally continent people are going to be wetting themselves."

He switched on the engine. "I'd give you dinner, Calder, but I think you should get back to our KGB chum as fast as you can. Anyway, keep me in touch, through Amberley, of course." The last words were a tactical afterthought.

Calder nodded as Meade drove off.

"What about Galina?" Amberley said.

"*What* about her?"

Amberley's nostrils flared. "I was merely asking out of concern."

"Thank you." The tone was abrasive. "She's used to coping on her own."

Amberley glanced at his wristwatch. "I'll call you at the warren in, say, two and a half hours."

Calder knew the bastard was testing him. It was a trial to make it clear Amberley knew he aimed to disobey Meade's order to get back to the warren right away.

"I shouldn't," Calder rasped.

Amberley frowned. "Something wrong with your car?"

"Phone calls can put the kiss of death on interrogations. I'd not like it if you stopped Pavel just when I'd got him in full flow. Neither would Meade."

He went to the Austin and drove out, waving to the policeman standing outside Number 10. To hell with détente and diamonds and the lot of them. He had every intention of spending the night in bed with Galina.

Sir Sefton Dykes took a pill and washed it down with a glass of water. His face was like parchment, and he had one hand on the edge of the kidney-shaped rosewood desk as though to steady his to-and-fro movement in the brown hide swivel chair. The room was swimming. His heart was going like a sledgehammer, and he kept belching. He was screwing up his face to make the tiny dark eyes find focus under the tight eyelids. He kept his gaze beyond the small memo on his blotter. He could make out the framed photo on the right hand far edge of the desk showing him and his family outside Buckingham Palace with him displaying his "K" insignia. But it was hazy. So was the massive oil painting on the far wall which a contemporary artist had been moved to paint after looking at cut diamonds.

As for Charlton his features were like a Francis Bacon face.

"Are you sure you're all right, sir?"

The news hadn't impaired Dykes' hearing. "Of course I am, dammit," he rasped. "Or at least I shall be in a moment. Stop being an old woman."

He ran a wrinkled hand over his dried-up face. The skin was so tight over the bones it could have been grafted, giving a skull-like effect. The pebble eyes lay in deep sockets. He blinked over his half lenses, then he picked up the memo. "If this is true, it could be the death of this company," he said gravely.

"I can well see that, sir," said Charlton, a lithe young man with short hair and a recent scar over a still-bruised right eye. He was standing almost at attention.

"It could destroy the diamond industry." Dykes ran a nervous hand over his mouth. "It could destroy it beyond hope of recovery."

Charlton just looked on, his mouth working. He was never at his best when Dykes was irate. He wanted to say something really stunning, but he always lost his tongue.

Dykes went over to the picture window with its panoramic view of the City of London. The green glass of the Commercial Union skyscraper dazzled him, but he put up with the glare. "I've always thought the Russians would get up to something one day," he said. "But it's only a week since we had their trade attachés here to lunch giving us all that balls about cooperation."

"It's just not on, sir."

Dykes spun round. "Not on?" His head was even more like a skull against the eerie green of the Commercial Union building. "This bloody memo says it *is* on. Very much on."

He came back and fell back into the chair. "Who else knows about it?"

"Only Edgeley, sir. He dictated the memo, and I typed it."

"He said nothing about this Russian?"

"Nothing."

"Nothing about where he's being held?"

"No, sir."

Dykes gazed at Charlton as if he were carrying some infectious disease. He pressed one of the intercom buttons and a husky voice came on, "Good morning, Sir Sefton."

"No, it's a stinker. Come in right away, Nobel."

Charlton's face twitched. He could see no reason why Nobel Bray should be the only one in the firm to get first-name treatment from Dykes. Bray had a fine war record, and Charlton had been no more than a postwar subaltern in the Household Cavalry when Dykes saw executive material in him for the Krueger Corporation. He wished Dykes would call him Simon.

There was a brief knock, and Bray opened the door. Anybody else, Charlton thought, would have waited Dykes' call to enter.

"Nobel!" Dykes' bluish lips parted in what could be taken for a smile.

"Sir Sefton." Bray came in with that slight limp, his alert eyes bright. He took in Charlton with a nod. He still had a military look and Charlton was a bit in awe of his reputation of having killed more Germans and Japanese, with bullets and bare hands, than any of the numerous ex-officers Dykes had brought into Krueger's. He took the chair facing Dykes. The sun was getting up, and he blinked in the glare.

"Put the blinds down," Dykes told Charlton, who let down the pale-blue venetian ones.

Dykes pushed the memo over.

"Christ Almighty!" Bray said, stroking his greying moustache.

"Precisely."

"So what's all this détente bullshit about?"

He looked militant. And that pleased Dykes. He'd made errors in his choice of key men in his time, but not with Nobel Bray. Nobel was a man for all troubles.

"Where's he being held, do we know?"

"All we know is what's there," Dykes said.

"No bother," Bray said. "I'll find out."

Charlton's face was a blank. Bray glanced at him as if he were a spare part.

"Thank you, Charlton," Dykes said dismissively.

With Charlton gone, Bray leaned back scratching his neck with both hands. "It's a bit like the kamikaze pilots."

Dykes looked baffled.

"Doing themselves in as long as they take a battleship with 'em."

"We're more than a damn battleship, Nobel. We're a multinational company with a vast industry."

"Which they're ready to knock out even if theirs goes with it."

Dykes was looking a shade better now. The pill and Nobel had helped. "I personally have found the Russians amenable to reason. I hope we can talk them out of this destructive venture. But with this chap on the loose. . . ." He put up his bony fingers in a gesture of despair. "If this gets out, Nobel, the consequences for this company could be calamitous."

Bray got up and went over to the rosewood bench under the other window, north-facing to give Dykes the perfect light for checking specials that were always sent up to give him joy.

Bray stood with his back to the bench his hands gripping the edge. "We have three options, sir," he said. "We buy his silence—and greed does seem to be his motive. Or if the Russians come to their senses after you've met them, we see that he's sent back. Or—well, there's no reason why I need to go into that."

Dykes was a new man already. He rubbed his dry hands together and swung to and fro in his chair. He really did find Nobel a tremendous chap to have round. And he found it poetic that Bray's father, a career officer in the Ordnance Corps, had named his son not out of respect for the Peace Prize but because Nobel invented dynamite.

"May I leave it to you then, Nobel?"

"Indeed," Bray said.

No sooner had Bray limped out of the office than Dykes put through calls to personal contacts in the Home Office, the Foreign Office and the Soviet embassy.

"I'm not your prisoner, Calder, not yours or your country's."

Pavel's outburst took him by surprise. It was late on Monday afternoon, and they were out for a walk in the warren grounds. Pavel had been pressing for an answer to his request for asylum. Calder had been evasive. He'd only got back at midday after his night with Galina, and Pavel had been pulling his leg about what he'd been up to.

Twice while Calder had been with Galina, Amberley had phoned, the second call coming just as Calder and Galina were into a simultaneous orgasm. Calder rolled off her, cursing and she reached out and took the bedside phone and said he had left. Amberley had not suggested taking her out for a drink. He knew bloody well Calder was there.

When he got back to the warren, Calder found Drabble loading the boot of the official car with asparagus and spinach and beans from the vegetable garden and tomatoes from the greenhouse. "I've left you a note with the duty officer," Drabble said with formality. "I must get home while these are fresh."

The note confirmed that Pavel's diamonds were all genuine. Drabble put their value at three hundred thousand pounds plus. "It could be a little less," he qualified. "It could be a damn sight more." The information shook Calder, but his job was to play it cool and squeeze all he could out of Pavel about the KGB.

Pavel made no secret of his dismay that Calder had not come back with a permit to let him stay in Britain. He'd hung about for two days now. He'd walked the grounds of the warren and knew a foxes' den and a badgers' set and had even got Sergeant Skeene to a point where she would soon say yes. But he wasn't in Britain for nature activities.

And now, as he and Calder went down between the lines of dying elms, he said, "You haven't given me a reply. Am I a prisoner here?"

"You're an illegal immigrant," Calder said. His mind was on Galina and that bloody clown Amberley.

"I still have a Russian passport."

"Sure you have," said Calder sourly. "Back in Moscow."

"I'm still a Soviet citizen."

Calder hated Pavel for causing him to be away from Galina. He hated Amberley. At this moment he couldn't stand his job. "I could get you a booking on Aeroflot any time you say."

Pavel's mood changed. "I'd rather go down to one of your pubs." He nodded in the direction of Wychfield, the nearest village snug in the valley beyond the warren's woods. Calder threw him a quick look. He thought Pavel was taking the piss.

"I mean it," Pavel said.

"There's only one pub down there."

"The Three Foxes." Pavel smiled. He'd been told about the pub by some of the SPs. "I'll play you at darts and buy you a beer."

"You mean I'll buy you one." Calder didn't like it, but he was warming to Pavel again. He was also fed up with caution. He stopped at the guardroom near the main gate and told the duty sergeant that he and Pavel would be in the Three Foxes. "One or two of your blokes might like to come down and I'll stand them a round," he said with a wink.

Wychfield is no more than half a mile from the warren. But on the way Calder and Pavel were overtaken by two RAF Special Police jeeps and a Mini in Army green.

Four locals were playing darts, but the Three Foxes' public bar was otherwise deserted except for a group of young men on half pints at the far end. Calder saw that one was the SP sergeant. Pavel caught on, too.

In the saloon bar a grey-haired man in tweeds sat in a corner with a brunette of no more than twenty. Pavel couldn't take his eyes off them as Calder got the drinks.

"I think *she's* beautiful," he said quietly, his gaze trespassing across to the saloon bar.

Calder took in the girl, who had a lovely oval face and wide calm eyes and long dark hair that cascaded down to her breasts. He saw that Pavel couldn't take his eyes off her.

"Don't make a bloody nuisance of yourself or it's straight back to bloody Siberia."

"I'm just looking a lovely woman straight in the eyes."

"Well, bloody don't." The last thing Calder wanted at this stage of Pavel's test was a public scene. "If her dad sees you winking, he might just come into the public bar and plant one on you."

"What's the difference?" Pavel asked. "Between the two bars?"

"It's like your party boys and your peasants," Calder said. "Only here you can make your own choice."

The long-haired brunette was also wearing a flimsy silk blouse that showed off her tits, and her legs were crossed in a way that gave an eyeful of thigh. Pavel was hooked.

"Keep staring at her like that," Calder said, "and her dad will surely come over and belt you one." ·

"He's not her father," Pavel said.

Calder just stared at him.

"He just kissed her on the mouth."

"Oh, that's common in Britain," Calder said. But his own eyes were on the couple in the saloon bar.

Pavel smiled.

He felt someone brush his elbow at the bar.

Lenkov said in Russian, "Think again, comrade. Come home." His voice was so quiet that Calder could not hear. "You were misled."

Pavel's instinct was to turn his back, but he said, "You're in the West, speak in English."

Lenkov ordered four light ales. Pavel turned to see three of Lenkov's comrades only a few feet behind them.

Calder's view of Lenkov had been blocked by Pavel. But he saw the square-set Russian now and he remembered him. He gave a slight nod to the sergeant in the public bar.

As the barman put the light ales on the counter, the SP sergeant and his corporals in civvies came over and stood behind Lenkov and his comrades.

Lenkov said to Pavel, "You'll come back with us?"

Pavel shook his head. Lenkov's left hand took his arm like a vise. Pavel stared at him. Lenkov held on. "I'm telling you to come back," he said in Russian.

95

Pavel was toying with his double scotch. Suddenly he threw it in Lenkov's face. He dropped the glass on the bar counter and hit out with his left fist, catching Lenkov full in the mouth. The first of Lenkov's aides went for Pavel now. Pavel butted him in the face. The others began to move in only to be staggered by rabbit punches and kidney punches. In a frenzy of fists and broken bottles, two were felled, one from a clout on the head with a beer glass; another staggered and hit his head against a barstool. The other writhed in a full nelson applied by a two-hundred-pound corporal. Calder threw a quick look at the publican, who was about to pick up the phone, and said, "Leave it, Frank."

He took Lenkov by his lapel. "Aren't you out of bounds?"

Lenkov dabbed at his mouth. It was streaming with blood.

"You know your limits out of London," Calder said. "On your way." He turned to the RAF SP sergeant. "See them safely away, Sergeant. If they play silly buggers, kick them in the goolies. Otherwise remember it's not officers who are gentlemen but proles like us."

The sergeant smothered a snigger. The SP squad led the Russians out.

"You *must* be bloody important," Calder said to Pavel.

His eyes were cold. "It's bad enough for a peasant to defect. It's worse for a writer or a ballet dancer. And worse still for an officer of the KGB."

Calder had begun to believe him. They finished their drinks and went back to the warren.

In the hall the duty officer, an army captain, took Calder aside and said, "You have a visitor, sir."

"I hope you searched the bastard," Calder said, irked by the night's events.

"Oh, he's a gentleman." The captain smarmed.

"This isn't the bloody Eton wall game," Calder

pped. That took the giggle out of the well-spoken tard.

Calder went over the drawing room. He opened the r, and the smell of Balkan Sobranie met him. He saw and knocking out a pipe in the ashtray on the side le near the fireplace. And then the caller got out of the h-backed chair and came towards him, holding out his t hand and stroking his trim moustache with the er.

'My name's Bray," he said amiably. "Nobel Bray."

el was asking the duty officer about Sergeant Skeene en Calder came back into the hall. He was asking how the sergeant's duties went. Her thighs were on his d, and he had images of their strength as she writhed h him inside her.

Calder's face was set. "I don't want our friend in there king to Pavel," he told the officer. "Just see they're t apart till I get back."

He went into the library to phone Amberley in Lon-.

He'd just had an awkward passage with Bray, who had n a bit smart. He'd first brought out his card which wed him to be industrial relations director of eger's.

"Then I doubt if you should be here," Calder said.

Bray then took from his crocodile-skin wallet a pass to er the warren signed by Jeremy Saunders, who ranked ween Amberley and Meade and who was in charge of day-to-day running of the warren.

"I would think"—Bray smiled—"you were still at uni- sity when I first helped your setup."

'I never went to university." It was a sore spot Bray l touched. Calder regretted that instead of going to Ox- d, he'd taken a job on a local paper before doing his ional service.

"It doesn't show," Bray said condescendingly.

He now gave Calder a note from Saunders which sa[id] that Bray should be given "total facilities."

"I just need a few moments with our Russian frien[d]," Bray said, tucking his hands in the pockets of his twe[ed] jacket. The smile had gone, and his eyes were hard. [It] seemed to Calder not only that Bray should not be giv[en] access to Pavel but that as an executive with a busine[ss] corporation he shouldn't even know of Pavel's presenc[e]. The warren was becoming like Clapham Junction. Th[e] Russians knew about it, that much was known, but it w[as] carrying open security to ludicrous lengths to let businessmen.

Bray's pipe was still smouldering in the ashtray. Cald[er] wafted away the smoke.

"I'm sorry," Bray said.

"It gets my sinuses," Calder said.

Bray snuffed out the stale tobacco. "May I see o[ur] friend now?"

"Not just yet," Calder said, going out.

"I'll come out for a bit with this," Bray said, picking u[p] his pipe. "Then I'll not foul the place up."

"I'd rather you waited here," Calder said. He didn't s[ee] why Bray should even set eyes on Pavel.

On the phone now, Calder said, "I have some blok[es] from Krueger's here. I don't know what the hell's goin[g] on."

"If it's Bray," Amberley said coldly, "give him all th[e] help you can."

"Should they know what's going on here?" Calder[']s tone was angry.

"Calder," Amberley rasped, "you don't draw up th[e] parameters."

"The what?"

"The parameters." It was a word he'd picked up fro[m]

secretary to the Cabinet Office. "I'm saying you don't
ke the rules."

Calder put the phone down and bit a fingernail. There
s more going on than he knew about. And he didn't
e it.

lina had Mahler on the hi-fi and Ladybird Johnson
eep in her lap when the doorbell rang. The Siamese cat
ang from her lap, startled. It was just after half past
e, and night callers were rare. For some time after she
l let the Russian team go back without her and had
yed to live with Calder she had known moments of fear
en Calder was away from the house and people had
led. But that was a long time ago. Calder had the spy-
le built into the front door and brought home the
alther pistol and showed her how to use it. Her sang-
id was one of the things he liked in her, but he thought
e was not aware enough of the hate some of her com-
les would harbour over her defection.

The only night caller in recent weeks had been the
wsagent with his bill.

But she felt a chill of fear now.

She sat still for a while.

The doorbell rang again.

She went over to the fake Sheraton drum table. She
ened a drawer and took out the Walther. She walked
wly to the front door and peered into the spyhole. In
e dim yellow light from the streetlamp she could make
t Amberley. He was biting his lip and he was about to
ess the bell again.

"Colin," she said, opening the door. "You really should
ephone first."

He kissed her on the cheek. "I was worried about
u," he said. Beads of sweat stood out on his forehead.
s glasses had misted up. He took them off and wiped
em as she led him through to the living room.

99

"Colin, whatever's the matter?"

He didn't even look at her.

"Colin?"

He looked up now, the eyes weak and moist as he po
ished his glasses. It was not the first time he had com
round when Calder was away. But Calder hadn't bee
away for months now and thought he was being froze
out till he was sixty. Amberley fumbled as he put h
glasses back on.

"Sit down, Colin, and let me get you a drink."

"Just coffee if you don't mind," Amberley said.

Now he had dared look at her he couldn't take his eye
off the small breasts under the green blouse. She sense
the urge in him. He was stripping her with his eyes. Sh
said, "You spend too much time on your own, Colin,
and went through to the kitchen to put on the coffee. Sh
turned to see him watching her from the doorway. He wa
biting the inside of his mouth, and his head was shaking.

"I do wish you'd phoned," she said for want of an
thing better to say. He was making her feel uneasy. H
gazed at her as if he were taking in every part of her, e
ery inch, every curve.

"Colin, do go and sit down."

"I couldn't stop thinking you were on your own," h
said. His voice was shaky. "With Calder having a Russia
to cope with now, I just wanted to make sure they weren
going to take it out on you."

It was a lie, and she knew it for a lie. But she sai
"That's very kind of you, Colin." He was so different no
from the remote bureaucrat who first tried to have he
sent back to Russia and then went out of his way to en
Calder's career because of their association. It was Mead
who had not only overruled him but had made such a fus
over Galina that Amberley's own attitude to her ha
taken a U-turn. She never had hated him. Now she fe

rry for him, though she wished he wouldn't strip her
th those desperate eyes.

They went back in the living room. She leaned over to
t down the hi-fi, and she was near enough for him to
ach the bare flesh between her blouse and her slacks.
t he didn't. He just gazed at it.

She sat facing him across the hearth. Ladybird Johnson
mped back on her lap.

"Ladybird," Galina said, grateful because she could
d little to say to Amberley.

"She's a lovely cat," Amberley said nervously.

"She's a he." Galina smiled.

"I thought its name was Ladybird?"

"Just one of Calder's jokes." She laughed. She always
lled Calder by his surname.

Amberley watched Ladybird digging his claws into
alina's thighs. His eyes were sad and intense under the
asses. Galina thought he was fighting an urge to rape
r.

In fact, he was thinking what a match she and Pavel
ould make.

obel Bray twirled the big special under the light from
e anglepoise. Just to hold it gave him a kick. He knew
utters in Tel Aviv and Antwerp who would have drooled
ith excitement at the very sight of it.

Pavel stood behind Bray at the baize table while Calder
oked on. He'd been well briefed for this moment, even
it had come sooner than Suslov had said it might at one
their meetings at 2 Dzerzhinsky Square. "The diamond
pitalists will try to ensure your silence one way or an-
her," Suslov had predicted. "It's up to you to see they
n't."

And with Vader dead it was all up to Pavel now.

Bray was still peering at the big special through a

loupe. "You must be the richest Communist on earth," he said.

"I'm no longer a Communist," Pavel said.

Calder studied Pavel, trying to see if his eyes backed up the words. They revealed nothing.

"How did you come by them?" Bray asked quietly.

Pavel went over his story about his work for Yukatulmaz at the Mir mine and in Mirny. Though he was checking closely for discrepancies, Calder heard none. The story was just as Pavel had told it to him.

"I admire your lot," Bray said, checking another diamond under the loupe. "The way you get the stuff out in those conditions."

"You mean the permafrost?"

"Where *I* learned the game," Bray said, "the heat was the killer."

Pavel leaned his elbows on the table. "At the Mir the ground freezes right down to three hundred metres."

"You're bloody marvels," Bray said, taking up yet another gem.

The mutual admiration was irking Calder.

"High-quality stuff," Bray murmured. "I hear you've been digging out a lot of it."

"Yes." Pavel nodded.

"Lots of lovely clean maccles in gem group one."

"Like these," Pavel said, fingering some thick triangles out of the pile.

Calder picked one up. He resented the expertise, but he was hooked.

"Maccles are twins," Bray said. He held one out for Calder to look at. He pointed to a line in it. "You can see where they fused a couple of million years back. They're like lovers."

Bray threw an impish look at Pavel. "Quite a lot of grade one maccles have been showing up in Tel Aviv."

"I wouldn't know," Pavel said impassively.

"Russian maccles," Bray said.

Pavel began to scoop up his diamonds.

"May I?" Bray took the big special again. He couldn't sist feeling it again. "Bloody fantastic," he enthused, ressing it in the palm of his hand.

He gave it back and Pavel put it in the pouch with the st.

Bray weighed him up and brought out his pipe and en, aware of Calder, thought better of it. "Just one ing," he said. "I hear you have some documents that ight interest us?"

Pavel shook his head. "Not any longer." He indicated alder.

"Official secrets," Calder said. He was on his own round now. He had a feeling Bray knew the contents of ose papers anyway. And he'd like to know who gave e nod for Krueger's to be tipped off about Pavel.

Bray watched Pavel put the pouch away. "You'll give s a chance to buy them?" He had the look of a simple an, but his mouth gave him away. It was set tight, the w firm.

"I want to sell them as soon as possible," Pavel said.

"I could take them in for valuation," Bray said. "We'll ve you a good price."

Pavel put on his slow smile. "You'll value them in my resence. And you will get them when one of the big anks has cleared your cheque to my account."

"And maybe not even then." Calder could not resist utting in. He thought they were both taking too much or granted.

Bray would like to have put him in his place. He nought better of it. Pavel just grinned. Bray left then—in steel blue BMW. He even won salutes from two of the P guards on the drive, which irritated Calder.

"Right," Calder said. "Let's get down to the real usiness."

Pavel looked puzzled.

"About the KGB."

"Could we get a bit of fresh air first," Pavel asked.

They borrowed a hand torch from the duty officer and went outside. The night was balmy, and Pavel breathed in several times and stretched himself and suggested a walk as far as the main gates. On the way they came across two pairs of SP guards with Alsatian dogs and a jeep with a searchlight mounted on its roof. Pavel wasn't planning to make a break for it yet. But he wanted to know what he was up against.

The Rolls Corniche was passing St. Paul's when Sir Sefton Dykes caught sight of the news placard. In crude black capital letters it cried KRUEGER'S SHARE CRASH. Sir Sefton felt the blood rush to his head. He went dizzy, and his heart began to bump so hard he thought he was in for a coronary. It was no new experience. He had been expecting his first coronary for the last twenty-eight years. He turned to catch a second glimpse of the placard through the back window. It was out of focus, and he felt grateful for that small mercy.

He leaned forward and switched on the two-way radio and said into the microphone, "You there, Charlton?"

"Loud and clear, Sir Sefton."

"Give me the latest."

"One moment, Sir Sefton."

God Almighty, Sir Sefton thought, why doesn't the idiot know it offhand? He must have the closed-circuit monitor staring him in the face, unless he was watching the flaming test match on the TV. Up to a few minutes ago they'd been watching the share flashes together in Sir Sefton's office in Octahedra House. Krueger's share price had moved down all morning. It had opened at 278 and shed 40 points in two hours' trading.

When Sir Sefton left the office the price was 216.

"Are you there, Charlton?" Dykes called into the radio.

"Sorry, sir," came Charlton's voice. "We've been getting interference." He meant on the closed-circuit TV.

"No need to tell me *that*." He snarled. "What's our price?"

There was a moment's pause before Charlton's high-flown voice came on. "We're standing at two hundred and nine."

"I'd not call that standing," Dykes snapped. "The word is falling. Do we know yet who's selling?"

"Not yet, Sir Sefton."

"Then get them to pull their fingers out and find out."

"Yes, sir."

"Any news of Nobel?"

"He does have a long way to come, sir."

Dykes's knuckles were white on the microphone. "We sent the helicopter to pick him up, didn't we?"

"Yes, sir."

Dykes switched off. He leaned back and took a grip on the silk tassel strap and gazed blankly at the back of the chauffeur's head.

"The world's full of cheats and creeps, Desmond," he pronounced.

"Yes, sir," said Desmond, without turning his head. The City was heavy with traffic.

Dykes was in no way leaving things to Nobel Bray. He couldn't afford to. Since that selling of Krueger's shares began when the Stock Exchange opened, he'd acted fast. He'd told Ogilvy to keep the public relations temperature down and the press calm. He'd given Maybon orders to fix support buying of Krueger's shares. "I don't want us to go below two hundred and fifty," he'd said. It sounded hollow in face of the later drops. But the price would have fallen much more but for Maybon's secret buying of large lines of Krueger's shares.

Dykes had not felt so unsure for thirty years. But one

thing he knew. He knew in his bones that the share fall could only be due to one thing—the arrival in the United Kingdom of one Russian. He racked his brain for any other explanation. It had to be due to Pavel.

The Rolls Corniche came off the Strand into the Mall. Dykes got out near the path leading to the Horse Guards. "Cruise round for half an hour, Desmond."

He found Mazarev near the lake throwing bread to the wildfowl. Young secretaries from Whitehall were taking early picnic lunches, and one blonde of no more than eighteen or so was lying out with her skirt so high that Dykes could see the pink pants under her tights. He was past the capacity to enjoy it.

He went up to Mazarev and said, "I'm a little late. The traffic was busy."

"That's all right," Mazarev said. He threw chunks of bread to a couple of Chinese geese.

"So what the hell are your people up to?"

The diplomat flipped open his briefcase. He took out a paper bag full of bread. He threw a handful of bits to the ducks and water hens. "The world's full of hawks and doves," he said. His high-domed head and thin blond hair gave him the look of a sporting academic.

"I'm not on about birds," Dykes said fiercely. "I'm on about this plot of yours to smash us."

Mazarev held out a crust to a mallard.

"I'm on about this man Pavel who's come over with a fortune in stones," Dykes said.

The mallard took the bread from Mazarev's hand, delighting him.

"Did you hear me?" Dykes asked. He preferred to shoot ducks, not feed them.

"Every word."

"So what about it?"

Mazarev took out the last handful of bread. He began to scatter it. "One defector doesn't make a policy."

"So those papers are fake?"

"Which papers?"

"The ones he came over with."

"I know nothing about them," said Mazarev, shaking the last crumbs out of the bag.

Two young secretaries came up to watch the ducks and drakes closing on Mazarev. One of the secretaries, a shapely twenty-year-old with long red hair, opened her sling bag and brought out a bag full of biscuits. She smiled at him. He watched her feed the birds he'd attracted. She gave him a warm smile.

He said, "We're spoiling them."

"I think we are." She laughed.

Dykes felt out of it. He knew Mazarev was a keen bird watcher who had given roubles to the Royal Society for the Protection of Birds, but this was too much.

"I thought we were going to discuss things," Dykes said, curbing his frustration.

Mazarev ignored him and said to the girl, "Even the great-crested grebes are more friendly."

Her soft wide eyes sparkled. "They like it here." She smiled. "They've settled in."

Dykes was wondering if the share price had gone below two hundred.

Mazarev screwed up his empty paper bag. He watched the girl feeding the mallards and geese and a couple of daring water hens.

"It really is urgent," said Dykes.

The young redhead threw him an innocent grin. Dykes put on a tight smile. He wished to hell that Mazarev would pull himself together. Mazarev watched the wildfowl crowding. He looked at the young redhead and said, "I think they know you."

She laughed and went on feeding them.

"Mazarev!" Dykes whispered.

He gave the girl a paternal smile, then moved away

with Dykes along the lake side towards Whitehall. They had only gone a few yards when he said, "You can take it that my country has no wish to disturb the present compact for world trade in diamonds."

"I'm glad to hear it," Dykes said.

He was feeling the midday heat. He would have liked to take Mazarev to his club for an iced drink.

"Should we walk back to the Mall and talk it over?" Dykes asked.

"I've told you all that matters," the diplomat said. "I'm not going back to the Mall. I have a meeting at the Foreign Office seven minutes from now."

He shook hands with Dykes, who went back to the Mall.

When he looked round, he saw Mazarev had gone back to join the young redhead. He thought he had simply got rid of him to avoid getting anywhere near the truth. But Mazarev had found a fellow wildfowl lover in the redhead, and they were enjoying the geese and mallards and the grebes, feeding them, seeking a common language with them. The young redhead was laughing at the antics of the wildfowl. Their plumage and movement, Mazarev thought, were pure art.

He glanced at his digital watch. He was due at the Foreign Office in four minutes. Moscow wanted Pavel repatriated.

And his orders were to see this was agreed to right away.

SEVEN

Nobel Bray paid off the taxi and went into Octahedra House past the two commissionaires and the special security men in civvies. It was sights week when dealers and brokers flew in from all over the globe to buy their boxes of rough diamonds. Bray was about to enter one of the lifts when he saw it was full of foreign dealers. There was the beefy Texas Bobby Liebling III and Asher Kleinman, the alert seventy-year-old genius who was such a legend at the Tel Aviv diamond bourse they called him King Asher.

Bray felt grim. But he threw them a tight smile and then took to the stairs. He couldn't face being cooped up in a lift with that lot on a day such at this. Their faces were already full of doubt and worry and Bray had no idea what line Ogilvy and his PR squad had put out to excuse the share slide.

Dykes' office door was locked. Bray pressed the button and tried to look calm. He knew Mrs Frensham would be watching his image on the TV monitor in the outer office. She pressed the door-release button to let him in. He was looking puzzled. Dykes normally kept the door locked only when he was checking special gemstones. "Do go through, Nobel," Mrs Frensham said, touching back her greying hair. She was a widow of forty-five who had been fond of Bray for years now. The passion was discreet, and no more had come out of it than the odd dinner in the West End. "It's one of those days, I'm afraid."

"Don't I know it," Bray said with feeling.

He went through into Dykes' room. The doomlike silence hit him. It was like joining some pious mourners at the reading of a will. Dykes had his bony hands pressed together against his face as if in prayer and was swinging gently from side to side in the swivel chair. Ogilvy sat in a corner of the sofa, wearing a purple shirt, his trouser creases looking sharper than ever. Maybon sat primly straight-backed with a clipboard on his knee. And Charlton stood to Dykes' right near the phones and intercom. They gazed at the closed-circuit TV screen as if it were showing Krueger's obituary. Krueger's latest share price flashed on. Two hundred and three.

"That's seventy-five points on the day," Dykes rasped.

"It means the value of our company has dropped by close to twelve million pounds," Maybon said, making a quick calculation.

"I know what it means, Maybon," Dykes snarled. "It's the arithmetic of disaster."

Ogilvy had told the press that Krueger's was investigating the affair, and he had hinted that speculators out for a killing might be behind it. Maybon had been buying Krueger's shares on behalf of the company through several brokers and nominees. But the slide had gone on. Dykes had ignored Bray so far. But he glared at him now. "It took you long enough to get here."

"I had a long way to come," Bray said. He threw glances at the others, wondering how much Dykes had told them of Pavel. Dykes had confided nothing. He sent them out now. "I don't want the price going below two hundred," he instructed Maybon.

As they got to the door, he said, "Don't leave the press to any raw bloody fools on your staff, Ogilvy. Deal with the lot yourself. I hope the bastards believe whatever it is you have in mind to tell them."

"I think we can hold the line," Ogilvy said with a half

110

smile that was meant to convey hope. He was another of Dykes' ex-army officer recruits.

"Hold the line." Dykes sneered when the door was shut and only Bray was left.

"The only way he'll keep the press in order on this is to take 'em prisoner," Bray quipped.

"Don't try to be clever, Nobel," Dykes said, glaring out of tight little eyes. "This is a time of blood, sweat, and tears, not funny jokes. Our company is being murdered. And this heavy selling can only be due to that damn Russian. Someone's blabbed. I want to know who. And I want to know who's been selling."

Bray lit up his pipe.

"How far have you got with the Russian?" Dykes was massaging the area near his heart.

"I was doing fine till you called me back."

"In what way?"

"Even Commies get greedy. I reckon he'd sell us the stones."

"And those documents?"

"They're out of his hands now. Somewhere in Whitehall. Official secrets."

Dykes glanced at the TV monitor. Krueger's shares had steadied and were at two hundred and seven. "*Some* secrets," he said.

He delved into his drawer and took out his pill bottle. He swallowed a pill and sat there deep in thought, his eyes on Bray. "This Russian of yours may not have those papers anymore. But he has a memory. He'll have to be silenced, Nobel. And likewise those slick Charlies in pinstripes who've been spreading rumours."

"I'd hardly call them rumours," Bray said. "Somebody's been putting out facts."

"I want him or them smashed," Dykes said.

Bray looked unsure. "Could it be the Russians who've put the story out?"

Dykes shook his head. "I've seen Mazarev. I reckon he's as shaken as we are."

"Or pretending to be."

"There's always that possibility," Dykes said. He was feeling a shade better. Bray was good for him.

But then the closed-circuit monitor flashed Krueger's latest share price. One hundred and ninety-eight. Dykes gripped the edge of his chair with one hand. He stared at the screen and said, "Stop it, Nobel! Stop it somehow." His lips hardly moved, and his bottom jaw was twitching. He would have been in even worse state if he had known what was going on that very moment in Sights Room 1 on the third floor.

Asher Kleinman sat under the north-facing window and opened the first of the row of packets from his box. He emptied the rough stones on the blotter—four specials, all of 14.7 carats and above. He needed no loupe to know their quality. He brought out his golden loupe all the same. He dallied over the stones, twirling them one by one between his thumb and forefinger. He pulled a face.

"Oh, come on, Asher," said Howes-Mallett, who sat next to him. "That's a packet and a half. They're superb."

Oliver Howes-Mallett was used to the fake anguish of rich dealers who felt the prices put on their boxes was too high. He quite liked to act himself and was a member of two amateur dramatic societies in Sussex. He knew Asher of old. The old sod would plead that he was being "bust" by the monopoly and real tears would come into his eyes. Asher thrust his glasses on top of his bald and freckled head and took another peek at one of the specials. It was an enormous opaque gem.

"I don't know how you can do this to me," Asher said, squinting down at the pencilled price on the box. Asher's box was never less than a quarter of a million pounds,

112

d these four specials would form quite a part of that to-
l valuation.

Howes-Mallett chuckled and drew doodles on his note
d. "Asher," he said, "those specials are fit for a king."

"You want to know something," Asher said. "I
ouldn't inflict these on Arab sheikhs."

It was one of Asher's older gags. He really did sell
ms to oil-rich Arabs. He turned his sad brown eyes on
owes-Mallett as if to show he felt deeply hurt that
owes-Mallett should try to palm off such trash on him.

"You get our best specials, Asher, and then treat me as
I were your enemy." Howes-Mallett loved this part of
s job. He was doing his misjudged English gentleman
t now.

Asher squinted through the loupe at another stone. He
gan to shake his head in despair. "Do me a great fa-
our, Oliver, will you? Look at this, please."

Howes-Mallett was leaning back in lazy elegance with
s long legs at full stretch. "I've seen it, Asher. It's a
eauty."

"Please," Asher said. "Do me a favour."

With a show of resignation Howes-Mallett put the
one under a loupe.

"See that inclusion?" Asher said. "It's right in the heart
f it. How do I cut a thing like that and make a profit?"

"Easy," Howes-Mallett smiled. "It's a bargain."

He pushed the stone gently back to Kleinman.

Asher shied away from it as though it were contagious.
e looked sadly at the array of stones.

"Aren't you going to look at the other stuff?" Howes-
Mallett said calmly. He thought Asher was just up to his
sual tricks to get the prices down.

"Shapes, cleavages, and maccles I never look at,"
sher said, shaking his head sadly. "But these prices! I
ever thought you would try to ruin me."

Cunning bugger, Howes-Mallett thought. He put another of the stones under his loupe. On occasion, when he thought Asher or any other buyer had a point, he would bring down the price by merely writing a figure on the blotter. But he rated this parcel of Asher's very special. Those four specials would have made some dealers' eyes pop out. Howes-Mallett shook his head. "We're giving 'em away at this price already."

"I come all the way from Tel Aviv to be robbed?" Asher put on his tragic look.

At this point Asher should have said, "Done!" and clinched the deal. But he wrung his hands and shook his head and then opened another packet and let some lower-quality stones fall on the blotter. "And what's this stuff?" he said. "I can't keep any more of this in stock."

Howes-Mallett grinned. It was one more of Asher's old games. "You know the rules, Asher. You take the whole box at valuation or not at all."

It was unheard of for most dealers to turn down a box. Asher Kleinman had not turned one down ever. But he tugged his glasses down from his head and got up and offered his hand to Howes-Mallett, who still thought it was bluff. Even when Asher left the room, Howes-Mallett thought he would come back. He waited for the door to open. He just couldn't believe that Asher Kleinman had turned down a box. He went to the door and was just in time to see the dealer enter the lift.

Baffled, Howes-Mallett went to see Sir Sefton Dykes right away. He would have to explain why one of Krueger's oldest and best clients had turned down a box and walked out. He tried to recall anything he might have said that had upset the old man. One thing Howes-Mallett knew for sure. Sir Sefton would be furious.

Meade was still smarting over the way the mandarins had just carved him up. "Sit down, Colin," he said as Amberley came in with a closing price edition in his hand. "And don't tell me about the bashing Krueger's shares are king. I've just had to endure all kinds of lousy insinuaons about that."

At the Cabinet Office meeting called by Girton, Sir arwood Caine had said the leak could have come only om Meade's setup. Girton himself had spoken cuttingly f "too many interrogators with busy tongues," and a buling creep from the Home Office called Menzies had said untly that Meade's men had got too used to doing their wn thing and lost all sense of their duty under the Offial Secrets Act.

"I think you'd better stop throwing dirt around till you ave some proof," Meade had said angrily.

"Never mind that now." It was Girton, and he looked ke a severe headmaster. "All that matters is that this ap should never have been brought in and we want him ut, back where he belongs."

"We have no extradition agreement with the Soviet nion over common thieves," Menzies said piously, with shifty glance at Meade. "But I'm sure you have your ays of filling the gap."

Meade knew lots of hard cases in Whitehall, but Menes was straight out of the scenario for 1984. He had a rpetual scowl and a way of staring at you sideways.

"There's still a lot we hope to learn about the KGB om Pavel," Meade said.

"I trust you're not asking him too politely." Menzies' ce was full of hate. Meade knew he was a sadist.

Sir Harwood Caine looked grave. "You'd better hurry , Meade. Find out all you can—but quickly." He now ld Meade what the others knew, that Mazarev had been see him to demand the handing over of Pavel to the ussians. He had stalled on that demand but had agreed let the Russians have access to Pavel.

"When?" Meade asked.

"It had best not be too long," Caine said. "Our masters

don't want a gigantic cockup so soon after the Helsink
agreement."

Meade came away feeling the three mandarins were
worse than the bloody Mafia. He loathed the idea of send
ing any man back to the Soviet Union, even a KGB officer. But now, back in his own office, he had to tel
Amberley to speed up Pavel's interrogation and get some
quick results.

"Thumbscrews?" Amberley grinned.

It must be the heat wave, Meade thought. It's turning
them all nuts. "I'm sure Calder will know how to cope,"
he said.

Amberley's brow furrowed. "That's just it, sir. I'm no
sure he can."

"You'd better explain."

"It's that old chip on his shoulder. He's been on twice
today raising hell about what he insists must be leaks
about Pavel and those KGB documents."

"I should say he's dead bloody right," Meade said im-
patiently.

"He seems more concerned about people selling their
shares in Krueger's than about what Pavel knows of the
KGB."

Meade watched Amberley twiddle the ring on his little
finger.

"I wouldn't put it past Calder to have leaked the story
himself."

"Don't be bloody silly, Colin," Meade said.

"All the same," Amberley said, "I feel someone else
should work on Pavel."

"Who?"

"I was thinking I'd have a go myself."

"Isn't that a slap in the face for Calder?"

"I have a task in Berlin that could be right up his
street," Amberley said. He was twisting the ring really
fast now.

116

"Calder seems to be on your mind a lot, Colin," Meade said, his eyes very steady on Amberley.

"He is indeed, sir." It wasn't true. It was Galina who was on his mind—Galina and Pavel.

For a long moment Meade was undecided. Then he said, "Very well, Colin. Have a go yourself. Get Pavel to give you all he can on that bloody Disinformation Department."

Amberley felt the adrenaline race. His mind was tumbling with images of Galina with nothing on. He had to rub his glasses with a handkerchief, they were so steamed up. As soon as he went out, Meade pressed his intercom, and a Scots voice came on. "Mac," Meade said quietly, "dig out Amberley's file for me, will you? I'd like specially to see the psychiatrist's notes on his annual medical report."

"Yes, sir."

Something was troubling him about Amberley. And he couldn't for the life of him work out what it was.

Calder couldn't find Pavel.

After looking in the drawing room, the dining room, the kitchen, where Pavel was now wont to visit Sergeant Keene, and finally Pavel's bedroom, he was told by one of the SP corporals that Pavel had gone out.

"Gone out?"

"Don't worry, sir," the corporal replied. "He's being well watched."

Pavel had disappeared when Calder had gone into the library to make three phone calls. Calder had spoken briefly to Galina, wanting to say he loved her but put off by her coolness. He'd then dialled out the number on which a prim tape-recorded voice gave the Stock Exchange report. His third call was to Amberley, asking what the hell was being done about what was clearly a serious leak unless you believed in Santa Claus.

The first Calder had heard of the Krueger's share drop was on the radio news when he was back in his room showering after a long walk through the grounds of the warren with Pavel. He'd phoned Amberley right away.

"Just get on with your job, Calder," Amberley said testily. "And let the moneymen get on with theirs."

He clearly thought Calder was rambling. But as the price fell steadily—and Calder had phoned the Stock Exchange report hourly—it seemed to Calder the link was beyond doubt. He now thought it would be a good idea to let Pavel hear the Krueger's share price news on radio or TV or the phone service and study his responses.

He found Pavel playing table tennis with one of the SP corporals behind the main guardroom. Pavel's shirt and slacks lay in a pile under the table, and watching the game with the intensity of an umpire was one of the RAF guard dogs. Both Pavel and the corporal were glistening with sweat.

Two corporals and a sergeant looked on.

Pavel misserved into the net. He cursed in Russian, his taut face full of self-disgust. His next serve the corporal hardly saw. It flew off the table through the open window of the guardroom. Pavel slapped his thigh with his bat in ecstasy. He was wearing nothing but his underpants, socks, and those moccasins. He threw a wink at Calder. The game went to deuce. Pavel threw himself into the battle as if nothing else mattered. His legs and arms were well muscled, but his girth was evident, and he tapped his belly in disgust when the corporal took the next point with a shot Pavel was not within a yard of reaching. The corporal took the game. Pavel went over to him and hugged him. The corporal blushed. The Alsatian jumped down from the chair and went to him.

"You had the umpire fixed." Pavel smiled.

The SP sergeant and corporals laughed.

118

Calder wanted to laugh. But he kept a straight face. He still found Pavel an enigma.

"How about a game?" Pavel was looking at Calder.

Calder shook his head. "We've things to get on with," he said feeling pompous.

Pavel shrugged. He pulled his slacks back on but chose to carry his shirt.

On their way back up the drive Pavel threw a glance at Calder, his eyes twinkling, and said, "You'd spoil the fun and games in a concentration camp." He was only being mischievous.

"It runs in the family," Calder said. "My father was a sergeant major."

This was a fact, though Pavel took it for a joke. Two can play this believe-it-or-not game, Calder thought.

Back in the house Calder led Pavel into the library. He dialled the Stock Exchange prices number and heard the grim male voice reciting the world exchange rates and then the gold and metal prices. Share prices would come next. Calder gave the phone to Pavel. He listened for a few moments, alert, his eyes bright, his shirt in his other hand. He began to smile not so much at the news he was hearing as at the way Calder had made such a ceremony of the whole thing.

"Krueger's?" Calder asked.

Pavel nodded. "But how can that happen?"

Calder just studied him.

"You think it's because of us?" Pavel put on a look of complete naïveté.

"You know bloody well what it's because of," Calder said. "It's because of you and your flaming diamonds and that bloody KGB plan."

"Secrets get out just like that?" Again that look of innocence. Pavel put the phone down.

"There's one consolation," Calder said, scratching his

face. "You've probably taken a few rich slobs out of the millionaire class today."

Pavel screwed up his face as if he didn't follow.

The phone rang now. Calder took it and heard Amberley's voice.

"Would you mind?" he said to Pavel.

Pavel went out.

Calder parked himself on the third rung of the library steps. "So who's making a bloody fortune out of all this?" he said brusquely.

"That's being gone into," Amberley said. "But we have other problems."

He told Calder of the Berlin assignment. He said it was urgent and that Calder was booked on a Lufthansa flight leaving Heathrow at half past nine.

"Tonight?" Calder held the phone tight.

"I did say it was urgent," Amberley said. He sounded full of poise.

"Why tonight?" Calder's voice was like a razor. "I'd like to get home for a few hours."

"I'm afraid that won't be possible," Amberley said drily. "I'll see you in the Balloon Bar at the Excelsior at Heathrow at eight o'clock."

Amberley hung up. Calder slammed the phone back on its rest. He felt sure the Whitehall Mafia was getting him out of the way.

He started to dial his number in Swiss Cottage. It was engaged. He put the phone down and waited.

In the drawing room Pavel sprawled in the corner of the sofa reading the *Times*. Sergeant Skeene came in with a tray. Pavel's gaze went over the paper and took in the wide hips and the strong thighs under the dark-green skirt. As she bent over to put the tray on the coffee table, the mound of her left breast was so close that Pavel could have touched it without moving. She lingered awhile, setting cups on saucers and laying out the plates of cucumber sandwiches and scones.

"Splendid," Pavel said with an eyeful of breast.

She looked at him and smiled. "I did them myself," she said, still bending over the table. "It's the cook's afternoon off."

Pavel put out his right hand to touch her upper arm. He let his fingers roam to her breast. It was large and firm and he squeezed it and stroked the nipple through the khaki shirt.

"You shouldn't do that," she said with a quick glance towards the door.

But she hardly moved, and when she did, it was a shade closer to Pavel. He could feel her heartbeats. She threw another quick look towards the door.

"I suppose," she said, "you'd like me to pour your tea?"

Pavel nodded. "Please."

Their eyes stayed on each other for a moment. She had strong blue eyes and the complexion of an open-air girl, and she had a quieter lipstick on the full mouth. She was on the heavy side, Pavel thought, and a bit thick round the neck as well as the waist.

She began to pour Pavel's tea. As she bent over the table, Pavel caught a glimpse of the back of her thighs. He stretched out his hand and touched the back of her left leg just above knee level. He felt her tremble, but she stayed where she was, slowly pouring the tea. His hand moved up the back of her leg. She put the teapot down and let him grasp her thigh. His grip tightened. Pavel felt the tension in her, and the strength. His hand was up her skirt when they heard Calder's voice from the hall. She pulled away, pressing her skirt back in place.

"You could have a drink in my room," Pavel said. He wanted her like hell now. He was imagining her violent movements as he thrust inside her.

"No," she said. "It's against regulations."

"Where, then?"

She shrugged. "They're all watchers in this dump."

"Outside then?"

"We'll see."

Calder's voice was close now. He was talking to the duty officer. She started out, turning to look at Pavel. He got up and moved after her. She was hardly very feminine, and she even walked a bit like a man, but his imagination told him she would probably give him a time to remember.

"Can't we break regulations?"

She had no chance to answer. The door opened, and Calder came in. Sergeant Skeene's eyes lost their glaze, and she went out past Calder without a word.

"Your tea's going cold," Pavel said, turning his back on Calder.

Those cotton slacks he had on were very thin. And he didn't want Calder to spot that Sergeant Skeene had given him an erection.

It was around six o'clock when Calder left the warren, driving himself in one of the official Rovers. He'd found it hard to tell Pavel that he was going and that someone else would be asking all the questions from now on.

"But why?" Pavel said. He looked genuinely upset.

"I don't make the bloody rules," Calder said.

"There are too many rules and regulations," Pavel said. He was still seeing Sergeant Skeene with only her army skirt on and nothing underneath. "Is it because I've not told you enough?" Pavel asked.

"Maybe," Calder said. "But I doubt it."

Pavel munched a cucumber sandwich. "You could stay if I say I'll talk to you and hold my tongue with anyone else?"

122

"No." Calder smiled. "It would make no difference with the bastard who tells me what to do."

Pavel passed over the plate of sandwiches. He seemed hurt. Christ, Calder thought, what goes on? We're neither of us queers or even semiqueers. But it's like a sort of parting. There was some emotion in the moment.

Pavel had said, "So you won't be showing me London and Edinburgh?"

He was on about what had kept coming up in their many talks. He'd developed this thing about the two cities.

"Why Edinburgh?" Calder had asked.

And Pavel had swished the dead elm branch he was using as a walking stick and said, "It's all granite. With a castle."

Calder couldn't make him out then. And he couldn't make him out now. As he drove out of the warren, Pavel stood at the head of the steps waving him off with a sad smile. It's dotty, Calder thought. But he waved back.

He was still thinking what a mad world it was when he drove through Ross-on-Wye a few minutes later. He would have thought it madder still if he had known that just four miles away at that very moment one of two men booking into a hotel called the Fisherman's Arms was the Russian from the Stockholm flight, Lenkov. Lenkov and his aide had canvas fishing rod holdalls. Lenkov told the redheaded receptionist with the dirty fingernails that they were Swedes taking a day or two off from business meetings in Cardiff. He was given Room 3.

Lenkov struggled out of his jacket and slacks. He was built like a wrestler with arms so thick they could have been those of a man twice his height. His pudgy hands were covered with black hair. And his head was nearly bald. He ran the cold tap into the cracked washbowl. He dipped his pink face into the water, then wiped it, and sat on the edge of the ornate old bed. He opened his week-end case and took out gun parts which he began to assemble. It took him no more than a few minutes to rig the telescopic rifle. He put it into the fisherman's holdalls.

They were walking along the pier of Terminal 2 at Heathrow. Calder's Lufthansa flight had been called for Gate 11. Calder thought Amberley seemed a bit high, yet all Amberley had drunk in the Balloon Bar were a couple of martinis, and Calder had never seen him sloshed in the ten years they had worked together. Surely the old sod couldn't be on pep pills?

"I think you'll enjoy this jaunt, Calder," Amberley said, his eyes afire under the glasses. "I like Berlin. One might say I love it. It has all the ingredients."

"The ingredients?" Calder frowned.

"It's still the hub of our conflicts. It's still an exciting enclave. It's as if Birmingham were run by the Soviets."

"So why not go yourself?" Calder said dourly.

Amberley's face broke out in the gap-toothed laugh that Calder so despised. "I have other concerns," he said. "You must accept that we do have our priorities."

"You mean this Berlin job's nothing?"

"It's vital, Calder," Amberley said. "Absolutely crucial. A senior officer of the Soviet Control Commission wanting to come over is hardly nothing." His face was flushed.

Calder had never seen him so full of *joie de vivre*. He thought, the old bugger *can't* be pissed. They were getting near Gate 11.

"I don't see why Patton couldn't have done the job," Calder said, his jaws set.

"Patton is away from Berlin just now on other work." Amberley's tone was condescending.

Just in front of them a German woman with three very

young blond children put down two heavy cases to pause for a rest. Her eyes took in Calder and Amberley. Amberley walked on. Calder saw the unspoken cry for help. He took one of the cases and got Amberley to take the other. The tired woman gasped her thanks.

They all walked on to Gate 11, where passengers queued for the baggage security check. She almost wept when she thanked them again.

Amberley took Calder aside. "Take your time on this one, Shay." The use of the Christian name was enough to shake Calder again.

"What's the bloody game?" Calder snapped. "You want me out of the way?"

"Your chip's showing, Shay." Amberley had the sharp-edged look of a man on the brink of some vast achievement.

"You want no nasty questions about who tipped off those sellers of Krueger's shares?"

"There's no evidence anyone did," Amberley said suavely.

"So who's taking over Pavel?" Calder was beginning to suspect Amberley might be behind the Krueger's share collapse.

Amberley adjusted his glasses and smiled. "I'm having a shot myself."

Calder wanted to punch his face in.

But Amberley said, "They're waiting for you, Shay."

Calder looked round to see the security checkers had cleared all the other passengers. He could see the woman going down the ramp with her kids to the waiting Boeing 727. He picked up his weekend case and went through the checkpoint.

Amberley watched him go, then strode out briskly back along the pier. He paused twice to see that Calder had not mutinied. He even went to Jayston's office to make sure that Calder had not left the Boeing. The plane took off with no change in its passenger list.

Amberley went air side to pick up his official car and set off for London. His face was aglow and he had not felt so elated for a long time.

EIGHT

Nobel Bray waited for Asher Kleinman to take his chair before he took his own place at the table. The candlelit dining room of Sir Sefton Dykes' town house in Belgravia looked even more lush than Bray could recall. Dykes had already taken his place at the head of the table.

"Do sit down, please," said Lady Dykes, still elegant in her mid-fifties.

Bray and Asher took their places. Two elderly maids came in with the first course. Lady Dykes watched them carefully.

"I'm so sorry I can't join you, Asher," she said. "But as Sefton told you, I'm chairing my charity committee tonight. And he *will* spring these surprises."

"My wife thinks she can rescue the fallouts of London," Dykes said.

"You mean dropouts, dear," she said.

She was still beautiful, Bray thought. Her dark hair was flecked with grey, and her neck had wrinkles, and her dark eyes were fighting the years. The skin of her cleavage was tanned but dry-looking. Yet he found her sexy. And he always thought how marvellous it would have been to know her during the war when all the girls thought him a hero. How she'd managed to keep her looks after thirty-odd years with Dykes was something he'd never fathom.

"I'm most disappointed, Ellie," Asher said, adjusting his skullcap. "But you have your work to do."

She forced a smile, wondering if Asher would see through the charade. Nobel would certainly know there was no charity committee that night. Sefton had always made a point of keeping her at arm's length from his business interests. And tonight was a business crisis. Their personal life was also sticky. For years now they had slept in separate rooms because Sefton feared some night activity might give him a terminal coronary.

Lady Dykes saw the maids serve the artichokes and pour the chablis. Then she went round the table to take Asher's hand in farewell. He stood up and kissed her on both cheeks. Bray would have liked to kiss her, too.

"I'm sure the girls will look after you," she said, going out behind the two elderly maids.

They fell silent for a moment or two. Asher knew the score all right. "Ellie should have a holiday with us in Israel," he said.

"Agreed," Dykes said, raising his glass. "I'm glad you should have said that, Asher, because I thought you didn't like us anymore."

Bray raised his own glass. But he was thinking, It's just like the tight-arsed bastard to use Ellie and a kind offer by Asher as a lead into the real nitty-gritty of the dinner.

"Shalom," Asher said, raising his glass.

"So what's wrong with us, Asher?" Dykes said, tucking into the artichoke.

Asher wiped his mouth with his napkin. "These are hard times, and I'm getting old."

"Moshe's not old."

The cold menace of Dykes' words even shook Bray.

"My son has nothing to do with it," Asher said.

"He's following you in the business," Dykes said.

"In time," Asher replied, savouring the artichoke. "In God's good time."

"You're prepared to lose his place on our sights list?"

Krueger's "sights" were for a chosen few. People on

128

that list were as privileged in their own way as those closest to the White House, the Kremlin, the Élysée and Buckingham Palace. They were a rare elite. And lineage had begun to count. Grandsons of some original dealers were now on the sights list. The diamond game was developing its own version of royal succession to riches.

Asher's face was full of anger. "I lose my son's place for turning down one box?"

Dykes was sucking at the last artichoke leaf. He gave a satisfied grunt and wiped his mouth.

"You'd take it out on my son?" Asher's face was cold.

"You of all our trusted clients!" Dykes said, his lips hardly moving. "You of all people turning down a box!"

Asher let the rebuke hang as he wiped his mouth. "Delicious," he said. "And I smell roast beef. I must take your cook back to Tel Aviv."

She came in with the beef trolley. A greying matron with a vast fallen bosom and flabby arms, she threw Asher a smile and reserved a sniff for Bray. Dykes fancied himself as a carver, and she knew it was a business dinner, so she went straight out again.

"You didn't say why you turned down the box," Dykes persisted while carving the beef.

Asher rested his hands on the edge of the table. He was proud of his hands, brown and strong with exquisite fingernails. And Bray knew that when Asher rested his hands like that, it was a sign of defiance. Where some men would seal their mouths and others fold their arms tight across their chests, Asher lay out his hands. Bray knew him well enough.

They had clashed when Bray had gone to Israel to find out how the Tel Aviv cutters were getting supplies of two-carat-plus gems that should have gone to Antwerp under the monopoly rules. And again when Bray was out to find the source of Russian-mined maccles that were showing up in Tel Aviv and distorting the monopoly market. Asher had given him a big cigar and put out his lovely hands on the edge of the table and told him precisely nothing.

Bray also found it hard to rid his mind of the stories that Asher had given hard cash to the gang, who had murdered some of Bray's best army friends in the days when Palestine was a British problem. But the hate had gone now. And Bray could even find merit in Asher's refusal to disclose the source of those gems that shouldn't have been in Tel Aviv.

Asher loaded his plate with sprouts and roast potatoes along with the beef.

Dykes was using a toothpick when he said suddenly, "We must know why you turned down the box, Asher."

"Or you'll take it out on my son?"

Dykes gave an eye sign to Bray, who said, "Not just Moshe. We'll stop your supplies from now on. I'll see that Levy takes your place on the list." Levy was Asher's great rival in Tel Aviv who could never overtake Asher while the gem supply status quo stayed the same.

"You'd do that to me?" Asher held a forkful of beef half an inch from his mouth.

Bray's jaw was set, and his eyes were hard. He began to hope Asher would hold out so that they could punish him. He wasn't seeing the kindly Asher who had just asked Ellie Dykes to take a rest in Israel. He was seeing one of the old backers of that murderous gang.

There was a long silence. Dykes refilled Asher's glass with the rich Corton he kept for special guests.

"All right," Asher said. "You will ruin me, but I'll take the box. I'll buy."

"Come off it," Bray snapped. "You're about as near ruin as the royal family."

"I'm carrying too much stock. I hold enough under-two-caraters to fill up the Suez Canal."

"I shouldn't use them as silt just yet," Dykes said, peering over his half lenses.

Asher threw up his hands. "Does it matter that Asher Kleinman is ruined? Okay, it doesn't matter."

Bray stifled a sneeze. "We don't wish to make you destitute, Asher. We'd not want to see you give up your villa in Herzelia. Or your house in Jerusalem. Or your New York apartment. All we want is to know why you turned the box down."

"I've just said I'll take it," Asher said coldly. "Isn't that enough?"

Bray made it clear it was far from enough. "We think you heard a rumour."

"What rumour?"

"You tell us."

Asher blew his nose. The horseradish was getting him, too. "If I didn't hear rumours in this business, I'd have to be deaf."

"A very special rumour," Dykes said, and got some meat from under his part denture.

"Asher," Bray said in a measured tone, "I mean what I say about taking you off the list. So what did you hear?"

It was another hour before Asher gave way. They were on their third brandies. He was not even slightly affected by the drink. It was when Bray said they could not only squeeze Asher out of the rich U.S. market but have his daughter and son-in-law picked up for offences under the U.S. antimonopoly laws that Asher began to open up.

Even then he was diffident. "I hear some vague story about large supplies of gem-quality stones coming on the market."

"It can't have been all that bloody vague to put you off taking your box," Bray said.

Asher gazed sadly at his Havana cigar. "It was worrying."

"And you heard they were Russian stones?" Again it

131

was Bray, and he had his pipe going so he was content to stick at Asher all night.

Asher shot a quick look at Dykes, who had begun to sag. His skull-like head drooped, and he stifled a belch and wondered if he'd overeaten and whether it would affect his heart.

Bray read Asher's thoughts. "*I'll* stay up all bloody night, Asher," he said. "Till you come clean."

Asher came out with it now. "I hear the Yukatulmaz plans to release very large supplies of gem stones for political reasons."

"And you believe it?"

"I think they'd be foolish. They're in this industry besides us. But the Russians have motives some of us will never share."

"And that's all you heard?" Bray asked.

"I was told that secret papers about the plan have been brought to the UK by a defector."

Bray blew out a great cloud of pipe smoke. "And who tipped you off?"

"I will not answer that." Asher spread his hands over the edges of the chair arms.

"You will," Bray said firmly.

Two minutes later Asher said his informant was his London broker.

"Pytchford?"

Asher nodded. Bray knew Pytchford well. He was a diamond broker with contacts at levels even Bray found hard to scale. Pytchford was an ex-SIS operator no less tough than Bray himself. He would go to the limit to protect his contact or contacts.

As Asher blew out a plume of cigar smoke, all Bray could smell was scandal and the scent of wreaths.

NINE

Galina was watching *News at Ten* when Ladybird Johnson growled and leapt off her lap. The cat had heard the caller even before the bell rang. Galina froze. Again she was expecting nobody. Olga Johnson, with whom Galina worked part time with the BBC Russian service at Bush House, had planned to come over for a chat but had phoned to say she had a cold. And surely Colin Amberley would not be fool enough to come again without calling first.

Galina was more jumpy than usual. Olga had said over the phone that she could not face the risks of being on her own as Galina was left. When Olga's salesman husband went away, his mother always stayed with Olga, whose fears of KGB agents were more acute than Galina's. But Galina had to curb a shiver. She took the Walther from the drum table and went into the hall as the bell rang again.

She didn't switch the light on and felt her way through the hall. She put her eye to the spyhole. Outside stood a squarely built man in his early forties with an open-necked shirt and a loose-fitting pale-grey jacket. He seemed tense. He looked right and left as if scared to be seen and then pressed the bell again. Galina went back to the entry phone on its cord near the living room door. "Yes?" she said. "Who is it?"

The man's reply was in Russian. "May we talk for a few moments, Galina?"

"What is it you want?" Her hand was shaking on the entry phone, and she felt the blood course up her chest and her throat felt constricted.

"I'll not keep you long."

She left the entry phone dangling on its cord. She went back in the living room and dialled 999.

"Just keep calm, madam," said a young man's voice. "We'll be with you right away."

He also told her to keep the line open.

She fancied she could hear the man trying a key in the door lock. But Ladybird Johnson sat in the hall facing the front door, and his tail didn't even thicken in alarm.

Galina threw a glance at the french windows with the tiny courtyard garden beyond. She went over and drew the curtains. She closed the door to the kitchen and still felt in danger. She went back into the hall but kept well away from the door and sat in the semidarkness on the stairs facing the door and with her elbows on her knees and both hands on the Walther. Twice she thought she could hear the man's breathing through the dangling entry phone. Ladybird Johnson came and rubbed himself against her, purring.

It seemed like hours, but it was actually four minutes before the bell rang and a voice called, "Police, ma'am."

She felt an enormous surge of relief and ran to the door. Then she paused and put her eye to the spyhole. Outside were two young policemen against a flashing blue lamp. Ten minutes later, after the police had put out a radio description of Galina's caller, a Special Branch car came with an inspector who was being turned on by Galina's smile and those small breasts under the flimsy green blouse. He was all for making the job spin out in the hope that he might come to know her better, when his prospects were blighted by another caller.

It was Amberley. It was agreed procedure that if ever Galina should run into this kind of trouble, the police would promptly inform Amberley or the duty officer in St. James's. They had found Amberley in his Marble Arch flat.

"Dear Galina," he said fussily, taking her shoulders in his hands and kissing her on the cheek. "It must have been terrible for you."

The inspector felt envious. He also thought Amberley looked like a randy old sod. He didn't like randy old sods. He thought randiness should be forbidden after the age of, say, forty.

Amberley saw his eyes raping Galina and dismissed him.

"What about this Russian chummy?" the inspector said. He was a lithe, athletic-looking man with vivid brown eyes and crisp dark hair.

Amberley weighed him up for a moment. Then he looked at Galina and thought of Pavel and said, "You can leave it to us now."

When he had gone, Amberley ran his hand through Galina's hair and said, "What an ordeal, poor thing!"

She drew away.

"One thing's for sure," he said. "You can't stay here at present. Not while Calder's away. And he's likely to be away for a few days yet."

She was still jumpy. He took her hand and squeezed it as if to give her reassurance.

"I mean why now?" she said. "Why should they try to frighten me now?"

Amberley hesitated. "I think you should know that Calder's been working on a Russian they would like to get their hands on. It's possible they have it in mind to swap you for him."

"You mean kidnap me?" It was beyond her that they should use her as a pawn after all this time—and in a period of détente.

"I think you'd better pack a few things," Amberley said.

Her green eyes were alight. "Colin," she said quietly, "I'm not coming to your apartment, and that's final."

"That's not what I have in mind," he said.

He told her now that he was on his way to the warren to continue the job Calder had begun. She could go with him. She would be safe there till Calder came back from abroad.

"I don't want to leave here," she said. "The police could put a guard on the house surely?"

"We're not in the advertising business," Amberley said. "It's not in Calder's interests to have police crawling all over the place. He's in a discreet profession."

Galina couldn't explain it, but she felt Amberley was not being frank.

Amberley ran a finger round his collar. "I could never forgive myself if anything were to happen to you, my dear. Besides, you might be able to help us with this Russian we have to cope with."

She looked puzzled.

Calder had said nothing of Pavel. But then he never would.

Galina said, "Isn't the warren full of Alsatians and Doberman pinschers?" She indicated Ladybird Johnson who was sitting on top of the TV.

"Oh, she'll be all right, don't worry," Amberley said.

"He," she corrected.

"He, then." Amberley chuckled. "They keep those guard dogs on leads."

He felt a surge of elation. He took in the small breasts and the brown skin of her cleavage and could hardly wait to get on the road. She felt his eyes going all over her. But she didn't much mind now. Maybe Olga was right. Perhaps she was less safe than she thought. And Amberley probably knew more than he could tell her. And she kept seeing the face of the man at the door and hearing his Russian voice.

"I'm supposed to be on duty at Bush House in the morning," she said.

"Never mind that," Amberley said confidently. "I'll fix things."

His eyes were full of concern.

She was feeling better. She craved an escape from the dread that man's face in the spyhole had filled her with. She leaned forward and pecked Amberley on the cheek. "Help yourself to a drink, Colin." She smiled. "I'll not be long."

She went upstairs to change.

Twenty minutes later they were on their way in Amberley's official Rover. Ladybird Johnson was in a cat basket in the back seat.

"Do you know, Colin," she said as they drove west along the M4, "I can still see that awful man's face."

"You never told me what he looked like." Amberley was casual.

She shuddered.

"He looked Caucasian," she said.

"Caucasian?"

"Some Russian men have the most sensitive faces like Nureyev," she said. "Some have faces more full of humour than you can see anywhere in the world—faces like Yuri Gagarin's."

She glanced at the speedometer. It was showing one hundred miles an hour, and Amberley was driving along the moonlit M4 like a man possessed.

"And this man?" he said.

She could see the face now as clearly as when she gazed at it through the spyhole. "He was a cold Caucasian," she said. "Hard eyes. Very blue and very cruel. His mouth was so tight he seemed to have no lips as

though he had never kissed anyone in his life, and h
must have been at least forty-five."

"That's a very good description," Amberley said, star
ing at the empty stretch of motorway ahead. Galin
thought it was a tribute to her use of English. Amberle
knew she would take that to be what he meant.

But he had chosen Helsby to call on Galina precisel
because Helsby could so easily pass for a hard-faced KGI
officer from the *mokrie dela* mob. Come to think of it
Helsby did look as if he'd never used his lips for any othe
purpose than covering his teeth.

The Rover was doing a hundred and ten miles an hou
now. But Amberley seemed not to notice. Galina wa
feeling scared again.

Amberley put down his brandy glass and said, "Well, you
two, I've got some calls to make. I'd prefer to take a strol
out there, but duty calls. So if you'll excuse me?" He go
up and went out with a nod for Pavel and a kiss on the
cheek for Galina.

When the door closed, Pavel said, "He makes me fee
uneasy."

Galina finished off her brandy. "He's a very lonel
man," she said.

Pavel put up his hands in bewilderment.

It had been a strange day for both of them. Amberle
had brought them together over morning coffee. He and
Galina had got to the warren at two in the morning, and
she had been given Bedroom 4. Only when she had gone
down to breakfast had she met Pavel. He had just finished
his breakfast and was going back to his bedroom, which
they found was next to hers. They exchanged no more
than a formal "Good morning." Pavel had a good look
at the small breasts and then turned to see the nubile
figure making for the stairs. She was wearing yellow

138

slacks, and he could make out the outline of her pants under them.

Amberley had made quite a ceremony of the introductions. "I think you two will find lots to talk about," he said, like a priest blessing a union. He'd spent the rest of the morning keeping out of their way on the pretext that he had many phone calls to make from the library. They had lunched together. Amberley kept up his avuncular role right through the meal. He said nothing about why Pavel was in the UK or why he'd brought Galina to the warren. He spoke about détente and Russian writers and the need for people to move freely across frontiers. And he spoke with a manic ecstasy, using his hands a lot. His eyes behind the glasses were never placid even when he was talking about people being nice to each other.

It was not till midafternoon that he even began to tackle Pavel about his defection and the KGB. And even then he'd been halfhearted. He gave Pavel the impression he was in no hurry to wrap things up, even when Pavel had said, "I want to sell my diamonds very soon." Amberley had told him there was plenty of time.

"Not the way Krueger's shares are going," Pavel had said sharply.

Amberley had put on that lopsided smile. "You just don't understand the market nonsense that goes on over here."

He was like a man with all the time in the world on his hands. It baffled Pavel; more, it frustrated him.

Amberley had then seen to it that Pavel and Galina were left alone. But Galina was feeling the effects of the late-night drive from London and had gone to bed for a couple of hours. When she came down, she found Pavel in the drawing room and they had talked of Russia and the effects of détente and of what might happen as a result of the Helsinki agreement. They were sitting at opposite ends of the chintz-covered sofa, and Pavel had be-

139

gun to make her laugh when Sergeant Skeene came in with the tea tray loaded with salmon sandwiches and scones.

The sergeant planted the tray on the coffee table and threw a quick critical look at Pavel. His face was a blank. The sergeant's eyes met Galina's.

"I'm sure you can pour the tea," she said to Galina.

"Thank you," Galina said.

She looked tiny beside the strong sergeant. Pavel wanted both of them very much. He was getting an erection, and he wasn't sure who was causing it. After that, it was Galina all the way.

They talked nonstop. She wanted to know all about Russia since she'd left. He wanted to know all about living in the West. Two subjects never came up. Neither Calder nor Pavel's purpose of journey was mentioned. They were on about individual liberty when Pavel had the urge to feel her small breasts. He moved closer to her on the sofa.

And then Sergeant Skeene came in to collect the tea debris. As she leaned over to pick up the tray, her tits were like mountains against Galina's molehills and her thighs in those tights were magnificent and powerful and Pavel longed to get lost in there. He shot a quick glance at Galina and caught her looking at him. And she was smiling. Her eyes were subtle and her tits so neat under the thin blouse.

Pavel thought, Who cares about bloody diamonds?

Sergeant Skeene went out with the tray, an Amazon in tights, her hips swinging. And again Pavel thought what it would be like to have them moving to and fro and not from side to side.

The moment the door closed Galina burst out laughing.

"What is it?" Pavel said.

"Nothing," Galina said.

"You found something funny."

140

She clapped a hand to her mouth, and tears were rolling from the soft green eyes.

"So what's so funny?" Pavel said. And he was beginning to smile.

"It was nothing." She laughed.

"It must have been something?"

Galina was still giggling. "It was the way you looked at each other, that's all."

Pavel looked baffled. "How do you mean?"

Galina was about to explain. But once she had caught Pavel's slightly pained expression she couldn't. She began to laugh again. Her laughter infected Pavel. He started to chuckle.

"She could devour the Red Army!" He laughed.

Galina was wiping the tears from her eyes. "With you for starters!"

She was laughing again, wiping her eyes with a hankie.

Pavel was laughing, too. But he noticed her mouth with those sharp eyeteeth.

Dinner with Amberley had been a dull interlude. But now that he'd gone they went outside. It was not only warm but still. The only sound was the urgent spluttering of wood pigeons in the tall elms. They walked down the drive towards the guardroom, talking about Russia. They were aware of the SPs with their Alsatians not far behind. But they could not see Amberley watching from an upstairs room at the warren.

Pavel pointed to a narrow path that gave a shortcut to the meadows and woods. As they set out along it, their hands brushed against each other. "So what's this about you and Calder?"

She turned in surprise. "I suppose Amberley told you about us?"

"Not much."

"It's personal anyway."

"I'll not mention it again."

141

A squirrel came into their path and sat bolt upright for a long moment eyeing them. Then it raced up an elm.

"You must be very fond of him?"

"I thought you weren't going to talk about it?"

"I was just thinking it's better to cross over for love than for greed."

He stooped to pick up a fallen horse chestnut and began to dig into the green skin with his fingernails. "Aren't you going to ask me what I mean by that?"

"I don't interfere in Calder's work," she said. "It was part of our deal, and you must see it makes sense."

"So why have they brought you here?"

"*They* haven't," she said. "Colin Amberley thought I'd be safer while Calder's away."

"And useful in finding things out from me?"

Her eyes weren't soft now. She gazed at Pavel with a kind of contempt. "It doesn't interest me at all why you're here."

Pavel put on a pained look. "I'm *that* dull?"

"No," she said easily. "I'm not specially curious, that's all."

He laughed now. "Surely you care why people choose to defect?"

She shrugged.

"You're too intelligent not to care," he said.

"Most people change sides for idealism or freedom."

"I came for wealth," he said.

"Poor you."

They were passing the rose bed on the fringe of the meadow, and she paused to sniff at a large pink one. Pavel broke off another and gave it to her.

"I'd rather you'd left it growing," she said. But she took it and held it near her nose, enjoying its fragrance.

They walked on a few yards in silence. Then Pavel said, "You mean you don't know I came over with diamonds?"

There was a light breeze, and she threw her head back to get her hair in place. Her candid amused eyes were almost laughing at him.

"I worked for the Yukatulmaz," he said. "In Siberia."

Even that news had no effect. She sniffed at the rose and gave him the first warm smile since they'd come outside. He was beginning to like her. But she must be part of the game to be with him at the warren, and he thought her lack of interest in his story was a put-on.

"I brought a fortune in diamonds," he said.

"Good," she said casually. "It makes you an instant capitalist." Her face said she didn't believe a word he was saying.

"Would you like to see them?"

She nodded. He turned his back on her and began to unzip his slacks. For a second she thought he was going to turn out to be nothing but a flasher and she glanced backwards to see that the SPs were still shadowing them. They were about thirty yards behind on the path, coming to a stop. Pavel undid the loop round his waist and brought out the pouch and did up his zip. "I'm sorry about that," he said. "Only I don't have a safe deposit in England."

His face was serious, and he looked down to check that his slacks were done up properly. Galina started to laugh. Bewildered, he looked down at his zip yet again. It only made her laugh the more. She caught his pale-blue eyes fixed on her, and she found herself liking them.

He knelt on the grass and opened the pouch and felt for a handkerchief to lay the diamonds on. He had left it in his jacket back at the house. Galina saw his problem. She untied the pale-yellow silk scarf from her neck and gave it to him. He laid it on the grass and poured out the diamonds. She knelt facing him and took one of the mid-sized stones. It was like two pyramids joined together,

143

almost perfect in form, less opaque than most of the others. She twirled it inexpertly between her fingers.

"This is a diamond?" Her manner was changed now. Her face was alight with pleasure and amazement. In that moment Pavel thought she was a woman totally without guile, but he smothered the notion as naïve.

"It's a very good one," he said.

"But it's just like Perspex," she said, still gazing at the stone and holding it with the fingers of both hands as if afraid to drop it.

Pavel smiled. "It won't break if it falls."

She was still fumbling with it when he took the stone and held her right wrist and put her finger and thumb round the stone in the experts' hold. He then showed her how to swivel the stone with her middle finger. She was entranced. She chose another stone, again ignoring the big special, which Pavel took to mean something about her nature. She got into a mess trying to swivel it, so he took her hand in a gentle grip which she found gave her pleasure and trained her middle finger to touch and turn the stone.

The light was starting to fade. The two SPs pacing with their dogs some thirty yards away had an embarrassed air.

"You should look at them under the loupe," Pavel smiled.

"The loupe?"

"Come on," he said, giving her a hand to pull her to her feet. "I'll show you."

He tied the scarf carefully round her neck, and they began to go back to the house. The two SPs smiled. It was a relief to them. They had begun to feel like peeping Toms in lover's lane.

In the drawing room Pavel was about to lay out the stones on the baize table when he had a better idea. He took an embroidered table mat from the stand under the window, put it in the middle of the sofa, and poured the stones on it. Galina sat down, and he gave her the loupe, showing her how to use it. It was a joy to touch her. She now picked out the same stone she had first chosen in the meadow. She peered at it through the loupe. Puzzled, she drew back. Pavel laughed.

"You've not got it right," he said. He knelt on the old carpet that was threadbare in places and put her hand with the loupe close to her left eye and the stone between her fingers and then manoeuvred the stone into focus. "You should be able to see right into it through the 'windows.' "

He twirled the stone till she had a good window in focus. And she was suddenly excited. "It's beautiful," she exulted. "It's really very beautiful!"

He was still holding her wrist, though there was no need.

"See how clear it is?"

There was something awesome about its depth and colour. "It's like a star at night," she said.

"No bubbles, you see," he said, enjoying her delight. "No inclusions. It's flawless."

She put the loupe on the sofa and rolled the stone in her left hand, her head on one side.

"Keep it," Pavel said. "It's yours."

Shaking her head, she put the stone back among the rest.

"Why not?" Pavel said. "You think I stole them?"

"No," she said, avoiding his gaze.

"You do," Pavel said. "You think I stole them and you disapprove."

She fixed him now with candid green eyes. "I don't know what the state did to you, Pavel, but you must have good reason for what you've done. Who am I to make judgements?"

"Then please take it."

He was leaning against the sofa near her legs. He put a

hand on her ankle. She studied him for a long moment. Then she drew her foot clear and stood up, being careful not to disturb the diamonds on the sofa.

"I'm sorry," Pavel said. "You're offended."

The smile was tolerant. "I'm tired, that's all."

Her eyes stayed on him for a while before she said, "Good night, Pavel." She went to the door without turning round once. Her mind was churning. She had an urge to help him. He seemed so lost and mixed up. And she could still feel those gentle hands. But Calder's face kept imposing itself on her mind.

"Galina!"

She turned at the door. He was still where she had left him with his hand on the cushion she'd been sitting on. "I don't know why you're here," he said. "But I'm very glad you are."

She looked very cool. "Good night, Pavel."

He could have stayed up all night with her.

In Bedroom 4 Galina looked at herself in the dressing-table mirror. In the reflected background was the antique four-poster bed which had come with the house unless some Ministry of Works official had gone mad. It didn't go at all with the contemporary built-in wardrobe and dressing table. But Ladybird Johnson found it all right. He was curled up on it fast asleep.

Galina kicked off her patent-leather shoes and took down the zip of her slacks. They'd felt tight all night. She would have to watch her diet. She sat at the dressing table and studied her face in the mirror.

No more than four feet away, behind the two-way mirror, Amberley was staring at her. He was so enraptured he didn't notice that his cigarette had burnt low. He felt the stab of pain as it burnt his fingers. He stubbed out the butt and rubbed his fingers without once taking his eyes off Galina. His eyes were glazed. He rubbed his glasses with a tissue without taking them off.

146

Suddenly a shaft of light blazed into the gallery where he was sitting forward in an armchair. It startled him for a moment. But then he saw it was coming from the next two-way mirror. He saw Pavel cross Bedroom 3, switch on a bedside lamp, and flop on the bed with a copy of *Pravda* graciously supplied by the Foreign Office. Amberley now lost interest in Bedroom 3. He even put up a hand as a shield against the light coming from it.

For in Bedroom 4 Galina had begun to unbutton her pale-green blouse. She took it off and threw it on the dressing-table chair. She put hands behind her back and released the bra, letting it slide off her arms. Amberley put his face almost against the glass as her small breasts were bared firm and with strong nipples darker in tone than his mind's eye had ever pictured. She came right up to the mirror now, evaluating her looks, supporting her breasts with her hands, though they needed no support. Amberley gazed unblinking at the mirror. He felt for his cigarette case. It was just out of reach of his fingers on the cheap plywood bench. His gaze was riveted on Galina, but he felt thwarted by the close-up now. He wanted a wider angle as she began to take down her tights.

His fingers found the cigarette case. He put a cigarette in his mouth and felt around the bench for his lighter. Again it was within inches of his searching fingers. He groped around as Galina stepped out of her tights and began to take off her pants. His hand found the lighter. He held it close to the cigarette in his mouth. But he could not bring himself to flick it for fear the flame would cost him a moment of the sight of Galina's body. He wanted her to go back a bit. She was too close to the mirror. But being a woman, she would surely want to look at herself not just from the waist up but from tip to toe? He saw her hands go down to take her pants off. Then she stepped back, and he could see the pants were pink. His hand was shaking on the lighter. She eased the pants down her legs and stepped out of them. He had the lighter poised near the cigarette. She moved back a little to see more of herself in the mirror. Amberley looked petrified. He stared through the glass at Galina's Venus mound and the auburn pubic hair. His mouth fell open. The unlit cigarette dropped on the bench which he was gripping tightly.

He was gasping.

Calder was sprawled out in Room 407 of the Berlin Hilton with the German papers all over the double bed. It was a hot night. He wore only his underpants, and he had a lager on the bedside table straight from the freezer. He also had bowls of peanuts and stuffed olives, and he reckoned it wasn't a bad life except for being away from Galina. He was reading about the way the European Common Market bureaucracy in Brussels could become corrupt. German wasn't his best foreign language. He was reading so slowly he got fed up and threw the paper aside.

He wouldn't mind trying something new like flogging exports to the Russians. It would be better than this dead end. And at least he'd be free to call Galina. Twice in the last two hours he'd felt this urge to phone her. Why the hell shouldn't she know he was in West Berlin? After all, nothing was happening. The way Rumbold had put it was typical. As they strolled along the Kurfürstendamm, Rumbold had run an elegant hand through his silver hair and said, "Our clients aren't yet quite ready, Calder."

"Clients?"

"Candidates then," Rumbold had said. He loved to play with words.

"I mean," Calder snapped, "I was told there was only one."

"Two for sure," Rumbold said, striding out. It had been his idea to take a long walk. His army training had left him with the conviction that a good walk was the best civilian equivalent of a long route march to keep up one's virility. Rumbold was an old hand. He was near pension age and had opted to leave early since they'd brought in inflation-proof pensions.

They were looking at the Berlin Wall. It always looked a bit more evil every time Calder went to Berlin.

"Christ," he said. "What a monstrosity."

"Yes indeed," Rumbold had said, scuffing the ground with one of his handmade shoes. A wall was a wall was a Wall.

They walked on a bit.

"So when will our comrades be ready?" Calder asked sharply.

"It could be any day," Rumbold said lazily, eyeing Calder up and down. "We need patience, dear chap. And Berlin's no bad place for a virile young fellow like you."

Calder wanted to tell him to piss off.

"I can't think why you're in such a hurry," Rumbold said. "Our exes aren't exactly puny."

"I'm not mad about the gravy train," Calder said.

Rumbold allowed himself a short laugh. "You sound like a puritan, Calder."

"That's me," Calder said. "It's the way I was brought up."

He couldn't take pension-hunting nits like Rumbold who had done more to bugger up Britain in the world than even its old enemies from the days of empire. He shook off Rumbold as fast as he decently could. They agreed that Rumbold would phone as soon as the clients showed up.

Now in Room 407 Calder went over to the dressing table and poured himself a strong scotch. The lager was only making him burp and doing nothing for his morale. He leaned back with his shoulders against the headboard. It had begun to worry him that the KGB might try to recover Pavel *and* settle an old score by snatching Galina. He put a call through to her. The operator came back efficiently in a couple of minutes. "Your call is ringing out, sir."

It rang for a long time.

"There seems to be no reply, sir."

"Thank you," Calder said, hanging up.

He decided he was being irrational. He'd made thirty-odd trips into Europe since they had shacked up together. She had probably gone over to Olga's with Ladybird Johnson. He thought of calling Olga Johnson's number in Windsor, but that would amount to driving coach-and-horses through the bloody rules. He sat up against the headboard and downed a couple of stuffed olives and a gulp of scotch. And he thought of Galina and murmured, "I love you, Russky."

TEN

The hired Vauxhall sped off the moment Lenkov left it. He was almost invisible in the moonlight. He wore a navy-blue windbreaker over a black crew-necked sweater. He had binoculars slung round his neck and carried a hand torch and a coil of rope. He could have been taken for a poacher.

He took the ditch in his stride despite his short legs. He squeezed through the vandal-made gap in the fence which he had seen during a daylight reconnaisance. The moonlight was piercing the beech trees. He had no need to use the torch. He knew from his studies of the ordnance maps that he had some four hundred metres of beechwoods to cross to the point where a Douglas fir tree would give him an owl's-eye view of the warren.

The ground was hard from the heat wave, and every footstep seemed to carry through the night. His arm snapped a branch and it sounded like a gunshot. He paused. He came out from the beeches to the edge of the meadow. An owl drifted across his eyeline. He began to run now, keeping low. His left foot snagged in a burrow. The pain shot through him. It was an agony to put his left foot on the ground. He was across the narrow meadow now. He went down on one knee, listening. A fox moved stealthily to the cover of the beeches.

Lenkov saw the Douglas fir rearing some thirty metres to his right. He hobbled across to it. He gazed up at the vast fir. He hurled the rope at the lowest branch, but it fell back. He tried again. The rope went over. He shook it so that more rippled over the branch. When enough was over, he made a knot in it, slipped the rest of the rope through it, and drew it tight so that the knot soared towards the branch. He climbed the rope now, hand over hand, helped by stumps in the trunk, his face twisted in pain from that ankle. He made his way up through the branches now.

He was seventy feet up before he saw what he wanted. Over the lane and the tree fringe he could see the warren. The house stood out clear in the moonlight. He had a clear view of the entrance and a long section of the main drive. He picked out two moving lights in the grounds which he took to be SP patrols, then he focussed on the house and saw one of the first-floor lights go out.

Lenkov had found a sniper's paradise.

It was Wednesday afternoon, and for the third day running Krueger's shares had taken a tumble. Nobel Bray left his evening paper with its stop-press City prices in the back of the taxi and hurried into Octahedra House. He wasn't looking forward to his meeting with Dykes, who would be in a vile mood. And he was late.

He had been kept waiting for half an hour in a small café off Stepney Broadway by an underworld middleman whom he had briefed on Pavel and his present whereabouts but not about Pavel's diamonds or his purpose of journey. Bray had also given him a photograph of Pavel taken at Heathrow without Pavel's knowledge. Saunders had passed over the print to him that morning. Bray gave the middleman two thousand pounds in cash as an advance payment. The balance of three thousand pounds was due when the hit man had done the job and Bray had proof that Pavel was a corpse.

Bray paused outside Dykes' office door and went to use the private lavatory first. His mouth tasted foul, his tongue was coated, and he felt dirty. Sweat had dried into his shirt during the long hot day, mainly spent chasing from one brokerage house to another, cornering contacts to find out who were the chief sellers of Krueger's shares.

He'd also called on Pytchford, the diamond broker.

"I don't know what the hell you're on about," Pytchford said when Bray began to ask questions.

"You told Asher some loony tale about a Russian plan to swamp the market."

"You're getting hysterical in your old age," Pytchford said. But he had to be careful. Bray had the power to have Pytchford's clients taken off the sights list.

He offered Bray a drink which he refused. "All right," Pytchford said, "I overheard the story at an embassy reception when a couple of Russian diplomats got half pissed."

"Which embassy reception?"

"The French embassy." Pytchford smiled.

Bray remembered that there had been a reception at the French embassy on Monday night.

"Which diplomats then?" he said.

Pytchford shrugged. "I only know the trade attaché, and he wasn't one of them."

"So you scare the hell out of Asher on the basis of some drunk Commies' party chat?"

"I have a responsibility to my clients," Pytchford snapped.

"You also have a responsibility to *my* company and the whole bloody business."

Pytchford nodded. "I hope that Russian pair will be proved wrong."

"So do I." Bray got up and went out. He knew Pytchford was lying.

Now, in Dykes' personal lavatory, Bray found what he was looking for among the vast hoard of patent medicines and toiletries.

The door opened, and Dykes came in.

He put on a look of surprise that Bray should be using the place, which was sacred. He went to his personal stall and started to urinate, screwing up his face in anguish as if he had drainage trouble.

"Any luck, Nobel?"

"We're getting somewhere," Bray said.

"How about Pytchford?" The old devil would have to pick on the one man Bray had had least luck with.

"He's a bloody liar."

They went out across the corridor to Dykes' office.

"Very well, Nobel. Let's hear the worst."

Nobel faced him across the huge rosewood desk which was not defiled by even a single memo. The first major selling order had come from Simon Drew, an investment expert who advised sheikhs and a few governments. "He sold heavily through four brokers on Monday morning."

"How much?" Dykes narrowed his eyes.

"Around twelve million?"

"Shares?"

"No," Bray said. "Pounds' worth."

The other big seller was one of the major Swiss banks acting on behalf of special clients. They had begun to unload Krueger's shares on Monday afternoon. "They were at it again today," Bray said.

"And they've sold what?"

"Around twenty million dollars' worth."

Dykes was drumming the edge of his desk with his fingertips so loudly it got on Bray's nerves. The day had taken it out of him.

"So who's the Swiss insider?" Dykes said.

"There isn't one," Bray said. "They were tipped off by Tony Lintas."

"Lintas!" Dykes exploded. "I gave him his first leg up in the City!"

And now he's cocked it, Bray thought.

Loyalty was never Lintas' strong suit. He was the kind who'd point an accusing finger at his grandmother in the Old Bailey.

"So what about the other sellers?" Dykes said, still angry over Lintas, whose name should have been Judas.

Bray shrugged. "They just hopped on the bandwagon."

"Some bandwagon!" Dykes spluttered. "You got to Drew and Lintas?"

Bray nodded. Both had lied to him. Drew had said he thought the state of diamond sales across the world was flashing a "sell" warning. Lintas had said there was a buzz that Krueger's planned to step up gem sales to placate dealers and cutters, and he thought the market could not digest such quantities. Both claimed to have heard rumours that some unnamed state in South America had found a big new diamondiferous zone. Other people Bray had met in the City that day had come out with the same fairy tale. Bray had phoned in and got the PR people on to it. They had been going hoarse ever since putting out denials of a story they had started themselves as a smoke screen.

"So we have Drew, Lintas, and Pytchford," Dykes said, crossing to the window and looking out at the dome of St. Paul's. "So who tipped *them* off?"

"Pytchford reckons he overheard some Russians talking," Bray said.

"Balls," Dykes said, sitting on the ledge. He pointed to his desk. "The right-hand drawer, Nobel."

Dykes was nearer the desk than Bray. But this was just another of the old man's tricks, and Bray opened the drawer. It was empty except for one memo.

"Read it."

The confidential memo reported two incidents.

In Zurich an expatriate U.S. millionaire named Bradley J. Sagar had in the last two days broken up one of Europe's finest diamond hoards and sold out to a number of dealers.

In London Lady Naphill, the twenty-eight-year-old widow of the ninth baron, who had died aged eighty-three, had called with private security guards to recover from one of the major auction houses her collection of diamonds. They were due to come up for auction in two weeks' time. But she had changed her mind on Monday and sold them to dealers and other collectors privately.

"It's getting around, Nobel!" Dykes said, tight-lipped. He ran his hand over the Epstein head of a black boy on a plinth near the window. Corporation myth had it that he was a sculpture buff. Bray knew the head was a public relations piece meant to show guests the love Dykes felt for the black who mined diamonds in Africa.

"You and I, Nobel, don't want to preside over the death of this fine company. I want a list of every single man and woman who could possibly know about this damn Russian and his bits of paper."

His face was almost hideous, and the cheeks were even more sunken than Bray had seen them.

"I'll get it out tonight," Bray said.

"They will all have to be discredited," Dykes snapped. "Or otherwise silenced."

He was running his bony hand over the patina of the black boy's head.

Nobel Bray would have liked to tell him of the deal he'd done with the middleman to rub out Pavel. But he knew that Dykes chose not to hear such details. Sir Sefton hated the trivia of big business.

Pavel winked across at Galina and raised his glass.

"To both of you," Amberley said, swirling the Armagnac.

There was nothing especially odd about such a toast. But he had gone out of his way to make the dinner memorable, even romantic. He had insisted on the silver candlesticks being brought out. He had lit the candles himself, and knowing the red plonk they kept in the warren's cellars, he'd brought his own Corton. They had got through two bottles.

"The best to both of you," Amberley repeated. His eyes were glazed behind the glasses.

He still made Pavel feel uneasy. Yet he was a marvellous host and had Pavel and Galina laughing all through the meal. Sergeant Skeene had served the first course of shrimp-stuffed avocados. She had glared at Galina and then gone off duty in a fit of jealousy, leaving the service to two WRAC corporals. Over the roast lamb Amberley had made fun of Galina's on-off vegetarianism. Pavel couldn't make him out.

Amberley had done all he could to make such an occasion of the meal. He wore a green velvet smoking jacket with a matching bow tie and kept up a flow of funny stories. He told of the Soviet diplomat who put on a wig and a fake moustache every time he went to a Chinese restaurant in the West End, and he had Galina giggling over a story about the two fattest women in the world who were trying to get into the *Guinness Book of Records* and tried to bribe the referee at the weigh-in.

Then from his place at the head of the table he'd glanced left and right, first at Pavel and then Galina, and said quite solemnly, "I think you're marvellous people, I really do."

Galina laughed, thinking he'd drunk too much. Pavel wore a faint smile.

Amberley had given him an easy time. They had met three times during the day. And on each occasion Amberley had made it clear that Pavel should take his time to come clean about the KGB. Their last session was around five o'clock, and Amberley told Pavel that the Russians were pressing for access to him.

157

"I don't wish to see them," Pavel said.

"That's what I thought." Amberley smiled. "We'll have to let them talk to you, of course. Otherwise they might raise a yell that will be heard all over the world. And that wouldn't do. But don't worry. There's lots of time."

Amberley had asked Pavel about some of the goings-on in 2 Dzerzhinsky Square. But he had pressed no questions until Pavel said he knew little about the chain of command of Department A.

"Surely you know your own masters?" Amberley rasped.

"Not all of them."

"A few will do for now."

Pavel was tight-lipped. "You haven't let me sell my diamonds yet."

"Let's have a few names and roles first," Amberley said, taking off his glasses and polishing them. "Then we might persuade someone in the Home Office to put pen to visa and let you stay to make a fortune."

Pavel then reeled off the names and duties of half a dozen key KGB officers he knew were already known to the West.

"You haven't mentioned Suslov." He said it so coldly that Pavel thought he'd seen through the whole operation.

"Oh, yes," Pavel said as if reminded. "There's Suslov. He's mostly busy on administration."

"That's the trouble," Amberley smirked.

"I'm sorry?"

"They're all so bloody busy."

Amberley drained his brandy glass now. "I have calls to make," he said and began to rise. "I don't know why you two don't make the most of such an evening." He studied Galina for a long moment. He thought she looked very young. The thin dress with the flared collar and the deep neckline reminded him of what he'd seen the night before. He gave her a peck on the cheek and went out, reminding Pavel that they would have to talk a lot in the morning.

As the door closed, Pavel said, "He's supposed to check on me, but he does nothing but stare at you!"

"He's lonely," she said. Her eyes were soft, and she'd drunk rather a lot.

Pavel said, "He would very much like you."

"The word is 'fancies.'" She smiled, her green eyes alight. "In English they say somebody 'fancies' somebody."

Pavel was about to finish off his brandy. "I fancy you," he said. His eyes never left her as he spoke. "I fancy you more than any woman I've known."

Galina picked up the half-empty bottle of Armagnac and held it near his face as if to say that was the cause of what he was saying. He put a grip on her wrist and drew her hand close to his face.

She tried to wriggle free of his grip. But he held on gently.

"Please," she said. "You're hurting."

"No, I'm not," Pavel said. "I'm not hurting you at all."

"No, you're not." She put her other hand to her mouth to smother a giggle.

Pavel had forgotten all about Sergeant Skeene. He blew out all but two of the candles, and she snuffed those out.

"Why did he ever light them?" she said, indicating the windows. The daylight was still good.

"He's a romantic," Pavel said. "Or something."

She threw him a sharp glance of reproof.

"All right, he's a civilised man."

"And very lonely," Galina said.

"And lonely."

There was a pause.

"As you are," she said.

"I'm not lonely," Pavel said with a grin. "I'm the most unlonely man in the world."

She looked at him over her brandy glass. She liked his eyes and his touch, and so much about him had started to bother her. "You're lonely," she said firmly, the glass to her mouth. " Don't argue."

He didn't know what made him suddenly want to take her to bed, but he was aware of the shape of her mouth and the way her teeth turned him on when she spoke.

They went out now. They crossed the terrace, two SP corporals with their Alsatians following. Amberley was watching from the library.

He was not the only watcher. Seventy feet up in the Douglas fir Lenkov squinted into his rifle sights. He had one of the SP corporals dead centre. He panned the rifle slightly left until Galina's head filled the sight, her nose right at the intersection of the cross. He gazed over the rifle and saw the distant figures of Pavel and Galina. Another three seconds, and he had Pavel almost in the centre of the cross. Pavel's high cheekbones were just above the horizontal sight bar.

The shot cracked the evening. Pavel grabbed Galina and pulled her to the ground. Alsatians barked, and there was a loud flapping sound as birds broke from their nests.

Lenkov nearly pressed the trigger of his own rifle, it came as such a shock. He snatched at a branch and got his balance.

Pavel lay flat on the grass with Galina with one arm over her. He could feel her shaking. He could see the spot on the nearby gravel scuffed out by the bullet, and from that he worked out an eyeline to the sniper's position. He moved his body over her as she lay face down. He was on top of her for only a moment, and then he was between her and the sniper. He began to wriggle towards the cover of an elm, urging her to keep level with him. When they got to the elm, they were both trembling. He took her hand in a tight grip and kissed her on the forehead.

"He can't hit us here," he said, though he wasn't sure.

160

They could hear the voice of one of the SP corporals speaking into his walkie-talkie. "The shot came from the Lucas estate."

Pavel hugged Galina tight into his body. He could see the SP corporal with his dog speaking into the walkie-talkie. "He's somewhere between Tyberton Road and Stockley Lane."

Galina stirred against Pavel. He could feel her soft small breasts against him. Her hands were clenched tight under his chin. He pressed closer against her, knowing it had nothing to do with protection. She pressed her hands against him, making to move away.

"Stay still," he said. "We don't want you shot."

She smiled back at him. "Or you," she said. "I wonder which one of us they'd prefer?" It made him want her more than ever.

They heard a voice come over the corporal's walkie-talkie. "We're near Stockley Lane now. Deposit one, over." The voice was from one of the SP jeeps.

It sounded reassuring, and she began to edge away from him, but Pavel shook his head and had his arm so far round her waist that his fingers were pressing into her abdomen. He took in the scent of her and liked the feel of her breasts against him. He didn't think it right to move just yet.

Lenkov had come down almost as far as the lowest branch of the Douglas fir when he heard footsteps below. He froze among the foliage. He took off the safety catch of the rifle. Coming through the trees was one of the SP corporals with an Alsatian on a lead. The Alsatian was pulling hard, and the corporal murmured, "Easy, Mick. Easy." He had a pistol in his right hand.

Lenkov noticed the rope now. The thing was still dangling where he'd left it. And the corporal was heading straight for it. He could hardly miss seeing it.

161

Lenkov lifted the rifle and began to aim. He got the corporal almost in his sights but then changed his mind. It was one thing to shoot a defector. He had no brief to kill British corporals. He lowered the rifle and resigned himself to capture.

But there was suddenly the sound of someone running through the woods. A young man with long brown hair that grew down over the shoulders of his suede jacket ran into view. His face was terror-stricken, and he was trailing a rifle with a telescopic sight. He and the corporal saw each other almost in the same split second. The corporal challenged him to stop and let the dog loose. The young man fired in panic without having a chance to sight the rifle as the dog leapt at him. The bullet struck, and the dog twisted and howled in midair, but the force of its leap carried it into the young man. The young man was bowled over. Blood was coating the dog's ruff and staining the young man's suede jacket, but the dog was holding onto his arm.

The corporal stood over the young man. His face was full of contempt. "Right, Mick!" he commanded the dog. "Leave him! Leave!"

The dog let go. It sat obediently upright, blood pulsing from the neck wound and running down its front legs.

"On your feet, you bastard!"

The young man grimaced in pain as he eased himself on to an elbow. The corporal could see the dog bleeding just beyond him.

"You bastard!" he said, suddenly putting out a hand to grab the young man. The man grabbed the rifle and, using one hand, fired at the corporal. He hit him in the stomach. The impact sent the corporal reeling into the stubble under the tree from which Lenkov was watching.

The young man scrambled to his feet. His eyes were wild, and he was gasping for breath. The dog had another go at him, but it was weak from loss of blood, and he

162

fended it off. He turned the rifle in his hands and held the end of the barrel and began to swing the rifle like a club at the dog's head. But the swing lost its impetus as the bullet smashed through his brain.

The SP sergeant lowered his pistol and called into his walkie-talkie. "Depot Four here. . . ."

"Loud and clear, Depot Four."

"Corporal Kennedy's copped a bullet. I need a quack and an ambulance. I'm thirty yards in the Lucas estate from Stockley Lane."

"Understand, Depot One."

He stooped to comfort Kennedy, who was twitching in dazed agony in the stubble. Both Kennedy and the sergeant were in their summer rig of shirts and slacks without tunics or battle dress blouses, and Kennedy was shivering. The sergeant went over to the young man's body and peeled off the bloodstained suede jacket to put over the corporal. He took off his own shirt and made a pillow of it which he put under the man's head. "Keep still, Jimmy. You'll be all right."

Kennedy passed out, but his heart was going and his pulse not bad.

The sergeant glanced at the dog. It was still in that upright "sit" position. Blood ran down its right flank. Its fur was matted red and the moss near its front paws was stained with its blood.

"Lie down, Mick!" the big sergeant said, tears in his eyes. "Lie!"

The Alsatian was finding it hard to keep its eyes open.

"Lie, for Christ's sake!" the sergeant commanded.

The Alsatian lowered itself into the red-stained moss. Its eyes opened and took in Kennedy's inert body and the sergeant. "You big daft bugger!" the sergeant said affectionately. He went over to the dog now. He checked the deep wound searing the neck. He said to the walkie-talkie, "Depot Four here. . . ."

"Loud and clear, Depot Four."

"I suppose you couldn't get a vet here as well. Mick's copped a bad one."

"Doing all we can, Depot Four."

The sergeant knelt by the dog and gently stroked its head with an enormous hand. "Well, you are a daft bugger, aren't you? Copping one like that?" The dog's tongue was lolling, and it was panting. Its eyes were on him now like great opals. He ran a gentle hand over its muzzle. "Trust you, Mick," he said. "Trust you to cop one." Tears were running down his cheeks. The dog's eyes kept closing, but it barked once, very quietly. It was more a cough.

It seemed like an hour, but it was less than ten minutes before the doctor and ambulance got there. They were putting Kennedy in the ambulance when the vet arrived in a Jaguar. He put the needle into Mick's front left leg to kill the pain. The dog lifted one of its enormous paws slightly, and those opal eyes glazed over. The big sergeant carried it to the vet's car. He laid the dog gently on the rubber sheet the vet had spread over the back seats, and the dog licked his hand. The sergeant's nostrils flared as he tried to hold back tears. His shirt was still back there in the bracken, and his bare chest was smeared with the Alsatian's blood. The dog gazed at him for a long moment; then its head flopped over the edge of the seat. The vet leaned into the car. He turned round and said, "I'm sorry, Sergeant. He's had it."

The big sergeant turned away back to the wood.

In the clearing where it had all happened SP corporals were swarming. The young man's body lay where the sergeant had rolled it in taking off the jacket. "Cover his bloody face with something," the sergeant told a corporal SP. "Before I kick it in."

There wasn't much of the young man's face left anyway.

164

Another corporal SP began to climb the rope Lenkov had left hanging from the Douglas fir. Lenkov had climbed higher into the tree now. He froze as he saw the corporal coming hand over hand up the rope.

"What the hell are you doing?" the sergeant called to the corporal.

"I was going to get it down," the corporal said.

"Leave it," the Sergeant said, putting his shirt back on. "The civil police will want to look at it." In the distance they could hear the wails of police sirens.

Lenkov's ankle was giving him hell. He was in for a long hard night whether they found him up there or not.

Pavel lay on his bed going over the night's events. He could still feel Galina's body against his out there under the elm. But he was still unsure why she should have come to the warren when Calder left and whether she was no more than a come-on to break his story. All he knew was that he wanted her. And they couldn't have been given adjoining bedrooms in such a big place for nothing.

And that sniper's shot still puzzled him. It could have been a clever miss arranged by the KGB to make his defection seem authentic. It would have been an inefficient miss either by a section of the KGB kept in ignorance of his mission—and Suslov had warned of this risk—or by a killer hired by diamond interests.

Amberley had been solicitous but not forthcoming. He'd been called by the police to check the young man's body in the mortuary at Ross-on-Wye. It meant nothing to him, and it would have meant no more to anyone who knew him. His face was like a hunk of meat in an abattoir. Amberley had come back pale and withdrawn, but he'd shown special concern for Galina, saying it proved he was right to bring her down to the warren.

165

"I don't see what's safe about it," Pavel had snapped. "That bullet missed by inches."

"It would be easier for them in London," Amberley said.

Pavel found him weird. Stranger even than some he knew in Department A in Dzerzhinsky Square.

In Bedroom 3 now, Pavel turned his eyes off the ceiling and glanced at the mirror. He felt sure it must be a two-way job. And ever since he'd come to the warren, his every action in his bedroom had been geared to his suspicion. He had hurled *Pravda* across the room as if in disgust at something he'd just read. He had read the *Times* and *Time* magazine with hints of pleasure and approval. He had spread out his diamonds on the bed like some greedy miser checking his hoard. He would put the loupe to his eye, put down a valuation on each stone, and then tote up the total on a piece of paper on the dressing table against the mirror.

He let his mind dwell on two things now—that mirror and Galina. There was still work to do. He couldn't just go on shaking over that sniper's bullet that had kicked up the gravel within two metres of him. He gave the mirror no more than a casual glance. He lay back naked on the bed and closed his eyes and let his mind fill with images of Galina with only her pants on and knee-high leather boots.

Beyond the mirror Amberley stared as Pavel got his erection. Pavel got off the bed and went over to the wall between his bedroom and Galina's. He put an ear to it as if to eavesdrop on what she was doing. He thought this might not look too convincing because the walls, being so old, were also very thick. He couldn't hear a thing, of course, but he might convey that he hoped to.

Amberley watched Pavel with his ear to the wall, then peered at the two-way mirror serving Galina's room. It was in darkness. He'd seen nothing there for twenty minutes. Galina had gone to her room, frayed by the shooting incident, and had not lingered. Amberley had watched her take her clothes off and put on a pale-blue nightie and apply her night cream at the dressing table. Her small dark nipples under the thin nightie had riveted him. But then she had gone straight to bed and put out the light.

Pavel moved from the wall with his back to the mirror. He'd lost his damned erection, and he had to get it back. It didn't take him long. He went into the bathroom and made himself think of Galina with her legs wide open under the elm tree. Thus restored, he went into the bedroom and crossed to the mirror as if in self-admiration. It was taking him all his time to keep his penis erect, and when he felt the blood ebbing away, he turned and put on the knee-length dressing gown provided by the Foreign Office. He went out of the room now.

The bedside light went on in Galina's room. She rose to open the door and saw Pavel in the corridor beyond. Amberley began to shake. Galina kept herself behind the door.

"I want to talk to you," Pavel said.

"No, Pavel," she said. "Tomorrow."

"I must talk now."

She shook her head. "No, Pavel."

He looked beaten.

"All right," she said. "If you must."

He came into the room behind her. He saw her trim body under the nightie as she pulled on a towel dressing gown.

"It's no use, Pavel," she said, tying the dressing-gown belt round her. "I'll talk to you, nothing else."

"That's all I want to do," he said, sitting on the edge of the double bed across from her.

Her eyes were coming alive with amused disbelief.

"Really," he said, his face aglow. "I just want to talk."

"Talk then," she said, tucking her hands into the dressing-gown pockets.

He switched on the other bedside lamp and cast a swift look at the mirror.

"They wouldn't always shoot at us," he said.

"Whatever are you talking about, Pavel?"

He put a hand across the bed and tried to take hers. But she pulled away.

"You're not married to Calder?"

"No."

"You're free."

"I think that shot's frightened you into silly thoughts." She smiled.

He could see the brown circle of her left nipple under the gown and the nightie.

"You know what I'd like?" he said. "More than anything in the world?"

"I think you should go back to your room," she said.

"I'd like to sell my diamonds very soon," he said, "before they're worthless bits of stone. And then buy somewhere to grow vegetables and give you two children and not have any bureaucrats to fight."

She was relaxing a bit. She shifted on the far edge of the bed. He could see the whole of her left breast now.

Her face was warm, and her cheeks were flushed. "You'll never escape from bureaucrats wherever you run to," she said, and her voice was almost caressing. "They have the highest birthrate in the world."

Pavel laughed. He didn't really care where or how bureaucrats were spawned. He'd made his point, and whoever was behind the mirror must have taken it. They must believe now that all he'd said about the plan to swamp the world market with diamonds was true. He was feeling pleased with himself, and he didn't look at the mirror once.

"I'll see you at breakfast," Galina said, sitting on the edge of the bed.

He gazed at her across the bed. He was aware of that bloody mirror, which Galina took to be just another bit of glass one saw oneself in. He wanted her and thought she might respond. And that was something he wouldn't want anyone to see. He switched off the bedside light on his side and then crawled over the bed to turn off the other. In the darkness he felt for her, but she had moved away.

"Please, Pavel," he heard her say. "Please leave me now."

He couldn't even see her, though a sliver of moonlight was piercing the curtains. It was enough to make him feel that whoever was behind the mirror might be able to see them, however dimly.

"I'm sorry, Galina," Pavel said. "I really am sorry." He went out.

She sank back on the bed, gazing into the darkness. The trouble was that she had wanted him and wanted him now. In the gallery Amberley had his fists clenched on the bench. He saw Pavel go back to his room, and then all was darkness in both rooms.

ELEVEN

It was just after eight and the sun was already strong when Amberley came out to find Pavel on the terrace. Pavel had intercepted a corporal with the morning papers. He was giving them the once-over for stories about the diamond scare and the tumble in Krueger's share prices. Most of the press carried quotes from Krueger's spokesman about "wild unfounded rumours of a major diamond find in South America." One City page pundit said that in spite of Krueger's denials there had been a plan to put out more gemstones. He thought this plan had been dropped.

Pavel was suddenly aware of Amberley, who took in Pavel's concern for what the papers had to say. There was not even a hint of his arrival or the KGB plot. Amberley's face was solemn. "I really can't imagine what's got into her," he said.

Pavel looked at him sharply.

"Galina's decided to leave right away."

She had been down for an early breakfast. Amberley had just met her on the stairs, and she told him she was going up to pack and asked for a car to get her back to London. He had warned her of the risk. She would be an easy target in London.

"I seem to be a bull's-eye here, Colin," she had said. He thought she had looked more brooding than scared. He had tried to dissuade her, but she had been adamant.

All this he told Pavel now. "I can do no more to make

her change her mind," he said, his eyes cautious. "But I think you can."

Pavel's mind raced. He worked out the pros and cons of Galina's going in *his* interest. She would be one more person on the outside to know of his presence with diamonds. He would want that. But she was circumspect. He knew little or nothing about her relationship with Calder even now. If she stayed, he could still use his meetings with her, which he was convinced were not only bugged but quite likely watched through two-way mirrors. In what would seem to the watchers very private moments between him and Galina he could give her enough hints of the KGB plot to corroborate what he had told Calder and Amberley officially.

There was something else. He wanted to get her into bed. And he fancied she was on the verge of saying yes. He thought of Suslov and remembered the briefing. He thought of Galina and remembered the feel of those small breasts against him, and his mind had her just watching him with cool green eyes as he took all her clothes off.

"Why not pop up and see if you can't make her see it's safer for her to stay here?"

Pavel shrugged. "Why should I be able to influence her?"

"You're fellow Russians."

Pavel's shrug was cover for a churning brain.

"I also think she feels for you."

"You mean pity?"

"It could be no more than that," Amberley said. He tried to be casual, but it meant a lot to him that Pavel might prove able to get Galina to change her mind.

Pavel leaned on the stone parapet, idly turning over the pages of the last paper. Then he said, "All right. I'll see what I can do." With a sharp glance at Amberley he gave the paper to the corporal, who had heard all this with a blank look on his vast face.

As Pavel went off, Amberley took the papers. He began to scan them as Pavel had done. He took in the Krueger's share price stories. But what he was really after was some report of the sniper who'd had half his head blown off and the SP corporal who had died in the ambulance on the way to hospital. He felt some relief that the papers weren't on to it yet.

Pavel knocked once on Galina's door.

"Come in," she said, folding a dress and stacking it neatly into her case. It came as a surprise to see Pavel. She had thought Amberley had come back to give her more chat about her safety.

"I hear you're leaving," he said.

"I was going to tell you when I got downstairs," she said, without looking at him. Her green shirt was on the bed with a pair of jeans. But she left them and began to pack her well-pressed black slacks.

"Where's Ladybird Johnson?" Pavel asked, playing it easy.

"Getting fat in the kitchen, I should think," she said. "They're ruining his figure down there."

"Why are you going?" he said, moving closer.

She still did not look at him.

"I suppose it's no business of mine?" He was so close now he could have reached out and put his hands on her waist as she stooped over the bed packing.

"I'm going," she said, "because I'm free to make up my own mind." She made herself busy with a pair of shoes she put into the case.

"You think you'll be safe?" It was almost a whisper. He longed to take hold of her.

"I've been safe in London for three years," she said.

She still kept her back to him.

"They might try to get me back for you."

"You've been talking to Colin," she said, tucking her toilet bag into the case.

"He's not the only one who thinks you should stay." He let some warmth come through his voice now.

"I know that only too well, Pavel," she said.

"I'm sorry?" It was her tone that made him pause.

"You want me to stay for the wrong reasons."

He was so close now she could feel his breath on her neck. And he felt she was more afraid of her own drives than of the risk of another sniping attempt at the warren. She still would not even look at him. He eased round her and handed her the green shirt to pack.

"I'm wearing that for the trip," she said, keeping her eyes off him. So he gave her the jeans.

"And those."

He bent almost double over the bed and tried to peer up at her face.

"It's no use, Pavel. I'm going."

She made a thing of rearranging her clothes in the case. She would not look at him. But she did not move away.

"I'd like you to stay, please," he said. She was pressing the clothes tight into the case.

He stroked her stiff right arm with a finger. He felt her shiver.

For a while she didn't move, just letting him run his finger up and down her forearm. "I know you're lonely, Pavel. I like you very much. But you must go somewhere else."

The thought flashed through Pavel's mind that she might go and he would find himself with Sergeant Skeene. It seemed like going from ballet to kung fu.

"Why won't you look at me?" Pavel said quietly. He perched himself on the edge of the bed and leaned over her case to put his face in her eyeline. She stifled a laugh. He put a hand up to her mouth and ran a finger over her lower lip, trying to curl it back.

"Please, Pavel," she said.

He touched her thigh with his left hand. He felt the

173

slight tremble run through her. She was looking at him now. Her eyes were aglow with warmth, and she ran her tongue round her mouth. Pavel felt her thigh, taut and firm under the black nylon tights.

"It's no good, Pavel," she said, without taking his hand off her and making no move away from him. "We really mustn't."

He knew she would not move away from him now. He saw her eyes close as she leaned over the case, and he felt sure she was almost there now. He lay still, his elbow on her case, his hand squeezing her thigh. She glanced round and saw the mirror. He squeezed her thigh, and she let out a sigh, closing her eyes. Her mouth fell half open, and her hands were shaking on top of the packed clothes.

Quite suddenly he let her go. He took his hand off her and sat bolt upright on the edge of the bed, smiling. The change in his mood took her by surprise. She couldn't make it out.

"So you'll stay?" he said.

The moment had gone. She shook her head. "I must go, Pavel. I really can't stay here."

She studied him now, her eyes warm for him, her head shaking a little. "I'll see you downstairs," she said firmly now. "I have to change." She indicated the green shirt and the jeans on the bed.

Pavel's eyes never left her as he stood up. He made no move towards the door.

"Pavel."

He still made no move.

Galina put her hands behind her neck to unclip the zipper of her dress. "I told you I have to change," she said. She was having trouble undoing the hook.

"Let me."

He moved near her, and she hesitated and then smiled and turned round so that he could attend to the zipper.

She thought he might try to take it right down, but he just unclipped the thing and left it at that.

"Thank you, I'll see you downstairs." She went over to the dressing table. She could see his reflection.

She had her left hand to the zipper behind her back when Pavel moved quickly towards her. For a terrible moment she thought he was about to lose control. But he said, "No, Galina!" and instead of grabbing her, he eased her gently aside. He picked up the dressing table stool and flailed it at the mirror. The glass shattered. Galina clapped a hand to her mouth in horror as she saw Amberley's face.

He reeled back, raising an arm to protect his face. But the glass smashed his spectacles, and two splinters tore big gashes in his face. The blood gushed from under his left eye. He stumbled out of view, still holding up his arm to hide his bloodied face.

Galina sat on the bed shaking. She felt sick and near to tears. Pavel went to comfort her, but she shook her head. "I'll be all right," she said. "In just a moment or two I'll be all right."

She closed her eyes and could still see Amberley's shocked features. His face was grotesque and lopsided, with one eye staring and the other a red mess from the flying glass.

"Just stay where you are," Pavel said. "I'll not be a second or two."

She sat there gazing at the shattered mirror and the dimly lit gallery beyond. "Leave the door open, Pavel," she said, shuddering.

He came back with a brandy and a bottle of pills. She drank the brandy, and he poured out a couple of pale-blue tablets. "Tranquillisers," he said.

Galina shook her head. "This will do," she said. She was still shaking. She heard a click and looked round in

175

time to see Pavel taking his hand off her handbag. She studied him a moment and he smiled.

Opening the bag, she saw a pill bottle which was not hers. She opened it and tipped out a diamond. It was the medium-sized clear-white she'd first picked out.

"I'd like you to have it," Pavel said.

It took her some moments to make up her mind as she rolled the gem around her hand and peered at it in the way Pavel had taught her to check a diamond. Then she put it on the bed. "I couldn't, Pavel," she said. "I couldn't take it, much as I want to."

He looked disappointed. What was bothering him was that he was not playing a game this time. He really wanted her to have it. And he wanted to kiss her and keep on kissing her till they neither of them had any breath left.

His bounce had gone, and he knew this was nothing to do with any feeling he'd known before—either at Moscow University or in the past day or two for Sergeant Skeene. He was in love with Galina.

She pushed the diamond near him on the bed. When she got up, she was not shaking anymore. But her face was flushed, and her eyes glistened with tears. She put the green shirt and jeans in the case, shut the lid, and tried to clip the zipper back on her dress. "I'm not going to change." She smiled. "I'm going as I am. Now. I can't spend any more time here."

He saw she was having difficulty with the hook. He did it up for her. His face was full of sadness. "I don't even know where I can get in touch with you."

"You think that would be wise?"

He shrugged.

She picked up her case, but Pavel took it from her to carry down. They had got to the door when she said, "One moment." She went back to the bed, opened her bag, took out a piece off paper, and wrote something on it.

176

When she gave it to him, he saw she had written her address and telephone number. "Only if you're in trouble," she said.

If only she knew it, he was in serious trouble now. He was in love with her.

They paused at the door as he stood aside to let her go first. "Pavel, wasn't that awful!" she said. "Poor Colin! Poor, poor Colin!"

"Poor Colin?" Pavel said incredulously.

"He must feel awful about it," she said.

Pavel just stood there gazing at her. He had lost all interest in his mission. There was no place in his mind for diamonds. He was trying to work out why he'd had to come so far from home to find a Russian he loved. She even seemed able to read his mind. She put her face up to his and kissed him on the cheek. He put up a hand to stroke her face.

"I must go now, Pavel," she said.

He went down with her to the hall. And he was beginning to feel the greatest sense of loss in his life.

Coming off the Lufthansa Boeing at Heathrow, Calder saw Meade waiting and knew there was more to his recall than routine. Aglow with bonhomie, Meade beamed. "You're ten minutes early." He threw a look at Calder's zip bag. "If you're not smuggling hash or too much duty-free plonk, I suggest we skip the formalities."

They moved away from the rest of the passengers. Meade's Mercedes was near the terminal offices.

"We'll have a jar on the way into town," Meade said.

Calder was weighing him up.

Alert to the stare, Meade said easily, "I trust Berlin wasn't too exhausting." It was meant as mild sarcasm.

Calder threw his bag into the back seat and said, "I'm exhausted from bloody boredom waiting for spooks."

"I trust you're not referring to our friends in the CIA," Meade chuckled, closing the driver's door.

Calder still had him under scrutiny, trying to work out what lay behind the joky pose. "I've loafed around an expensive city in great style at the taxpayers' expense," Calder started.

"Don't let that crucify you." Meade chuckled, driving off. "The taxpayers are never likely to know."

Calder put his back against the door and watched Meade. Not only had Berlin been a bloody waste of time with Rumbold boring the arse off him, but he still felt bitter that they had got him out of the way because of his anger about the leak involving Pavel and the diamonds. Someone up there in Whitehall had been looking after his own. And Calder was still bitter.

They were coming out of Heathrow by a security exit when Calder put the question that had been on his mind since he'd first set eyes on Meade. "Did we find who put the shits up those holders of Krueger's shares?"

Meade didn't even blink. "It could have been coincidence," he said. "Krueger's claim there was a buzz about new diamond finds in South America."

"I saw that guff in the German papers."

"Then you know as much as I do."

There was the sound of bottles rattling in the back.

"What have you got there?" Meade grinned. "A distillery?"

"Two scotches and two bottles of Armagnac."

He chuckled. "You'll get us a bad name with customs."

Calder delved into the back seat and brought out a bottle of scotch and said, "This is for you."

"I couldn't possibly accept smuggled booze." Meade laughed. "Tuck it in the seat pocket, will you? And thanks."

All the way into London Meade kept up the light pater. Calder saw it as evasion. "So what the bloody hell's going on?" he asked.

Meade chose to tell funny stories about the CIA and the KGB and the way prostitutes were forming a union and trying to get affiliated to the Trades Union Congress. Calder kept giving him the chance to open up about the recall from Berlin.

He got nowhere until Meade took the Mercedes off the Cromwell Road and Calder realised they were not going back to the office. He threw an enquiring look at Meade, who caught it from the corner of his eye.

"I'm taking you home," Meade said tersely.

"You don't usually act as chauffeur."

There was a long silence. Presently Meade said, "Shay, I want you to listen carefully."

The use of his Christian name warned Calder that something nasty was up.

"Let me say at once that Galina is fine."

"Eh?"

Calder glared at Meade, and his stomach did a somersault. His mind wheeled with images of Galina's Mini crushed under a double-decker bus, of her being mugged on her way back from Bush House, and fighting off some KGB thug who hadn't yet heard of détente.

Meade's eyes took in Calder's mood.

"Don't panic, Calder. It's nothing serious."

Calder said, "If it's not serious, why you as bloody chauffeur?"

"I just want to advise you to keep your head and your temper."

"What's happened to Galina?" His tone was piercing.

"She's fine and well and waiting for you at home."

When they reached Calder's house, Meade would not go in with him. "Call me at home whenever you like," he said. "I don't mind at what hour. But call me before you call anyone else."

As he went up the small path, Calder was full of dread. Meade had made such a point about Galina being all right that he felt sure the opposite must be true. It even ran through his mind that she had found a lump on her breast and they had diagnosed cancer and that this was the reason for his sudden recall. He fumbled in his pocket and couldn't find the damn key. He was rummaging through his jacket pockets when the door opened. She had seen him through the spyhole.

She was wearing only a towelling bathrobe. Meade had phoned her from Heathrow to say that Calder's flight had landed and he was on the passenger list. She had showered, and she was ready. She put her arms round him and kissed him so hard he dropped his case on the concrete.

"You're all right?" he mumbled through her hair. "You *are* all right?"

He pressed her close against him, and she said, "Of course I'm all right."

"So what happened?"

Her eyes were afire, and she thrust into him kissing him on the doorstep.

"We're on view," he said through her hair, nuzzling her neck.

"I don't care if it's Piccadilly Circus." She was so tense and full of urge he knew this was no normal welcome. Galina was never sparing with her love, but she had never gone overboard quite like this before.

"What's wrong, love?" he said, and felt her hand unzip his slacks.

She looked up at him and said, "We've got caviare for starters, then steak and chips."

"Galina!" He tried to look stern. But her hand was inside his pants.

He stooped to pick up the case, and she went down with him. "You're breaking my wrist." She laughed. The bathrobe was loose. He could see the small breasts and down to her navel. They went inside and closed the door.

"Let's go to bed, Calder," she said.

He shook his head. His mind was still churning. What the hell had been going on? But his eyes met hers, and that bloody bathrobe was *very* loose.

"Calder," she said with a calm smile, untying the bathrobe belt. "I hope you're not going to be bloody-minded."

He moved to her and slid off her bathrobe and put his hand to her, and they went down on the carpet. They were in too much of a hurry to go upstairs.

Three hours had passed since Calder's return before Galina could bring herself to tell what had happened at the warren. When they finally got up off the carpet, she had gone to the bathroom. He followed, and they made love again in the shower. Now they sat facing each other across the dining table, and Calder's face was black with fury. They had drunk a bottle of good burgundy and they were on the Armagnac when Galina yielded to Calder's hundredth query about what had been going on.

He gulped down his Armagnac and refilled the glass. The news left him dumbstruck. When he found his tongue, he said, "So what the fucking hell was Pavel doing in your bedroom anyway?"

His lower lip had come out over the upper. His grey eyes gave off a tired sparkle, and his fists were clenched.

"I just told you," she said. "He was asking me to stay on."

"I bet he was."

"For my own safety."

"Balls!"

She put a hand across the table to cover his. He pulled away.

"He was out to lay you!"

"He's lonely," she said coolly. "He was very lost."

"And he found a cosy bosom to lean on!"

"He didn't lean on mine," Galina said.

There was a pause.

"Did he ask to come in your room? Or did he just barge in?"

She said nothing. Her mouth was tight, and she felt like throwing her glass at Calder.

"I said, did he ask?"

"He asked," she said as if wearily.

"And you said yes?"

"Don't be contemptible!"

Galina got up and started out. She was wearing only her pants and knew that a huffy exit from a dinner table dressed like that was hardly the way to make Calder angry. It was more likely to make him randy. He moved from the table after her, wearing only his briefs. It had been that sort of dinner.

"I'm sorry," he said, waylaying her at the door.

She put on a look she hoped would convey annoyance.

"I'm not blaming you, darling."

"Thank you," she said with sarcasm.

He put his hands under her arms and took hold of her breasts.

She stayed statuesque, as if just putting up with it.

"And it's not that bugger Pavel's guts I should hate. It's Amberley's."

He kept thinking of the smug old sod peering boggle-eyed at Galina as she undressed in her room.

"How long were you there at the warren?" he asked.

"Two days and nights." Her body was as quiet as her voice. She hardly moved as Calder held her close from behind.

"I bet the dirty old sod was behind there every time you took your clothes off."

"Possibly." She shrugged.

182

"Possibly?" he said. "What do you mean—possibly? You sound as if you didn't mind."

She pulled his hands off her breasts and turned to face him. "I mean he must be an unhappy man."

"Unhappy?" Calder's voice rose. "He was bloody drooling back there!"

"Anyway it's all over," she said, kissing him.

For some moments he just gazed at her. He began to shake his head. He took her face in his hands and put a tender kiss on her mouth, then he went upstairs. She followed. Calder dressed and kissed her again before going out of the bedroom.

"Calder!" There was a hint of alarm in her voice.

She heard the front door slam. She ran downstairs and went out to try to stop him. She was still wearing only her pants, and an elderly couple and a young boy stared in wonder. But there was no sign of Calder.

Back in the hall she took the phone and dialled. When Amberley came on, she said, "Colin, I think you should know Calder's on his way over to you. At least I think he is. He knows about what happened, and he's in a rage."

"Thank you," he said quietly. "And Galina, I'm very sorry."

"I'm sorry for you, Colin."

She had no further words for him and hung up.

With an eyepatch over his left eye, adhesive bandage across his face, and one hand heavily bandaged he was in no state to defend himself. He put some daphne into the fish tanks and watched the little fleas being swallowed by the black mollies and swordtails. The Siamese fighter swam in among the rest, tough and purposeful.

It would take Calder at least quarter of an hour to reach the flat, but Amberley pulled on his short raincoat with its fur collar and went out. The gardens in the square were locked, so he walked right round until he was on the opposite side of the square with a view through the trees of the entrance to his block. He patrolled up and down so that to any casual watcher he would look like an elderly resident out for a stroll before turning in. He saw Calder's ageing Triumph turn into the square.

Calder leapt out, slamming the door and leaving the car double-parked. He pressed the left button marked P for penthouse. He turned left out of the lift and along the rich grey carpet that ran down the middle of the wood block floor. He pressed the bell at a door marked P2. He gave it only a few seconds before pressing again. Then he put his face close to the mahogany door and called, "Colin!" His face was very pale, and he was glaring at the door. He felt the blood rising in him.

"Colin! Open the door, you bastard!"

For a moment or two he stood staring at the door. He moved back and barged his shoulder against it. The door held. He threw himself at it again, and the lock gave way with a loud crack. He prowled into the elegant flat, saying, "Come out, Colin! Come out, you bastard!" He searched the drawing room with its exquisite Georgian pieces. He checked the bedrooms, flinging open wardrobe doors and going down on his knees to peer under the ornate gilded bed with its lace drapes in the main bedroom. He flung open the lavatory door and then ripped the shower curtain aside in the bathroom. He caught a glimpse of his own bitter face in the wall mirror.

He paused, breathing hard. His eyes fell on a large red jar of bath salts. He hurled it against the mirror and glass flew as the jar and the mirror shattered. He went back into the main bedroom and picked up a metal-based bedside lamp. He threw off the shade and aimed the lamp at the dressing-table mirror. It splintered, and slivers of glass fell away. The mirror on the inside of the wardrobe door was next. Calder smashed it with a marble ashtray which he threw from right across the room with such accuracy that it hit the mirror dead centre.

In the drawing room Calder took up one off Amberley's most prized pieces, a mid-nineteenth-century bronze of a young nude with small breasts, and flung it with all his might against the rare Louis XVI mirror in its intricately worked gilt frame. The mirror exploded into fragments.

Calder's grey eyes blazed and roved the place for more mirrors to smash. His lips had parted, and he was breathing heavily through gritted teeth. He retrieved the nude and wrecked an *haute époque* mirror in the hall with it, leaving only small jagged fragments of glass protruding from the lines of the frame. Again he picked up the bronze. He found a vanity mirror on the dressing table in the small bedroom.

He laid it horizontally on the dressing table and then hammered it to bits with the figure. He opened the wardrobe door and found a full-length mirror on the inside. He hit it with the bronze, splitting it diagonally. He prowled with the bronze in his right hand, seeking more mirrors. He remembered there was one on the lavatory wall above the washbasin.

He was crossing to there when he found two people in his way.

"I'd like to know what you think you're doing?" said the man, moving to block Calder's progress. He was taller than Calder, in his early thirties, and he was in full dinner dress. He had a short upper lip that put his teeth on permanent show and gave him the look of one who was reacting to a bad smell. His voice and manner both implied privilege to Calder. He'd met a lot like this twit in his professional life. He tried to push the young man aside. The young woman gasped in fear. The young man stood firm. They glared at each other for a while before Calder said, "Piss off out of my way!" He made to go into the lavatory. The young man moved to block him and snatched his lapels. Calder butted him in the face, and the girl screamed. He went into the lavatory and swung the

185

bronze nude against the mirror. The crack as the mirror burst was like a gunshot.

The young man, dazed and bleeding from the mouth, stood against the hall table with a hand to his mouth. He made no effort to intrude as Calder went back into the drawing room, and there was no sign of the young woman.

"I suppose she's gone to call the police," Calder said.

The young man shook his head. "They're on their way now. We dialled nine-nine-nine right away. You'll not get away."

Calder was in no hurry, which puzzled the young man. He made a final check to make sure he'd smashed every mirror. Suddenly he spotted a framed photograph of Amberley standing outside Buckingham Palace in topper and tails with a smirk on his face and his Honours List award in its velvet-lined container in his open hand. It was his CVO, and Calder could think of some more applicable conversion of the initials in Amberley's case than Companion of the Victorian Order. He broke open the frame, took out the photograph, which he ripped into shreds, and went back past the young man who wanted to be brave. Calder dropped the bits of photograph into the lavatory bowl and flushed them away.

Then he walked out back to the lift. He could hear no police sirens and felt indifferent whether he did or not. The young man watched Calder press the lift button. He then went up the stairs by the side of the lift shaft. Calder got into the lift and pressed the G button. In the lift housing at the top of the block the young man saw the lift start down. He was brighter than Calder had thought. He knew those lifts as well as he knew the fire escapes and the small print of his insurance policies. He pulled the power switch.

The lift stopped between the second and third floors. Three minutes later Amberley saw the flashing blue lights of the police cars. Moments later the flashing blue light he saw from across the square was on a fire engine. The night was warm, and Amberley's raincoat was of thick gaberdine with a fur collar, but he was shivering.

Calder sat in a corner of the dead dark lift with his legs spread out. He was twiddling his thumbs, and he had a quiet smile on his face which stayed even when he heard the police sirens and saw the reflections of the blue lights penetrating the gloom of the lift just below the top of the gates.

Suddenly the lift light came on, and the lift was on its way down. Calder could hear excited voices. He was still sitting in the corner with his hands clasped over his stomach when the lift got to ground level. He felt like a zoo animal. It seemed hordes of people were peering at him beyond the bars. He could make out police and there were two firemen in helmets. Beyond them, he could see the stern, piqued faces of civilians, mostly men in dressing gowns.

Two heavies from the Metropolitan Police grabbed Calder. They propelled him through the crowd in the foyer like sheriffs taking Jesse James through a lynch mob. Some of the crowd threw abuse, and he could see the hate in their faces and he realised they were mostly from flats in the block and saw the young man who had tried to baulk him.

"What would you call that?" Calder asked the two police heavies who were taking him off with such force that his feet never touched the ground. "A rental of tenants?"

Their faces were blank. One of Calder's pleasures in life was to make up collective nouns and he thought that one wasn't at all bad. It's no use being literary with cops, he thought as they bundled him into a police car.

He wound up in an interview room in the Savile Row police station with a detective inspector who was trying to look like Hercule Poirot and behave like a cop with brains who knew all about Pavlov's dogs.

"I could throw the book at you, you know," he said, offering Calder a cigarette.

"I have little time for reading these days," Calder said calmly. "And I don't smoke." He gazed up at the inspector who was halfway through a filter tip. "You wouldn't either if you had half a clue about what it does to your insides."

The inspector said Calder might like a drink brought in.

"I'm not thirsty," Calder said. "I've had enough for one night."

"You're telling *me*," the inspector rasped. "You were pissed when you drove up to that place."

"You don't know that, Inspector," Calder said. He was feeling better than he'd felt for some days.

"You were pissed when you got there," the inspector said. "Then we have breaking and entering, and malicious damage, and theft, and assault that some might say was attempted murder."

Calder grinned.

"You think all that's amusing?" The inspector felt he could break Calder though it might take most of the night.

"I don't get the theft bit, that's all," Calder said. And he smiled as he spoke. The inspector was used to cheeky buggers, but this was ridiculous.

"You were making off with that valuable bronze statue," he said, taking a deep drag at his cigarette to show Calder hadn't scared him.

For a moment Calder went on the defence. It came back to him now that he must have held onto the bronze nude. The police had found it in the lift beside him. It was no business of cops to know why he had held onto that bronze. He wasn't even sure himself. He had theories, but he wasn't sure.

The inspector ran his finger and thumb through his tidy

moustache, thinking he now had Calder by the short hairs. "Let's get you some food," he said, forcing a smile that was meant to be kindly-looking.

He wasn't very good at the Pavlov's dogs bit, and Calder knew it.

"I'm on a diet," Calder said. "I have to get down to twelve stone."

The inspector's face hardened. "You'll be down to a skinny sod-all like those beggars in Bombay unless you tell me what tonight was all about."

Calder put on the most tolerant smile he could muster and laid his hands palms up on the simple deal table. "Nothing to declare," he said.

The inspector brushed an imaginary speck of dust off his trousers as he sat on the edge of the table. "I don't mind staying here all night, mate."

"Of course you don't," Calder said, smiling. "You're on overtime."

But for the fact that the police were being checked on so much these days, the inspector would have kicked his balls in. He lit another cigarette instead.

"I keep telling you," Calder said quietly, "I'll be out of here in half an hour or so. And you'll be clear to go home to your wife or mistress or boyfriend or whatever it is you have to while away your off-duty hours."

The inspector came round the table with the lighted end of his cigarette pointed menacingly at Calder's face.

"Don't get reckless, Inspector," Calder said.

The inspector paused. He was used to dealing with Soho thugs and pimps and hit men and thieves, and he had his ways with vicious men. But he was worried about Calder. Right from the start Calder had asked to be allowed to make one phone call.

"You mean you want to call your lawyer?" said the inspector, smirking contempt.

"I haven't got one," Calder said.

"Who then?"

"May I make the call?"

"Not yet," the inspector had said, letting the flame of his lighter flicker between them.

Calder had shrugged off the denial. "It's only a matter of time," he said.

Now the inspector was on his fourth cigarette since they had gone into the room, which had four walls and little else. He resumed his seat on the table edge. "Can't we be sensible?" he said, putting on his social worker's look.

"Yes." Calder smiled and went over to open a window.

The inspector glared at him.

Calder said, "Lung cancer's a conveyable disease in a room like this."

The inspector's face went taut with anger. He marched over to the window, "We've got you on so many bloody counts, mate, I shouldn't worry too much about the state of your health."

He was just about to close the window when there was a knock on the door. A young sergeant with a frown came in. He handed a note to the inspector, whose nostrils flared. His head began to shake. And when he had recovered enough to look Calder in the face, his eyes were heavy with frustration.

"You're free to leave," he said.

The young sergeant trotted over to open the door for Calder. Calder grinned at the sergeant and threw a nod toward the inspector. "Can't you find him a cuddly toy to kick?"

Calder thought he might need a taxi. But he was told that a car was waiting for him outside. Meade threw open the door of the Mercedes, "I did tell you to call me first, Shay."

TWELVE

Pavel screwed up his face in pain. Through the slits of his eyes he could make out the army doctor with his ash-grey hair and purple-veined nose. The major wasn't pleased to have been called out at two in the morning to a blasted Russian with a bellyache. He put his toper's face close to Pavel's. "You feeling rotten, old chap?"

Pavel managed a moan. The major pressed his fingers into Pavel's groin. He winced. The major prodded him in several places and his face twisted in agony. The major turned to the duty lieutenant at the warren and said briskly, "Get an ambulance and notify the hospital at Ross-on-Wye we have a rush appendix."

As the lieutenant went out, the major said, "And while you're at it, you might call my wife and tell her I'll go on to the sick bay at Donnington and won't be back for some hours."

"Yes, sir."

"Oh, Lieutenant," the major said. "She sleeps like she's dead, so you may have to be patient."

"Sir."

"And Lieutenant . . .?" The lieutenant paused. The major smiled. "A generous double brandy wouldn't come amiss."

"I'll find one, sir," the lieutenant said.

It was at this moment that Pavel changed his plan. With Galina gone and more delays likely in view of Amberley's departure he felt he had to move things on. And this meant an escape from the warren. He'd intended to make his break either from the ambulance or hospital. But he could not keep his eyes off the major's car keys on the bedside table. He'd watched from the window as the major drove up in an army green Princess car.

With the duty lieutenant committed to several chores it seemed to Pavel the moment was now. He clutched his abdomen as if in agony. As the major bent over him, Pavel put a sleeper lock on his neck with one hand and clamped the other over his mouth. The major went limp, his bloodshot eyes popping.

Calder leapt out of bed and stripped the major of his military cardigan with its crowns on the shoulders. He put it on over his pyjama jacket. He pulled on his slacks and moccasins but felt there was no time for socks. He moved out to the landing and saw the hall was empty and the duty officer's desk vacant. He moved down the stairs so fast he got a friction burn from the banister on his right hand. There was no trouble with the Princess, which the major had left unlocked. Pavel took it slowly down the drive to avoid undue attention from the SPs on patrol in the grounds and because he needed to get used to the car.

Suddenly in the headlamps' beam he saw an SP corporal with his Alsatian. Pavel froze. He prayed to no god he could ever know that the corporal would not stop him. He drove on with the driver's window half open and the crunch of the tyres on gravel was like an alarm signal. Just for a second it seemed that the corporal might step into the car's path and put up a hand. But he moved aside and threw up a salute. Pavel raised a hand as if in salute but to hide his face.

His headlamps were on full beam, and he had no idea where to find the dip switch. His hand fumbled madly about the dashboard. He was near the guardroom now. His probing fingers found what he thought to be the dip switch. He pressed it, and the wipers started whirring madly over the windshield. He saw one of the SP corporals in the headlamps and hoped he had not seen the wipers sweeping. He decided to leave the headlamps on full beam. If it was Corporal May on duty, he was done. May had seen him often enough over the table tennis table. But Pavel was in luck. The corporal in front of the barrier was no one he'd ever seen on the estate, a gangling SP of six feet plus with a long, thin face.

His throat went tight as the corporal put up his hand. In the full beam the SP looked like the one who would rumble his disguise.

Pavel braked as gently as he could with a car he'd never handled. The corporal put his head inside the window and shone a torch into the back seat. "Would you mind if I look in the boot, sir?"

"Go ahead," Pavel said.

He had no idea if the trunk was unlocked. In the mirror he saw the corporal at the back of the car. If the boot was locked, Pavel would have to give the corporal the keys. He daren't step out in grey slacks and moccasins. To his immense relief the lid flew open over the rear window.

"Okay, sir," the corporal shouted.

The barrier operated by another SP in the guardroom began to rise. Pavel's heart raced at a hundred times the speed of the barrier's ascent. One call from the house now, and he was done. The barrier rose higher than the Princess' roof.

He was away. He drove hard for twenty minutes, growing used to the feel of the car and its instruments, putting as much distance as he could between him and the warren, and taking minor roads by instinct. His eyes kept scanning the mirrors. His ears were sharp for the sound of police sirens. But the night was quiet. He was calming down.

He could see the amber glare of a motorway in the distance. Near a village named Horton his lights caught a man crossing the narrow road. The man turned to blow a kiss to a woman at an upper window of a stone cottage. He then began to climb into the cab of a lorry parked in a layby. Pavel drove past it as its lights flashed on. He slowed. He saw the lorry's lights grow in his mirrors.

As it got closer Pavel began to swerve the Princess left and right. He held the crown of the road for a while until he saw a lane to his right and braked hard with the Princess on track for a turn down the lane. The lorry skidded to a stop.

Tasman Davies had seen some idiot drivers in his time. He got down from his cab, his anger mixed with class fury. The bloody Princess was clearly being driven by some army officer who'd got pissed at a mess party. But he had to be careful. He should not have been on this road at this time of night or any other time.

"What's up, mate?" he said, keeping control and taking a good sniff at Pavel's breath.

It smelt of onions, not spirits.

"I think the steering's gone."

Tasman opened the driver's door and saw Pavel's pyjama trousers. "You all right, Major," he said, knowing bloody well the major wasn't.

"Let's get it off the road," Pavel said.

The last thing Tasman Davies could afford was some incident so far off his route between South Wales and London. He had a wife and four kids in Swansea. He helped Pavel push the car into the lane on the right. Pavel put the brake on. With luck it would not be found till dawn.

"I should walk it off, mate," Tasman said, making off. "Good night."

"How far are you going?" Pavel asked.

"Oh, I'm going a helluva way," he said, still moving away. "London."

194

"So am I," Pavel said.

"Nothing doing, Major," Tasman said firmly. "My firm won't let us pick up hitchhikers."

"I'm not a hitchhiker. "I'm a broken down motorist."

"Or a pissed one."

Pavel shrugged. "I'll see if they can put me up at the house then."

"Which house?"

"The one you just left." He was only playing a hunch.

Tasman studied him for a long moment, knowing that this major had the number of his lorry and had seen him leave Annie's cottage. "Why the bloody hell," he said, "are you still half in your pyjamas?"

Pavel's brain worked fast. "I had a row with my wife."

It took Tasman no more than a few seconds to decide it was in his interests to give Pavel a lift. He knew Pavel was a queer sort of major, and Pavel knew that Tasman was a driver who strayed off the route shown in his log-book.

Tasman thought he might give Pavel the slip at the first motorway service area on the way to London. He saw him as a nut case, and the last thing he could face was being involved in some public scandal over a nut he'd picked up in a place he should never been near.

In the cab Pavel sniffed deeply, and his nostrils twitched. "Cabbage," Tasman said. "I've got three tons up."

Pavel grinned. Now he knew it was cabbage he had no objections. "I wish our Russian farming was as efficient as yours."

Tasman nearly lost control of the lorry. They had gone half a mile before he said, "Russian?"

He was sure now that Pavel was a nut. What worried him more was what might happen if the nut became news and Tasman's diversions for reasons other than roadworks were to become known. They were on the M4 motorway

195

when Pavel told him he was a Russian seeking asylum in Britain after working in the Siberian diamond mines.

Tasman said nothing. Every glance he cast at the pyjama jacket under Pavel's British army major's cardigan made him even more sure that Pavel had got out of some asylum. Tasman drew the lorry into the first servicing area they reached. He had it in mind to lose his passenger. Pavel sensed what he was up to.

As he was about to leave the cab, Pavel grabbed his wrist. "Hold on," he said. He brought out the pouch and spread some diamonds on Tasman's palm.

Tasman leaned forward to gaze at them under the dashboard light. His shrewd dark eyes shone. "Don't tell me they're diamonds?"

Pavel confirmed that they were. He picked one out and put it on the dashboard shelf. "Get me to London and a change of clothes, and that's yours."

Tasman gave Pavel the rest back and put the small opaque maccle into his purse. They never even left the cab and were twenty miles nearer London when he said, "What's my one worth?"

"Two hundred pounds at a guess."

He wasn't convinced, but he'd known stranger things occur on his night runs. He took an oil-stained coverall from the shelf. "Try that for size," he said with a chuckle. He was wondering what to do with the diamond, if it was a diamond. He thought first he might give it to Annie on his next call at the cottage. But it might be better to sell it and buy her a gold bracelet for fifty quid or so.

Pavel put on the coverall.

"Great!" Tasman enthused. "You look like a worker now." Fear then came over him. "If the cops catch you, don't forget I picked you up at a service area and not in that village."

"I promise," Pavel said.

It was predawn, but the vast wholesale market in London was busy with trucks and middlemen and porters. On every side were crates of cabbages and cauliflowers and beans, and Pavel had never seen so much produce in one place in his life.

"You'll not get far in that outfit," Tasman said. "I'll find you something decent to wear."

He was soon lost to view in the moving mass of men and produce. It was some minutes later when Pavel saw Tasman with two hefty men in sweat shirts and a dapper little man wearing a bow tie. One of the heavies had on an old commando beret, and the other had the flat features of an ex-boxer and a cauliflower ear. They were passing something round. Pavel guessed it was the diamond. The two heavies began to approach the lorry, and Tasman was clearly making a protest. He tugged at the ex-boxer's trunk of an arm only to be swatted off.

Pavel was suddenly seized with fear. It seemed they were on their way to mug him for his diamonds and that Tasman wanted no part of it because of the attention it could focus on him and where he'd spent half the night. Pavel guessed that's what was going on, and he was right. The two heavies came on purposefully, held for a split second in the headlights of a juggernaut loaded with vegetables.

Pavel stepped down from the cab and began to walk away from them. They quickened their strides, and Pavel saw their grim faces. He broke into a run. So did they. The heavy in the green beret was still very fit and began to gain on Pavel, thrusting his way through knots of workers and leaping over crates of oranges. Pavel was feeling the effects of two nights' lost sleep. He was panting as he went round a corner of the market buildings where porters queued at a tea van for bacon-and-egg sandwiches, blocking the way. Gasping, he was on the point of running back to try to dodge his way past the two heavies.

But the queue broke in the middle to give him a clearway. He couldn't believe his eyes.

"All the best, cock," said a muscular porter in shirt sleeves as Pavel tore past.

The queue closed ranks again to block the two heavies, who began to hustle their way through a commotion of shoulders and shouting.

Some thirty yards beyond the queue a young man in a T-shirt held open the rear doors of a van packed with crates of fruit and vegetables. With a quick gesture he indicated that Pavel should dive inside. Pavel sprawled into the van face first. His left cheek grazed a box of cucumbers, and his body skidded a couple of feet on cabbage leaves. The young man closed the doors. He'd seen the chase. He went round to the front of the van, and the two heavies rushed past, the man in the beret red-faced and wild, the ex-boxer white-faced and weary, with drops of sweat coming off the end of his nose.

Pavel got up and put his face to the small gap between the cab and the van. He could see the two heavies still running, more slowly now, and having to weave past porters and parked vans and lorries. As the heavies were lost among the busy chaos, the young man climbed into the cab. He didn't turn round but glanced at Pavel's face in his internal mirror.

"Thank you," Pavel breathed, puzzled.

"We don't make it easy for the fuzz around here."

"They were police?" Pavel couldn't believe they were.

"They looked like they could have been," said the man, who was about thirty-two. "That's enough for most blokes."

Pavel studied the young man through the mirror, wondering if it would be wise to say the heavies were not police but potential muggers. He chose to say nothing yet. His pounding heart began to settle, and his breathing eased. And his brain was clearing. The young man had an open and kind face with humor lines about the eyes. Pavel could see the Smiley motif on his T-shirt. As the van pulled out from behind a big truck on which men were loading oranges, he caught sight of the two heavies. They were walking back, arguing with each other.

"I should keep your head down, mate," the young man said.

Pavel took one last look at his frustrated pursuers. He knew what he had to do. He had to dispose of his diamonds in ways which would not only support his story in the eyes of the authorities but which would attract notice beyond their secret world. But he had to avoid being caught or mugged. It had been a near thing. And he had much to do before he called Reuter's and set up a news conference to let the world know of the KGB plan to swamp the market with gem diamonds. He sat back working it all out on a sack of potatoes.

"All right, mate," he heard the young man call. "They've gone."

Pavel put his head through the gap and took a good look at the young man's face in the mirror before he said, "They weren't police."

"Vigilantes then," the young man said lightly. "They come to the same thing."

"They weren't vigilantes either," Pavel said. "They were trying to rob me."

They were held up at some traffic lights in Kingsway. The young man turned to stare at Pavel. In that scruffy old coverall he didn't look like a suitable case for mugging for gain.

"I'm carrying about half a million pounds' worth of diamonds," Pavel said simply through the gap.

"And those Brussels sprouts back there are worth a million!" the young man joked.

All the way through Holborn and along the Euston Road Pavel told about his diamonds and his attempt to

199

stay in the UK. The young man kept challenging him with sharp questions meant to trip Pavel. He was a lot better at it than Amberley.

"Help yourself to a pear if you fancy one," he said. Then, "Diamonds," and he started to chuckle.

"You'll see," Pavel said, biting into a ripe pear. "I'll show you the diamonds when we get there."

The van was going through Islington. "Okay, Ivan," the young man said, "I believe you. Millions wouldn't." He hadn't swallowed a word of Pavel's story. But he liked him and to Jack Stepney that was all that mattered.

"It was stupid of you to take things into your own hands," Meade confronted Calder across the L-shaped desk. The rising sun was blinding Calder, but Meade left the venetian blinds open. He felt let down by Calder.

"The bastard was drooling over Galina!" Calder's face was a picture of pent-up fury.

Meade squeezed his nostrils. "He was trying to get something out of Pavel."

"He was getting kicks out of Galina. He's kinky as the Big Dipper!"

"We have to learn not to be too squeamish, Calder."

Calder glared at Meade for a second. He got up out of the chair. "I suppose he's on sick leave? Full pay and pension rights?"

"What he's on is my business, Calder. Just as it's my business when you go hell raising and have to be rescued from the police."

Calder was on his way out. "Thanks for lifting me," he snapped. "I suppose I'm in line for suspension and Amberley for promotion?"

"Do sit down and calm down."

Calder faced Meade squarely, pointing an angry finger. "This whole rotten scene stinks and you know it!"

Meade was calm. "You mean Amberley or the possible leak?"

"Possible leak! It was the golden tip-off of the year!"

Meade wagged a finger to say that Calder should sit down. It had always been part of his thinking that his section recruited too narrowly for a nation facing the last quarter of the twentieth century. And Calder had been a symbol. Now he was just a bloody-minded puritanical nusiance. The old school, he had to admit, *was* more reliable. But he still had to placate Calder somehow. It took another twenty minutes of cajoling and persuasion.

Then Meade said, "Come, Calder, let's clear the pitch. You'll hear Amberley's explanation?"

"You mean he's here?" Calder wondered if he'd heard right.

Meade laid a finger on the intercom and said, "Mr. Amberley can come in now."

Pale and tense, with a patch over his left eye, an adhesive bandage on his face, and a bandage on his hand, Amberley came in looking like a refugee from the emergency department of the Westminster Hospital. He sat down in the other chair facing Meade and avoiding Calder's eyes.

Calder had shifted his chair to dodge the bright sunlight. He gazed at Amberley with such hatred that Meade thought he had been premature.

"I feel you owe Calder some explanation," he said in a tone that was very tentative for Meade.

Amberley had his hands clasped primly across his middle. He didn't look at Calder once. "I asked Galina down to the warren for her own safety," he said, touching his glasses back a bit. "I was using the two-way mirror system for the purpose for which it was installed—as a device for the observation of people we check on."

Calder ran a clenched fist up and down his thigh. Meade watched the two of them. Amberley had still not

201

looked at Calder once. He leaned back in the chair running a hand over the bandaged one. "I merely felt we had not made enough progress on Pavel and that we had to try every method at our disposal."

"Like voyeurism?" It was taking all the self-control he could muster to keep him from going at Amberley.

"I think I can ignore that remark," Amberley said, turning his head slowly so that his clear eye could get Calder in view. He looked so smug and sure of himself that Calder couldn't take anymore.

He darted at Amberley and took him by the lapels, hoisting him out of the chair as if he were a stuffed dummy. Amberley went rigid, glaring at him through his one clear eye. Calder stood off him, and it seemed for a moment that common sense had taken over. But Calder's eyes were bright with loathing. He swung his right fist into Amberley's face. There was a sharp crack and his glasses flew. He reeled back against Meade's heavy steel safe, moaning with pain. His jaw seemed to come loose from his face and blood flowed down his chin.

Meade came quickly round the desk to stop Calder's attack. He needn't have bothered. Calder stood over Amberley with a look so cold and violent it even shook Meade.

Meade knelt by the ashen-faced Amberley. "He's out and his jaw's gone," he said. "We'd best get him to hospital." He looked up to see the door close behind Calder.

"It could be worse," said Nobel Bray, watching the closed-circuit TV monitor in Sir Sefton Dykes' office. It showed Krueger's shares down another eight points.

"It could be worse if nuclear war broke out," Dykes rasped. "It could be worse if London were razed by an earthquake." He washed down another pill.

And Bray himself felt washed out. He'd only got to bed at four after a night getting nowhere with those two big sellers of diamond collections, Bradley J. Sagar and Lady Naphill. He had made contact with friends of Sagar and phoned him in Zurich, but Sagar had flatly refused to see him. Her ladyship had been more brief. "Piss off!" she said, flinging back her long black hair.

Then Saunders had tipped him off about Pavel's escape. What he had actually said over his breakfast kippers in his Highgate flat, after summoning Bray by phone, was that Pavel was no longer at the warren. He looked very nervous.

"You mean he's free?" Bray could hardly believe his ears.

"I'm saying nothing more," Saunders said. "I think all hell's about to break and heads will roll for sure over some of the things that have been going on." He knew of the two-way mirror scandal, but that was no business of Bray's.

"So where the hell do we begin to look for him?" Bray was limping about the room, red-eyed from lack of sleep.

Saunders wiped his mouth with a napkin. "Anywhere." He shrugged. "But I imagine he'll try to dispose of those diamonds from what he's been telling us."

Bray was flabbergasted. "You mean he's still got them? You let him keep them?"

"They weren't the property of her Majesty's Government, Bray. We're not muggers."

Now Bray was having to sit out this doom watch with Dykes watching Krueger's shares slide while the man who'd caused it and could see that it got much worse was on the loose. The TV monitor flashed a new price for Krueger's shares: down another three to 166.

Dykes swung round to face Bray. The crevices in his face were in shadow now and made his head even more like a skull. "He has to be found, Nobel," he said menacingly. "You *must* find him!"

Bray had got his legmen on a phone marathon to warn

all major dealers that Krueger's should be told instantly of any approach by a foreigner offering to sell grade one rough stones including specials over 14.7 carats.

Dykes sat very upright, his mean little eyes dark in their deep sockets. "You know what Machiavelli said of his enemies, Nobel?"

Bray was too flaked to remember Dykes' last words, let alone Machiavelli's.

"He said you had the option to conciliate or kill."

Bray was trying hard to keep his eyes open.

Dykes said, "I doubt our capacity to kill him. And we can conciliate only with habeas corpus—if someone produces the body."

Bray stood there, very wooden. Dykes knew nothing of the sniper who'd had his head blown off at the warren and who had turned out to be an East Ender with a long record of violence called Albert Cousins. It had been put out that he'd been killed in a hunting accident. The SP corporal's death had not been announced.

"I want him found, Nobel," Dykes said harshly.

"It won't be easy," Bray said. "Even the police haven't been advised. Our friends in St. James's have orders to keep the whole thing under wraps. Their masters are as keen as the Russians to get him back to Russia. They don't want détente mucked up."

"And I won't have this company mucked up," Dykes snapped.

What Bray had just said about the Russians gave him an idea. There were hawks and doves in Moscow as well as in Washington and London. The Russian hawks would want Pavel's KGB story to get out and hence would not want him caught yet. The doves would want him back on the first Ilyushin out of Heathrow.

"Go and see Mazarev," Dykes said. "He might help."

Bray went to the Russian embassy and strolled through

the garden with Mazarev. "I think you should know that Pavel's escaped," he said.

"We know that," Mazarev said. His ascetic's face was frosty and unhelpful.

In a small bedroom of the flat over Jack Stepney's greengrocer's shop in Islington, Pavel wriggled into a pair of tartan trousers and zipped them up.

"Savile Row," Stepney said, delighted.

Pavel smiled. He was beginning to like Jack Stepney. When he'd shown Stepney the diamonds, the lithe little Cockney had been amused but not very impressed. He seemed to be a man totally without greed. Stepney had rolled the big special around his hand and then given it back to Pavel and said, "Let's get you some clothes." As Stepney's stuff would be too small, Stepney went out to round some up.

He had come back with his arms full of jackets and trousers and shirts and ties and cotton sweaters. Pavel found a white roll-collar sweater, and it was a good fit. He tried on two jackets that were too bulky and then a brown hopsack blazer with military buttons not unlike the one he'd been given in Stockholm. It had an emblem worked in red and gold on the top pocket.

"Fantastic!" Stepney raved. "You look like a young Conservative!"

He produced a clothes brush and began to run over the blazer like some manic valet. He never stopped talking. "Our yacht club Russian," he was calling Pavel. He stood back to admire Pavel's outfit. His success in spiriting Pavel out of the wholesale market seemed to have given him a high, and he mentioned the Scarlet Pimpernel twice to Liz when he got back to the shop with Pavel.

"Right!" Stepney chuckled. "I could take you anywhere now. What should it be? The Beefsteak Club?"

Pavel took the diamond pouch off the bed and took out

a medium-sized gem and offered it to Stepney. "Please take this," he said.

Stepney shook his head. "Forget it, mate."

"Have it polished and give it to your wife."

"Liz, you mean?"

Pavel nodded.

Stepney laughed. "Liz and me just shack up. We'll get spliced when we're eighty."

Pavel insisted and pressed him to take the gift.

As they went out through the shop, Stepney caught Liz bending over a box of tomatoes. He put a hand up her skirt and pinched her bottom.

"Oooh, you male pig!" She was a plump little brunette with a round dimpled face and a mouth made for laughing.

Stepney kissed her, and Pavel shook hands. She told him the apples he'd brought back were the best ever. "Have one," she told Pavel, and gave him a Granny Smith.

Pavel went off in the van with Stepney. The drive took about twenty minutes.

"Here we are," Stepney said, pulling into the kerb. Pavel looked at the street sign. Stepney took a scruffy introduction card off the dashboard shelf and gave it to Pavel. "My phone number's on it as well if you get in a mess."

Hatton Garden was busy and more chaotic than Pavel had been led to expect. He was back on programme. He knew precisely what he was looking for. He wanted 283 Hatton Garden and a dealer named Brussei. At the Moscow briefing Pavel had been told that Brussei would buy some of his gems and could then be relied on to be wildly indiscreet about the deal.

"Get lucky, mate," Stepney said, his pale, determined face breaking into a grin. They shook hands and Pavel got out. He started along the street checking the numbers on the shops and offices. The sidewalk was alive with young secretaries out for lunch. Some queued outside a sandwich bar across the way.

Pavel's eyes roved past them, and his heart missed a beat. He moved on to the cover of a parked post office van, his heart racing. A postman was loading mail. Through the hinged slit of the van's open door Pavel took a longer look at what had startled him. There was no doubt at all. There was no mistaking that stocky man with the nearly bald freckled head who was standing near another snack bar. It was Lenkov. He was keeping his eyes on something directly opposite.

Pavel followed his eyeline and saw a run-down block of old offices. The number on the front was 283.

Pavel's first instinct was to run. He could see Jack Stepney's van held in the line of traffic a hundred metres back. Pavel got to it just as the traffic began to move again. He felt terrified and showed it. His cheeks had gone white.

"Who's after you this time?" said Stepney, all serious now.

Pavel said nothing. He looked out from the van at Lenkov. Pavel knew enough about the *mokrie dela* mob to make him shiver even here in a van in the middle of Hatton Garden.

Lenkov still had his eyes on Number 283. He looked very alert and fit, having rested for twelve hours in bed after his ordeal up the tree at the warren. He'd been stuck up there all night, looking down on the police and SPs.

All had taken it for granted that the dead hit man was the one who had been up there in the Douglas fir. Lenkov had expected one or two of them to climb up for no other reason than to check the sniper's vantage. He'd hardly believed his luck when they all left. The answer was simple. It was already known that the fir did involve a sniping risk and an order had been given to fell it.

Lenkov's eyes were on the entrance to Number 283. He decided his surveillance was being upset by the slow-moving traffic. Pavel sat in the van next to Stepney and saw Lenkov move between a car and a taxi no more than twenty yards ahead of them. He watched as Lenkov took up a new position on the same side of the street as Number 283 to keep it in view while being far enough away to make it unlikely he would be seen by people going into it.

In the van Pavel offered another diamond to Stepney. It was smaller than the first and worth, Pavel reckoned, some four hundred pounds. This one he wanted to give Stepney in return for the cash Stepney had just handed him to tide him over a few hours. He had expected to get cash from Brussei.

Stepney refused the diamond very firmly. "Suppose they're just bits of Perspex." He laughed. "I'd feel a prize loony." He was pretty sure they weren't Perspex. But he didn't like to be rewarded for helping anyone out. "I tell you what, Pavel," he said. "If that one you gave me back home turns out to be Perspex, you can send me the twenty-five quid back when you've conned somebody to buy one or two of the others."

Pavel shook his head in wonder. He have never met a man in his life with so little greed in his nature.

"Don't forget," Stepney said warmly as Pavel got out of the van, "if you're in a mess, call me."

"I'll do that," Pavel said.

They were in High Holborn, and Stepney had stopped near a line of phone boxes. Pavel had a couple of urgent calls to make.

THIRTEEN

Galina studied Calder through the open windows. She looked taut as she watched him sitting in a deck chair in the small garden. He was on his sixth double scotch since he had come back from that violent meeting with Amberley in Meade's office.

"I'm going out," she called.

"Sure," Calder said without turning to face her. "You do what you bloody well like."

Her mouth set firm. "And I might have dinner out somewhere."

"Sure," he replied flatly. "Eat yourself stupid and get fat."

For a moment she looked round for something to throw at him. Her green eyes were on fire. They had just had their biggest row ever, over his attack on Amberley. When he told her what he'd done to Amberley, she had gazed at him with distaste, lost for words. He took in the look.

"I suppose you enjoyed what he did?"

"Don't be contemptible!"

"He doesn't do that to me and get away with it!" Calder said, his voice rising.

Her self-control went then. "He didn't do it *to you!*" she flared. "You don't own me. You didn't and you don't and you never will!"

"I think you don't mind the bastard drooling at the sight of you?!"

She hit out at him. Calder ducked away from the open-handed swipe. He was bemused by the scotch and was fighting remorse. And he had to come back to her. "Anyway, you and Pavel in your bedroom! I mean what the hell do you call that? A party meeting!"

His sneer was too much. She struck so fast this time with her right fist clenched he had no chance to duck. The punch from the inside of the fist caught him near the right eye. He put up a hand in self-defence, shaken by the power of the blow but even more by her fury. He tried to fend her off, but she lashed out with a foot and both hands, and she was a hazy whirl of flashing colours. She was so quick and he was so scared of hurting her in retaliation that he began to retreat and finally fell back over a chair arm. She gazed down at him in scorn for a long moment, her fury still unspent.

Then Ladybird Johnson leapt up on his knees. The phone started to ring in the hall. It was a good excuse to turn away from Calder, but she let it ring.

"Aren't you going to answer it?" Calder said, nursing his tender spots. She shook her head and was about to go upstairs to get ready to go out when she changed her mind. She took the call.

"Galina?" It was Pavel's voice.

She closed her eyes.

"Is that you, Galina?" The voice was urgent.

"You'd like to talk to Calder?"

"No," he said. "I want to see you."

"What's wrong?" she asked.

"Nothing. I'm in London."

"In London?"

"I'll explain when we meet."

Pavel told her he was in Holborn.

She hesitated, casting a quick look at Calder, who was pouring himself yet another scotch. "All right, Pavel," she said quietly. "I'll see you on the concourse at Euston Sta-

:ion." She went upstairs, ignoring Calder, and changed nto a light dress, all emerald and auburn. She was just zipping it up when she turned to see Calder in the doorway, glass in hand.

"Who was that then?" he said, leaning against the wall. "Meade?"

"You should have answered it, and then you'd know."

"All right, it wasn't Meade?"

She threw him a look and said nothing. Then she went past him, and as he turned lazily back to the stairs, he heard the front door slam.

Pavel saw her come from the underground in the spacious concourse at Euston.

He walked up behind her. "Galina?"

Her eyes were full of concern. "Pavel," she said softly. "What *are* you doing?"

He kissed her formally on both cheeks, then he steered through the throng of rush-hour commuters to the Pennine Bar on which he'd already done a reconnaissance. They found two corner seats, and he brought over two vodkas. For a long while their eyes never left each other. He raised his glass. He found her bewitching.

Her eyes, so hard a little time back, were warm now as she took in the flared tartan trousers and the blazer. He looked so un-Russian she laughed. He knew what had tickled her and began to smile. Then the smile faded as he let his eyes feast on hers and on her cleavage.

"Why me, Pavel?" she said, raising her glass.

Why her? Pavel's first phone call had been to Brussei, and he offered a few specials. Brussei had told him to come in tomorrow. Though Brussei was among those advised to tell Krueger's of any such offer, he had not done so. Pavel had then phoned Galina. He wanted to hear her voice again, so much he did know. But it was also in his mind to use her as an unwitting agent to spread the story of the KGB plan. Looking at her now, he knew he could do no such thing.

"I'm glad you came," he said, reaching out to touch her hand.

"It's no use, Pavel," she said, letting him keep his hand on hers. "I'll help you if I can, but that's all."

He looked straight into her. "Calder?"

She held out her empty glass to say he should get her another. Her eyes and mouth were doing all sorts of things to his mind. "And you can take me to dinner," Galina said.

They had dinner in an Italian restaurant with red cloths on the table where the lasagna was superb. She enjoyed the meal and Pavel's company, but she began to check her wristwatch around ten o'clock. Pavel noticed. "How *is* Calder?" he asked, his eyes very bright.

"Alive and well," Galina said defensively.

Half an hour later he saw her into a taxi. He kissed her formally on both cheeks and then, after a pause, on the lips. As she was getting into the taxi Galina turned, put a hand to Pavel's face, opened her mouth and kissed him as he would never have dared at this stage try to kiss her.

Pavel walked on air through the drizzle. He headed for the Paddington district, not really sure where he was going and having to ask a policeman the way and then a taxi driver who was dropping an old lady outside a block of flats near Baker Street.

"I'll take you there," said the taxi driver.

"No, thanks," Pavel said with a big smile. He was enjoying the walk, even though it was now pouring rain. He knew there were lots of cheap commercial hotels around Paddington.

He booked into a particularly seedy one. On the counter was a discarded closing prices edition of an evening paper. Pavel took it to his dingy room, which reeked of dust. He flopped down on the soiled bedspread and tried to check on the Krueger's share price. He found the City page, but he couldn't get the words or numbers in focus. He thought it was the low-wattage lighting in the room but then told himself it was the vodka and chianti. But he thought he could make out a headline about the fall in Krueger's share price. He tossed the paper on the floor.

The diamond job was tomorrow's problem. He closed his eyes tight and saw her face in close up as he went into her. "Galina," he murmured, and fell fast asleep with his clothes and the room lights still on.

Brussei took one of the big stones from among the cluster of diamonds Pavel had just poured on the blotter of the cluttered desk. It was not Pavel's big special. He'd held that back with most of the rest. Brussei squinted at the stone through a loupe and tried to look unimpressed, though he knew what he was holding was a true blue-white in the first colour category. It was an important stone, but all he said was, "Not bad." He twisted the stone between his thumb and forefinger under the loupe.

"You do know there's an inclusion?" he said sternly, looming over the desk. His enormous bulk nearly blotted out Pavel's view of the wall behind him, with its flaking paint and an old Pirelli girlie calendar.

"It's near one of the points," Pavel said. "It'll go with the bruting."

"I'm not so sure," Brussei said, his eye at the stone.

"It'll go," said Pavel with certainty. "It will be bruted out."

Brussei's sharp eyes under the thick black brows took Pavel in for a long moment. He heaved himself out of the vast chair, waddled across to the window, and rechecked the stone under the northern light. Pavel thought he had the most enormous backside in the world and he was shaped like a pear. His well-worn jacket was like a bell tent, and he looked hard up. He waddled back and put the stone in the Oertling. The illuminated scale showed 16.7 carats.

"It's not bad at all," he said grudgingly, and eased himself back into the chair with a grunt. "And the colour's not bad."

"Colour category one," Pavel said. "It's exceptional."

Brussei knew that perfectly well. He ran his fat fingers through the rest of the stones Pavel had put on offer. "I don't know where you got them," he said.

"Are you asking?" Pavel smiled.

Brussei made no reply. He heaved his bulk over the desk and began to check the other stones, measuring them with calipers, gazing at them under the loupe, and putting them on the Oertling.

After a while he said, "Well, no thefts of rough have been reported, so I suppose they're clean?" He was doing his damnedest to justify the decision he'd already made to buy them if the price was right, whatever their origin.

"I worked at the Mir mine in Siberia," Pavel said.

"Miners don't own the product," Brussei replied solemnly. "Not even in Russia." He didn't really want to know how they had come into Pavel's possession.

"I wasn't a miner," Pavel said.

Brussei weighed him up—and the risk. He would have liked to know a lot more, but life had taught him that the less you knew about some things the better. And he couldn't let this parcel of first-quality gems slip through his hands for lack of nerve.

It took him the best part of an hour to put a value on them. "So, how much do you want?"

Pavel looked very cool. "Seventy-five thousand pounds."

"You're out of your mind, son!"

"That's their value."

"I would have thought half that."

Pavel stood up and began to shovel the diamonds into a purse he'd bought on the way in. He still had the pouch with the rest of the stones around his waist.

"Don't do that!" Brussei said, shifting like some human hippo. "I don't like to see people doing that!"

Pavel moved his hands away but stood over the desk as if ready to take the stones if Brussei said the wrong thing.

"Fifty thousand in cash," Brussei said. "Take it or leave it."

Pavel paused for no more than a couple of seconds. "All right."

He thought Brussei might make some excuse about a delay in payment while the cash was brought from the bank. But Brussei pressed a desk button, and an athletic young man materialised who stood near the door while Brussei opened the heavy green safe and took out wads of sterling. It went through Pavel's mind that they might kill him on the spot and keep the stones. But Suslov's advisers had done their checks in London. Robbery with violence was not Brussei's scene. He dealt in diamonds, and that was his game. He could also boast quite a bit about his coups. Pavel made a gesture of holding the notes up to the light as if to check they weren't fakes. He knew they would be authentic from what he had been told of Brussei in Moscow. Brussei put them in a greasy-looking carrier bag, and Pavel went out with it the way he had come— via the fire escape at the back of the block.

No sooner had Pavel gone than Brussei picked up the best of his buys and held it out exultantly to the athletic young man. "Just take a peek at that, son!"

The young man went over the window with it and gazed at it through the loupe. "My God!"

"Mine, too!" Brussei's eyes glinted under those bushy brows. He took the phone and dialled urgently. When someone took the call, he said, "Pinky, my son, you'll never believe it, but I have a deal in specials that are so special they'll make your eyes pop out. Let's have some salt beef together, eh?"

Pavel made his way into Gray's Inn Road. He felt elated by the Brussei move and was in a mood for Galina's company. He phoned her from a call box. He held on hopefully as the call rang out twenty times before he dropped it.

He hailed a taxi. There were one or two personal satisfactions he had planned while in the West. Twenty minutes later Pavel was standing with the grubby carrier bag in his hand, gazing earnestly through the railings at Buckingham Palace.

"You want him found and got rid of. I want to know who tipped off those sellers of your bloody shares."

Calder studied Bray as they leaned against the balcony rail of a riverside pub near Tower Bridge. They had been there more than an hour, and it was Bray who was being cautious. Company secrets weren't for government men. And Bray knew from Saunders that Calder was in trouble, so how the hell could *he* help to find Pavel? It seemed a one-sided proposition he was putting. Bray gazed down at the sun-dappled Thames right below them and said, "You still haven't told me how *you* could locate the bugger."

Calder took a swig of lager. He was off spirits. He'd had too much of the stuff last night. When it was clear that Galina *was* staying out to dinner, he had gone to a trashy night spot in Soho, downing scotch and letting the throb of the disco music anaesthetise his brain. He'd picked up an eighteen-year-old blonde, only to be turned off her when they danced and her hips were like jagged rocks against his hands and her shoulder blades felt like chicken legs. Her perfume was vile and made him feel bilious. And she was soggy under the armpits. He'd walked back home to find Galina fast asleep. Still furious with

er, he went into the spare bedroom. He hardly slept at
ll.

His anger over what he knew could only have been a
p-off kept his brain alive. He saw the Krueger's share
ide as a case of the old elite looking after itself. The
oyeur incident still rankled, and he felt no remorse about
e rough justice he'd dished out to Amberley. By six in
e morning he had declared war.

He went down to make himself a strong black coffee.
e saw Galina was still asleep. And he wasn't sure he
ould have made her a coffee even if she'd been awake.
e saw the dawn come up.

Calder was draining his third coffee, which had gone
ld he had been so busy with ideas, when Galina came
wearing a see-through grey nightie. It was a moment
hen they might have made it up, but he made a false
art. "I found a super bird last night," he said, lying to
t back at her for the way she had left him on his own.

"Good," she said, going straight through to the kitchen.
enjoyed myself, too."

"Marvellous," he said with sarcasm.

"With Pavel."

He felt numb for a moment. He felt hurt and all the
ld ideas that had gone through his mind in the night
urs were a turmoil. He wanted to make love to her
ere and then. But he said not a word and went to
ower. He would never have thought he could feel so
alous. He kept seeing Pavel with Galina. Daft thoughts
ced through his mind. Could two Russians make love
tter than a Russian and a foreigner? Were Russian men
ecially virile? That's crap, he told himself as he turned
e shower on. The cold spray hit him, and his brain
ared. He knew just what he would do.

He called Meade first, then Bray. Meade was icily pre-
se when Calder went into his room in St. James's. He
ll saw Calder's attack on Amberley as stupid and unciv-

ilised. He was impatient that Calder should make h
point and leave.

"I've made contact with Pavel," Calder lied.

Meade's impatience vanished.

Calder leaned sideways in the chair as if at ease. "
think you should know that he admits he stole the di
monds and that he and others forged this paper about t
KGB plan to flood the world market." It was a bold lie.

Meade ran his eyes over Calder. "I see," he sa
calmly. "So where is he?"

Calder put up his hands in a gesture of ignorance.

"You can contact him?"

"No," Calder said. "But he said he'll contact me."

He had a notion that Galina had been telling the tru
about her meeting with Pavel and that they would mal
contact again. But that was not what was on his mind ju
now.

"He cooked up the whole bloody yarn just to cover t
fact that he pinched that loot." Calder's tone and mann
were so placid that even Meade could not dig into the lie.

"You do realise we have to find him?" Meade said.

"I'd be a bloody fool not to," Calder said.

As soon as Calder had gone, Meade began to pre
buttons.

Calder checked the time. It was just after nine o'cloc
He had three hours to kill before his lunchtime meetir
with Nobel Bray. He went into the Royal Academy
Piccadilly and strolled through the galleries. The paintin
gave him a bit of faith that there were others among t
human race than greedy bastards and voyeurs.

Now, four hours later, he was with Bray on the pu
terrace near Tower Bridge.

"I still don't see how *you* can find him," Bray sai
peering down into the river. "I mean you personally." F
was making it clear he knew of Calder's lapse or at lea
that Calder was no longer on the Pavel job.

The lager had got warm under the hot midday sun. alder tossed it into the Thames. "All right," he said as if ath to come clean. "I'm in touch with him."

It seemed anything but farfetched to Bray. "Officially?" e smiled.

"No," Calder said, putting on the best grim look he uld muster.

"Let's go back to the office," Bray said, hurling the last egs of his sun-warmed lager into the dappled river.

As their taxi drew up at Octahedra House, Asher leinman was getting out of a jumbo-sized Mercedes. He ssed a hardly smoked cigar in the gutter and put an arm und Bray. "Nobel, my son!" he said exuberantly. His ear eyes took in Calder, and he said jovially to Bray, "Is friend or foe?"

"I'm not sure yet." Bray smiled.

Asher thought it was very funny. He didn't realise that ray meant it. Bray let Asher take the lift and took to the airs with Calder.

Halfway up they ran into Charlton, trotting down like me snooty thoroughbred. He had a wide smirk on his ce. "Isn't it marvellous news, Nobel?"

Bray threw him a warning look. Charlton took in Calder, and his smile went off like grime in a detergent. Check your monitor," he said guardedly.

In the office Bray switched on the closed-circuit TV d as it warmed up, he gave Calder a list of the major llers of Krueger's shares since the Pavel crisis had be-an. "I can't let you keep the piece of paper," he said. alder sat down to copy out the names.

"Jesus!" Bray had just seen the latest share price flash the TV monitor. Calder looked at it. It showed rueger's shares had shot up over the 200 mark.

"That's forty points up this morning," Bray said. "And think I never believed in miracles."

Calder smiled and took down a few more names.

He knew one thing for sure.

It was no bloody miracle.

Galina knew she was being followed just after she left the house. Two men were trailing her, one on each side of Belsize Road.

She knew for sure when she recognised one of the men on the underground. He was of medium height with mousy hair, the most ordinary-looking man you could imagine, the sort of man no woman would give a second glance. He could have been a bank clerk in his mid-thirties. He was wearing a wristwatch with a heavy stretch gold band that Galina thought in bad taste. He was still a few yards behind her when she got out at Euston.

Pavel had called an hour before to ask her to meet him at the same place. She had demurred, but his voice was so full of need that she had consented. Calder had been out since first thing, and they had not said a word to each other. And this personal cold war had helped Galina make up her mind. But she also wanted to see Pavel again.

She went along the underground platform, sensing the man was still behind her. Instead of following the exit sign to the main line concourse, she took the tunnel heading for the Victoria line platforms. On the southbound platform she caught the mousy man's eyes on her and was pleased she had made the last-minute switch. She took the next train, got out at Oxford Circus, and made a show of waiting for someone on the north side near Upper Regent Street. The mousy man was watching her from across the traffic.

Galina lingered for a few moments and let a few taxis go by before hailing one. "Belsize Road," she told the driver. And she felt sad to be going home.

vel had waited for an hour for her at Euston. First anx-
us, then hurt, he had come round to the idea that she
d thought better of seeing him. He felt intensely jealous
Calder. He went straight back to the hotel suite in Park
ane. He looked at the big double bed and the pretzels
the rosewood coffee table and the bottles on the fridge,
d his face fell. He had taken some care to set them up.
e had even got in some of the women's magazines she
ked. He thought at a glance they were decadent rubbish.
ut he had laid them out neatly all the same—overlap-
ng each other on the dressing table.

He felt an urge to phone her. He crossed to the picture
indow with its panoramic view of Hyde Park. The sun
as just setting over it, and Pavel felt that Galina should
ve been with him to enjoy the view. He had put back
e programme for her. He turned back to the luxury
om, and the sight of the unruffled double bed depressed
m.

But his mind was made up now. He opened the
ardrobe and brought out a briefcase he had bought in
nd Street. He took from it a tape recorder he had
ught in Oxford Street. Lying on the double bed, he be-
n to rehearse a statement. "My name is Pavel," he said
owly. "I came here for asylum, and I still await a deci-
on from your Home Office. I worked for a year at the
ir diamond mine in Siberia, where I was a KGB
ent—"

There was a knock at the door. He froze. On the sec-
d knock he called, "Who is it?"

"Room service, sir."

Pavel was unarmed. He went to the door. "I didn't or-
r anything."

"It's a delivery from outside, sir."

Pavel opened the door cautiously. A teenage page
ood there with an enormous bouquet of roses in cel-
phane.

221

"Oh, just a moment," Pavel said, taking the bouquet.

He went back into the room and dug a wad of note from his new briefcase. He peeled one off and gave it t the boy. The page couldn't believe it. It was a twent pound note.

"Thank you, sir." He saluted.

Pavel held the roses in front of him for a moment. H nostrils flared, and he frowned. He thought it was a su perb bouquet. He had ordered it himself through Inte flora. "Oh, Galina," he murmured, sniffing the roses.

They weren't the only thing he'd bought during the da that now seemed to be a waste. He had also bought Jaguar, and the salesman had been only too pleased t give him a practice drive through Hyde Park. Pavel ha hoped that Galina might have agreed to drive off wit him to Edinburgh. The car was also a refuge for most c the cash Brussei had given Pavel. All but four thousan of the fifty thousand pounds Brussei had handed ove were locked in the boot. Pavel had wanted to entertai Galina in style in the best hotel room in Mayfair. But h tel guests' bags were being checked because of terrorist Knowing his case would be examined, and that fifty thou sand pounds would create almost the same alarm as bomb, Pavel had chosen to use the trunk of the car as bank. He had driven the new Jaguar only as far as th underground car park in Hyde Park.

Pavel tore off the cellophane and ran the washbasin ta until the basin was full. He put the roses into the wate Then he went into the bedroom to talk into the tape re corder again. He dictated the whole story of the KG plan to swamp the world market with gem diamonds. H played it back and was not satisfied. He erased the tap and redid the whole story. It was a better version.

He then called the hotel desk to reserve a special roo for a press conference. An undermanager called him fiv minutes later to confirm it on condition that Pavel, wh

d booked into the hotel in the name of James Lee,
ould pay half the price in advance. Pavel went into the
·yer and paid in full and in cash. Back in the suite ten
inutes later he phoned Reuter's and AP and two na-
ɔnal newspapers to let them know there would be an im-
ɔrtant press conference with a Russian defector in two
ɔurs' time.

Meade's men took little time to get there after the calls.
ɪt all they found were those exquisite pink roses in the
ɪthroom washbowl.

FOURTEEN

So many taxis were queueing to drop passengers at th
hotel in Park Lane it 'seemed the occasion might hav
been some royal reception. Most were newsmen, but oth
ers had joined the profession for this press conferenc
Sitting just inside the main doors in his elegant brow
blazer with its army-style buttons, Pavel saw Nobel Bra
cross to the lift among a group of newsmen. Pavel wa
well screened by the crowd in the foyer. Seconds late
Pavel saw Lenkov go through with Galkin, the KG
resident in the UK. He suspected Lenkov was carrying
Tass card. The next "newsman" known to him was Ca
der, who came in with Meade. Pavel studied the recedin
figure of Calder over an evening paper. He envied hi
desperately.

Calder would not have been there had he not gone
see Meade to explain that the story he'd given him ear
that day was quite clearly the reason for the big recove
in Krueger's share price. He was about to tell Meade t
story was a lie when Saunders came in with news of t
press conference called by Pavel. "Oh, Christ!" Mea
exclaimed. "That makes my day!"

He suggested that Calder might persuade Pavel to ho
his tongue "one way or another."

Pavel saw the lift go up with Calder and Meade amo
another load of newsmen. No one else he knew we
through, though there was at least one other "newsma
who had never penned a news story in his life. He was

224

Glasgow-born hit man on the underworld list, who had now taken over from the dead one. Under his armpit was a Walther PPK.

Some other "newsmen" were from Scotland Yard's Special Branch. Their only orders were to stop the press conference before the Russian had a chance to open his mouth. Not even the senior Special Branch men had been made privy to Pavel's claims. To them he was no more than a Russian who must not be allowed to talk to the press. Two of the Special Branch officers had special dart guns with silencers they might have to use on Pavel. The darts would do no more than put him to sleep instantly and would not cause any serious injury. The press would have no cause to yell "censorship!" Pavel would just have collapsed in the heat of the moment.

Pavel glanced at the foyer clock. He had called the press conference for eight o'clock. It was just after eight now. He let a couple of minutes go by to allow for late-comers. Then he crossed the foyer, which was still packed with American and German tourists, and picked on a youngish concierge he had made up his mind would prove the best of the three on the reception desk opposite.

The concierge had a well-scrubbed, eager face and knowing eyes and collected tips with such dexterity that most people would not even see they had been given. Pavel led him away from the crush at the desk and said, "I wonder if you could help me?"

"Certainly, sir." Pavel handed him a twenty-pound note.

The concierge made it vanish like a conjuror.

Pavel let the leather sling slip from his shoulder and put the tape recorder on a chair near the desk. He flipped it open. "Do you know how to use one like this?"

"It's a popular model, sir," the concierge said. "I doubt if there'll be any problem."

Pavel showed him the play switch and the volume control. "It's on full volume, so you needn't worry about that."

The man glanced sharply at Pavel. He was used to eccentric clients, but he'd never been handed twenty quid to take a lesson in working a tape recorder.

"You know about the press conference upstairs?" Pavel said trying to sound calmer than he felt.

He nodded.

"I just want you to go up and play this tape over to them."

"But somebody's booked the room to talk to them."

Pavel smiled and pointed a finger at himself. The man shrugged. He had known dottier things happen.

Pavel shook his hand and watched him cross to the lift with the tape recorder.

The lift doors opened and the man stood aside to let half a dozen people come out. One of them was Lenkov. He had a bulge under his left armpit, and his quick eyes scoured the foyer. The lift doors closed. Pavel was halfway to the main doors, trying to escape Lenkov's radar gaze but he was spotted.

He ran for the swing doors and was held up by an old woman who was moving it so slowly it was nerve-racking. If he pushed at the glass as they went round he might knock her off-balance and jam the bloody thing. He could see Lenkov within a few yards of the swing doors. Pavel came out past the old woman. He took the steps in one leap and ran out onto the sidewalk. His one instinct was to flee not left or right but right across the eight traffic lanes—four going each way—to the Hyde Park underground car park and use the Jaguar for a long-distance getaway.

He ran wildly across the south-bound traffic, pausing, dodging, weaving, and was just missed by a taxi. He could hear the cacophony of motor horns and the screech of tyres as brakes were slammed on by a score of angry and terrified drivers. A sports car swerved to avoid him and hit the central barrier, bouncing off into the path of a Citroën.

Pavel's heart was pounding as he made the central area. He spared a quick glance and saw Lenkov taking on the traffic. Horns blared and headlamps flashed, and there was a pandemonium of cars and taxis skidding and swerving. Cars bounced off each other, but Lenkov was still coming on.

Pavel took to the north-bound four lanes. At one moment he stood stock-still between a car and a van as they flashed past him in separate lanes. Amid the blaring of horns and squealing tyres he got across three of the lanes when the double-decker bus hit him. He had almost made it. But with the driver braking hard the nearside mudguard winged Pavel, and he was tossed into the air and fell just inside the slow lane.

It was, he imagined, like being in an explosion. He could hear the horns and urgent brakings as Lenkov took off after him across the four north-bound lanes. The world swam. Pavel got up and stumbled down the steep ramp leading to the underground car park. The pain in his left flank was crucifying him. And he seemed to be losing control of his left leg, dragging it down the ramp.

He could still hear the strident horns and skid sounds as Lenkov dodged running through the Park Lane traffic. Dazed, Pavel felt it was a miracle he had run the gauntlet of such fast and heavy traffic and still be alive. Surely by the law of averages Lenkov would never make it as well.

"Gentlemen!"

The hubbub died as the concierge laid the tape recorder on the dais of the conference room. In his smart grey uniform with it gold-and-blue lapel insignia he might have been a revolutionary general about to call for the people's support.

"I have been asked to play this tape over to you," he said, and began to flip open the tape recorder.

Meade nodded briefly to one of the Special Branch men with dart guns. The only sound was a faint plop like a cork going on a bottle of dead champagne. The concierge slumped over the baize-covered table.

In the pandemonium it was Calder who grabbed the tape recorder. He was going out with it when three newsmen, two heavyweights and a sharp-faced flyweight, barred his way. All three were snatched from behind by Special Branch men. The scuffle was brief and not very rough. By the time it was sorted out Calder was going through those swing doors. He had the feeling that someone was in the next section behind him as the doors swung. He didn't look round. But as he came out he turned to see Nobel Bray.

"I'd like to hear that," Bray said, with a look at the tape recorder. The swing doors were disgorging a third man, who had heard the request.

"Nothing doing," said Meade.

In his stationary Mercedes two minutes later he and Calder played back the tape. Pavel's voice burst into the car, and Calder turned the volume down. In a cool and sane voice Pavel said how he yearned for asylum in the UK. He confessed that he was a KGB officer. And he spoke clearly of the KGB plan to swamp the world market with Soviet diamonds.

"I have sold some of the diamonds I brought over," Pavel said. "I am prepared to give the proceeds to some deserving cause if I am permitted to stay in the United Kingdom."

Meade glanced across at Calder in the front seat of the parked Mercedes. "No wonder that Krueger's chap wanted an earful. This tape's worth a million dollars an inch to him."

Calder was still not sure whether Meade himself wasn't

228

the source of the leak that had saved fortunes for some and made them for others over the past few days.

"I think I'd like to hear that again," Calder said. He pressed the rewind button and kept his eyes on Meade.

Pavel heard the crack of a pistol and the zing of a bullet as it ricocheted off the wall of the long, narrow tunnel. He could hear oaths being screamed in Russian and the echoes of Lenkov's feet pounding the concrete. And though Pavel never once looked round, he knew Lenkov was gaining on him. Pavel's whole left side was stiff, and it was an agony to drag his left leg. Another shot rang through the tight tunnel and ripped an asbestos roof tile, bringing down a shower of plaster and dust on Pavel. Lenkov's coarse shouts were very loud, and Pavel feared he was closing the gap.

Pavel was still fifty yards short of the turnoff to the acres of the underground car park itself when Lenkov's third shot got him. It was only a snick and the pain no more than that from a shaving cut. But Pavel was out of breath. His left side was giving him agony and his left leg felt more like a heavy cargo than a limb. It amazed him that even in the dim light of the grey-green tunnel Lenkov had hit him with only one bullet. The *mokrie dela* mob was trained to hit moving targets with greater room for manoeuvre than Pavel had in the confines of the tunnel.

Yet another bullet pinged on metal, probably against one of the glass portholes between the pedestrian tunnel and the traffic exit. Pavel was gasping for breath when he got to the turnoff. He hurried desperately past the well-lit paybox and the three cars waiting to check out.

The paybox attendant had heard the shots and sat petrified in his box as Pavel shuffled past. Pavel saw there were still several hundred cars still parked in the huge area and felt some relief. He heard cars being driven out, and he zigzagged between the concrete pillars to the

Jaguar. The light was dim, which helped. Pavel could hear the echoes of Lenkov's running feet. Then there wasn't a sound in the whole area, not a sound, not an echo. Pavel put the key in the Jaguar's door and opened it slowly, scared it might even squeak. Then he had a lucky break. Another driver in the far recesses of the car park switched on his engine, and Pavel was able to close the Jaguar's door under cover of the noise.

Lenkov had never seen an underground car park so vast. He knew Pavel could not have got far. He moved from one concrete pillar to another, the pistol at the ready. The dim light was a handicap, but he put his face against the windows of every car, pausing now and then to listen when other cars were not entering or leaving the area. He went down on the concrete, lying full length in the oil slime, trying to see Pavel under a car or his legs beyond one.

For a while Pavel lost track of Lenkov, who had begun a methodical search block by block, checking every car. Some cars were still coming into the park from the far end.

In the paybox the attendant finished his 999 call and went out to check on the two men. Lenkov needed only one shot. The attendant, a middle-aged Pakistani, died on the spot as the bullet went through his forehead. Lenkov resumed his prowl.

In the Jaguar Pavel had let down the driver's seat so low he was lying almost prone. He was shaking with fear, and the blood from his wound was making the sleeve of his blazer stick to his arm. He saw that he was bleeding more than the sensation of the bullet's impact had led him to think. And his left side was giving him hell. He couldn't even feel his left leg. He had the driver's window slightly open. He was aware of people running back to the distant Marble Arch approach to escape from the shooting.

He heard the sound of an engine starting up, again as if miles away in the vast spaces of the car park. Lenkov crouched behind a pillar. His eyes tried to pierce the gloom. He could make out a Range Rover weaving between the pillars towards the exit. Lenkov was nearly dead with fatigue. His mind was not sharp any more. He felt sure Pavel was driving the Range Rover. As it turned into the lane leading directly to the exit, Lenkov crouched behind a pillar and aimed his pistol at the windshield. His first shot zinged off the hood. His second went through a side window and out through the windshield, missing the driver by inches.

Pavel sat up in the Jaguar and saw Lenkov get in a third shot. Then he heard the crash as the Range Rover hit the barrier and saw Lenkov dash towards the exit, which was out of Pavel's range of vision.

Pavel was in agony. Sitting up had made the pain worse. He knew Lenkov would return, and after a few seconds he saw the square bullock of a man come back from the exit, reloading his pistol.

Pavel was aware of total silence. Not a single car was coming in or out of the park, which seemed as vast as the Siberian tundra. He adjusted the seat so that he was only just high enough in the Jaguar to keep an eye on Lenkov, who had resumed his search in the dim light.

Calder said, "I don't mind going in with a Walther PPK."

"Nobody's going in," said the assistant commissioner from Scotland Yard. "We don't want a petrol explosion."

Meade knew why Calder wanted to go in armed, and because of this, he was on the Yard man's side. They were at the Park Lane approach to the Hyde Park underground car park. Armed police waited. Fire tenders and two ambulances were parked on the ramp. The Marble Arch approach was also blocked. Calder could see newsmen and sightseers at the top of both ramps leading off Park Lane. It had taken only a few eyewitnesses to put the newsmen on to the fact that the sterile press conference and the hairy chase across Park Lane were linked.

"I'd still like to go in," Calder said, peering into the endless tunnel.

"Don't be a masochist, Calder," Meade said stiffly.

The police cordon at the top of the southern ramp opened to let through an armoured car, which Calder reckoned some bright spark at the top had worked out from a safe distance was the right sort of vehicle to have round. The cordon had no sooner closed than it opened again to let through two police motorcyclists escorting an official three-litre Rover. Sir Harwood Caine lumbered out, brushing back his grey forelock. He saw Calder and Meade at the tunnel entrance, but he feared to go there in case some idiot should shoot from inside the tunnel.

Having dodged a war by joining the Foreign Office, Sir Harwood was in no mood at this late stage of his career to fall victim to some KGB man's stray bullet in London.

He beckoned Meade to join him. His face was flushed.

"Good Lord, Meade!" he blustered. "Did this have to happen? Park Lane's like Wembley Stadium. The press are up there in droves!"

"I can't very well wave them away," Meade said coolly.

Calder felt proud of him. He'd moved in close enough to hear what Caine had to say. He reckoned Caine might have a vested interest in dousing the Pavel affair and that it might have little to do with foreign affairs. Calder loathed him, all the way from his self-righteous jowled face to those ridiculous laced-up boots he wore.

The police cordon opened again. A police car came down the ramp leading a Soviet embassy Ford without even a CD plate. The Zises would never be used for such a job as this. Mazarev got out wearing an elegant medium-grey suit, and was greeted by Caine.

232

"I'm here to help, Sir Harwood," he said, his thin ascetic's face full of sincerity. "I'm prepared to go in there if necessary."

It was more than Sir Harwood Caine would do, even for a guaranteed peerage and an early pension. Caine glanced at the assistant commissioner, who had heard Mazarev's offer. The assistant commissioner shook his head.

"Nobody goes in there for the moment," he said.

Caine laid on a gracious smile for Mazarev and held him back from getting too close to the tunnel entrance. "Nothing is about to happen yet, Andrei," he said with a smirk.

Calder saw and heard. He had no time for well-bred geriatrics in key jobs.

FIFTEEN

Pavel watched Lenkov move from car to car in Block C. Lenkov was getting so close now that Pavel was breathing in gasps, he was so scared. His left leg was numb, and he was in agony from the injury to his hip where the bus had hit him. And he saw now that his gunshot wound had left a trail of blood that run through the oil patches on the concrete floor right up to the Jaguar. It could only be a matter of seconds before Lenkov spotted the red trail. Pavel made up his mind. The Jaguar was automatic and didn't need his dead left leg. He put the car in drive and switched on the ignition and sped out.

Lenkov's first shot pinged against the offside mudguard. His second smashed the rear window into frosted glass. Pavel had to make two right-angle turns to the exit. Lenkov saw this and ran through gaps between the parked cars to cut him off. The Jaguar nearly went over at the second turn, so fast was Pavel driving. He put his foot down and aimed for the exit only to see it was blocked by the Range Rover which was wrecked. He swerved the Jaguar violently only to find Lenkov right in his path with a pistol pointed straight at the windshield. The bullet shattered the windshield, and it fell in, fragmented.

Lenkov put up his arms as if to protect himself as he ran backwards. He loomed big and grotesque to Pavel beyond the holed windshield from which slivers of glass were still dropping. And behind Lenkov was one of the concrete pillars.

Pavel tugged madly at the steering wheel. The impact was violent, and his head hit the remains of the windshield. He blacked out for a moment and then saw Lenkov—or what was left of him. Lenkov's body had acted as a bumper between the Jaguar and the pillar. It was crushed flat with only the head and shoulders intact. And Lenkov's head hung like some grotesque twisted mascot over the Jaguar's grey hood, which was streaming with his blood. Pavel shook his head and saw the dead gargoyle face staring at him through the open windshield.

Calder was first to turn away from the press conference the assistant commissioner was giving at the top of the ramp. He found the AC a bit twee, and the evasive answers that had to be given called for a good lying politician, which the AC was not. He threw Meade a look or two beyond the TV camera lights for reassurance.

Meade had nodded. It spurred the AC to enjoy his evasions. All he would admit was that two men, one known to be armed, occupied the underground car park. No, he couldn't confirm that one of the men was the Russian who had called the hotel press conference that never was.

Calder watched the AC smile benignly at a tough TV reporter and gave a nonanswer as if he fancied himself as a clever politician. And when a pygmy-sized reporter peeped through the inner ring of newsmen and asked if he denied that both men in the car park were Russians, he smirked and said, "I haven't seen their passports."

It was too much for Calder. The AC was lucky that none of the newsmen knew Mazarev as a first secretary from the Soviet embassy. Sir Harwood Caine's face meant nothing either. He was the perfect specimen of the faceless bureaucrat. One final look at the AC in his immaculate uniform trying to become an instant folk hero made Calder want to throw up. He joined the gaggle of Special Branch men and police snipers near the gasoline pumps at the foot of the ramp.

Some moments later, peering into the tunnel, Pavel thought he saw a distant movement. In the faint light he could make out a figure hundreds of yards back inside the tunnel. The Special Branch were on to it now and moved to each side of the entrance for cover. They were head-on targets where they had stood. The police snipers took up position, the left-handed marksman crouching at the right-hand edge of the tunnel.

One of the Special Branch men shouted, "Sir!"

The AC put up a hand to the newsmen to imply their privilege was over and went back down the ramp.

Calder stared into the gloom and had no doubt who it was reeling and falling his way along the tunnel. He turned to see Meade coming down the ramp with Caine and the heroic AC. The police cordon closed ranks behind them. He knew that both the AC and Meade would forbid him to go in. So he went in now.

"Hey, mate!" one of the snipers yelled in alarm.

But Calder was already two paces into the tunnel. He didn't look round once. Pavel was his business. He saw Pavel stumble and pick himself up and stagger on. He had a case and he was dragging his left leg.

Calder heard Meade shout, "Calder! Come back! Come back at once!" The voice echoed through the tunnel.

Calder never even changed his pace. As the gap between him and Pavel closed, Calder saw Pavel's face was a mass of blood and that the sleeve of his blazer was stained dark red.

The snipers wanted to go in to cover Calder. But the AC shook his head. "If he wants to get himself killed, that's his affair." His smugness over the way he had coped with the newsmen had been wiped off his face.

Even when Calder and Pavel had cut the gap to ten

yards, Pavel had still not made out that the blurry figure looming towards him was Calder. He fell down again and was desperately trying to reach his feet when Calder got to him. Calder just stood over him and watched him slowly force himself up off the concrete. He thought Pavel was almost dead, and he felt cheated. Only now, with their faces a couple of feet apart, did Pavel see it was Calder. Calder's eyes were grey marble. "You thieving bastard!" he said.

Pavel was rocking. He tried to focus Calder, but the image kept fading, and Calder's face seemed to swirl like liquid.

"You lousy thieving bastard!"

Pavel tried to offer him the case. But Calder was not on about diamonds or cash. He was on about Galina. He would have liked to kill Pavel. But now his need for revenge ebbed as he studied the wrecked face. Pavel could hardly keep his eyes open, and blood was pouring from his nose, and an ugly lump was coming out on his forehead.

"Are the press out there, Calder?" he said, swaying.

"Fuck the press!"

"I want to see them," Pavel said, trying to hold out the case. "I want asylum, that's all."

"I want you back in bloody Moscow!" Calder's look was pitiless, but he was churning inside.

Just for a few moments Pavel had Calder in focus. "Give this to Galina," he said. Again he tried to give Calder the case.

But Calder just stood absolutely still, full of hate but with pity taking over. The case fell out of Pavel's grasp.

"Where's the other bastard?" Calder said.

"He's dead," Pavel said, and his eyelids would not stay open any more. "And there are two people in a car." He began to sway.

Calder reached out and took him before he could fall.

It took all Calder's strength to lift Pavel over his shoulder. He left the case where it had fallen. He would be no errand boy delivering Pavel's gifts to Galina. When he had carried Pavel to within fifty yards of the entrance, Calder called, "The other one's dead!" Only then did ambulance men and police come to relieve him of Pavel. "And he says there are two more in there."

Meade's face was severe. Calder just stared him out.

The police snipers were going in now, cautious as infantry in spite of the information that the other man was dead.

As some Special Branch men went into the tunnel, Calder said to Meade, "There's a case back there he was carrying. I suppose we ought to have it."

"We'll recover that," said the AC sharply.

Meade shook his head. "I'd rather we had our hands on it and no one else."

The AC looked down at Meade from his great height. "It could be a bomb!" he said stiffly.

"Don't be bloody silly!" Calder said irritably. He'd had his bellyful of this immaculate hero, and he felt like a mess with Pavel's blood all over him. He saw Meade go into the tunnel to fetch the case. And he turned and began to walk up the ramp.

Ahead he could see the flashing blue lamp of the ambulance as it rushed Pavel to hospital through a gap in the crowd of media men and women. He walked past the assistant commissioner and Mazarev and Sir Harwood Caine without so much as a glance.

Then he heard Caine's pompous voice behind him. "May I give you a lift, Calder?"

"No, thanks," Calder said. "I'm fine." He would rather have walked.

He got a couple of policemen to see him through the media crowd. As he walked up Park Lane looking for a taxi, a second ambulance raced past with the two from the wrecked Rover. They were both dead by the time Calder found a taxi to take him home.

Galina was reading *The Gulag Archipelago* with Ladybird Johnson on her lap when she heard Calder come in. She heard him go through the hall and straight upstairs, which was not his way. He had left no message when he had gone out to see Meade. Before, he would always let her know if he would be back late. But their personal cold war explained such behaviour.

She had dined with Olga and since her return had not switched on the TV. She knew nothing of the siege of the underground car park.

Solzhenitsyn's words were a blur now. It was time she and Calder began to thaw things out. She went upstairs and heard the shower being run. In the bathroom she could hear Calder puffing and blowing behind the plastic curtain. Then she saw the heap of blood-soaked clothes on the floor.

"Calder!" she called in alarm, and flung the curtain back.

The spray came out at her. "Calder!"

She could see almost right away there was nothing wrong with him, and the feeling of relief was intense.

"You'll get wet through if you don't close it," Calder said.

But she just stood looking at him with the water spurting all over her.

"It's not my blood," Calder said.

She closed her eyes in relief.

"It's Pavel's,"

She studied him for a while as he put his face up to the spray and made faces, blowing out water.

"He's dead?"

Calder kept his face up into the spray. "He wasn't when they took him off."

239

She hardly moved but stayed rooted with her eyes on Calder under the shower but not really seeing him. For a moment Calder thought she had gone. He took his face out from the jets and saw she was still just where she had been with those vivid green eyes on him and yet seeing something a million light-years away.

"Well, aren't you going to ask where he is?" Calder knew it would hurt her, yet he still came out with it.

She said nothing for a moment or two. Then, "Yes, I'd like to know where he is."

"St. George's Hospital," Calder said soaping himself.

Galina's eyes stayed on him for a while. She glanced down at the bloodied clothes.

He heard the door close. Calder let the sprays splash his face. He kept seeing Pavel with Galina in that room at the warren and somewhere in London, wherever it was they had their rendezvous. He saw Pavel touching her, embracing her, kissing her, and he hoped Pavel was dead. He took his face clear of the water. And he saw Pavel's face in its bloody agony. He didn't hope he was dead. He hoped he was out of pain. He dried himself off and went downstairs.

Galina was back into *The Gulag Archipelago*. He saw that she had poured him a large scotch. "Well, cheers," he said. "I must say you're in a better mood."

She looked up and he tapped a finger against his glass.

"I suppose you phoned St. George's and they told you he's doing fine?"

It was for no more than a split second that she hated him. She let the question hang and made a point of going back to her book.

"Well, you *did* phone?"

"Yes," she said coolly, without looking up. "I telephoned."

"And he's fine?"

240

"He's still unconscious and can't have any visitors."

"Ah!" Calder gulped down the scotch in one. "That explains why you're still here?"

Not many minutes ago she still thought she was in love with Calder and merely liked Pavel. Now she was not sure anymore.

Meade was in his office with Sir Harwood Caine and Humphrey Girton from 10 Downing Street when Calder came in uninvited. They were thrashing out ideas about how to cope with the Hyde Park incident. The press was heavy with stories that Pavel was a Russian dissident who had been denied asylum and that Lenkov was a KGB officer sent over to take him back. There was not a single word to connect Pavel with diamonds.

Calder had also read all the papers—in a black mood. Jaded by the strain of the tunnel encounter with Pavel and his fears of losing Galina, he had gone to bed early. He had taken a sleeping pill and spent a night of oblivion. When he came to, he found that Galina had not shared the bed but had used the spare bedroom. He went down and saw that Galina had already been through the papers. She left him to see to his own breakfast and went out without saying where she was going. He felt it might be St. George's Hospital. He brooded till midmorning. His mind was full of Galina and questions.

He took the phone and dialled the Stock Exchange news report. What he heard made him angry. He drove to St. James's right away and parked on a double yellow band. Meade ordered him out of the office, and Caine went a shade of purple. But Calder held firm and dialled the Stock Exchange news report and gave the phone to Meade. Meade's composure was shaken. He took the phone. The deadpan voice said, "Krueger's were a feature in the first hour of trading. At eleven o'clock they were forty-two points down at a hundred and sixty-six, losing all the gains made yesterday."

Meade was aware of Calder's accusing eyes on him. He put the phone down and, with glances at Caine and Girton, said, "I think we'd best let Calder have his say."

"Somebody's leaking official secrets," Calder said with venom. "And probably making a packet!"

He waved aside Caine's and Girton's interruptions and gave them a rundown on the Krueger's share scene. The shares had taken a beating right after Calder had told Meade about the KGB plan to swamp the world market. They had come back with a big jump when he told Meade that the whole thing was a put-up job by Pavel to cover his theft of gem diamonds. "But that was a lie," Calder said. "It was a downright lie invented by one person."

"And who was that?" Sir Harwood was trying to stay cool, but his face colour was giving him away.

"It was me," Calder said. "I made up that story."

Calder let them stew in the silence before saying that the morning's fallback in Krueger's share price must be tied up with the tape recording Pavel made the previous night in which he told of the KGB plan. Calder was gazing hard at Meade. Caine and Girton also fixed Meade with accusing looks. Meade's face turned fierce. His eyes roved from Caine to Girton. It was like the accused suddenly becoming the judge. "You, Sir Harwood, and you, Girton, were also privy to every one of the developments Calder has just told us about. I put both of you in the picture within minutes."

Caine squirmed under the implied charge.

"This is absurd," Girton said. He got up with a show of disgust.

Meade was like a prosecutor now. "I want to know who else was put in the picture."

"I informed the prime minister naturally," Girton said stiffly.

"Anyone else?"

Girton was indignant. "No one."

Meade turned on Caine.

"I told the foreign secretary." Caine was so angry he seemed about to propel his bulk out of the chair and snatch Meade across the desk. It took more than Caine's menace to scare Meade, who had throttled an SS man twice his size in the Battle of Arnhem. "Anyone else?"

Caine shook his head. There was a chance, Meade pointed out, that either the prime minister or the foreign secretary had brought up the matter with their senior officials.

"Not a chance!" Caine sniffed.

His quick eyes rested on Calder as if to imply that he was also a suspect.

"I personally put one other person in the picture on each occasion," Meade confessed. "Saunders."

They all knew there would have to be a harsh internal inquiry now. And Calder felt they hated him for having opened up the skeleton's cupboard in the first place. Nevertheless, Meade took him to lunch at his club.

Sir Harwood Caine felt he needed fresh air. He drove out for a round of golf at Moor Park.

Humphrey Girton went back to the Cabinet Office and tidied his desk and packed his briefcase with its embossed gold initials EIIR on the flap. He took an early train home to Hampshire.

After a long lunch when they did not discuss the Pavel affair even once, Meade and Calder went back to the office to question Saunders. Meade was just about to begin when the phone rang. His hand shook as he listened. And it took a lot to unnerve Meade.

"Thank you." He put the phone down and turned to Calder. "I hope you're satisfied," he said. The body of a man had just been found lying against a bag of peat moss in his garden shed with two empty bottles nearby. One had contained scotch, the other barbiturate pills.

It was Humphrey Girton, MVO.

SIXTEEN

It was forty-eight hours after the Park Lane incident before anyone other than doctors and nurses came to see Pavel. He was up and about in his private patient's room, but his phone was cut off, and there were always two Special Branch men in the corridor beyond.

Meade came in briskly. He crossed with a smile to join Pavel at the window, where he could see the lights of Buckingham Palace shining in the distance through the trees.

"I hear you're feeling much better?" Meade said, introducing himself as one who worked with Calder.

"A little," Pavel said cautiously. His left side still felt stiff, and he felt the odd stab of pain from his arm, but the lump on his head was going down, and his nose which had been so swollen was almost back to normal size.

Meade noted the two dozen roses in the vase on the coffee table near the bed and the splash of mixed flowers on the window ledge. He knew all about them. The roses had come with a get-well note signed by Galina. The card on the mixed flowers had baffled him and Calder—and Amberley, who was also consulted. They had no idea who Jack and Liz could be.

The doctors had kept Meade away so far. And Meade in his turn had made sure that nobody else should get anywhere near Pavel. The media were still on about what one paper had called "the mystery Russian" and another "the defector the KGB missed."

But both the Whitehall and Krueger's public relations operators had worked hard. It was Meade's idea that Whitehall should leak hints that Pavel was a military defector whose life was in peril and that he should not show his face to the media. And Krueger's had blown up their lie while also denying it about rumours of a big diamond field in South America. Pavel had almost burst the stitches in his face when he read the papers and saw the quote from a Krueger's spokesman. "We'll get rumours next that there are diamonds under the North Sea." Pavel thought the spokesman was very clever to have mentioned the North Sea and not Hyde Park.

He had not been kept from the papers. They had blocked his phone and would not let him out of his room. And he hoped that the only reason Galina had not been to see him was that they had denied her access. Ever since the moment he'd come round he had been unable to keep his eyes off her roses for long. And that bouquet from Stepney and Liz had made his throbbing brain think of the real people who were not part of the dirty tricks being played on the world.

Meade let his eyes wander off the lights of Buckingham Palace and focus on the battered Pavel in his National Health dressing gown. "I don't know if you feel well enough to talk yet?"

"It depends who to," Pavel said guardedly.

"Well—me for one."

"And the other?"

"One of your comrades from the Soviet embassy."

Pavel shuddered. He was reminded of that blood-spurting gargoyle with its popping eyes over the Jaguar's hood.

He turned from the window, urging his mind into some sort of order. He felt that Meade was there to trick him. "I have asked for asylum," he said quietly. "Why should I see someone from the Soviet embassy?"

Meade had to be careful. The Russians had been

pressing for some days for access to Pavel, since before the Hyde Park business.

"It's a formality," Meade lied. His brief was to see Pavel out of British airspace on the first Aeroflot flight he could be humanely put on.

Pavel had never felt so mixed up in his life. A lot of things still confused him, all the way from the killing of Vader in the Gulf of Finland to Meade's appeal now. In a way he knew he must push on with his task, for the impact of his arrival was waning. Krueger's shares were back again over the 200 mark, and the media had still not caught on to the link between Krueger's ups and downs and the Hyde Park sensation. The complication was Galina. He was in love with her.

He made up his mind now. "What does this comrade want to see me about?" he said, pouring a glass of barley water and offering Meade one.

Meade pulled a face at the thought of the drink. "He wants to help you."

Pavel recalled what Suslov had said at the final briefing. "It might seem our own comrades will try to stop you. But don't let them stop you, however real their attempts."

It had all been too real for Vader in the Gulf of Finland and for himself in the Hyde Park underground car park. And Pavel couldn't make out why Meade should be in league with the Soviet embassy. Maybe détente really did mean something to the British? Maybe they really did see him as an embarrassing pawn in the new game?

In his mind's eye he saw Galina—her hair, her eyes, her buttocks as she walked in tight jeans.

"Very well," he said to Meade. "I'll see him."

Relief came over Meade's intelligent boxer's face. He was moving to the door when Pavel said, "On one condition."

Meade paused.

247

"I want my diamonds back." Pavel's second reaction when he came round in the hospital was to think of those diamonds. His first reaction was to worry about Galina. It was all very blurry. But he had searched the bedside cupboard and then stumbled to the dressing table to open up one drawer after another. He went to the door and told one of the Special Branch guards to find the ward sister. He complained that a leather pouch of his was missing. The sister said his clothes were in such a state that they had been sent to the laundry.

"And the pouch?"

The kindly sister had checked with the almoner to learn that almost one thousand pounds found in Pavel's pocket was in the hospital safe, but that a Special Branch officer had called to sign for the pouch. The way the sister had put it to Pavel was that the authorities had taken the pouch away for forensic checks to find clues about the attack on him. It was a lame excuse, but the sister believed it. What had happened was that Nobel Bray had tried to get hold of the diamonds on behalf of Krueger's and Meade had forestalled him.

In Pavel's room now Meade chose not to play dumb. "Well, we can't have you going around flogging valuable gems, Pavel."

"Why not?"

"It's not in the interests of our two countries," Meade said. "It's not in the interests of the world."

"It's not in the interests of the diamond industry," Pavel said. His head was aching so much he felt it might burst. "It's not in the interests of a lot of very rich people."

Meade was shaking his head. Pavel lay back on the bed, leaning against the headboard. He looked very stubborn and closed his eyes.

Meade said, "May I bring in your comrade from the embassy?"

"You can bring him in," Pavel said, his Arctic blue eyes alive in spite of the pain behind them. "But I won't talk to him."

Meade crossed back to the bed. "Pavel," he said simply. "It will help all of us."

It was going through Pavel's mind now that he didn't really want all the diamonds. He knew just what he wanted now. He wanted only the big special.

"Get me the big special back," Pavel said. "And I'll talk to Comrade Whoever-he-is."

Coming out of such a wounded face, the words found a response in Meade. He thought Pavel had guts. "I'll see what I can do," Meade said, going out. He had an idea what Pavel was up to. But he wasn't sure.

He was back an hour later with the big special. He was insensitive to its beauty, and it meant nothing to him. Pavel caressed it for a few moments. Its opaque mysteries were a joy and he was reminded that he had not yet seen the Tate Gallery, which was on his list of places to visit.

Meade's eyes were saying, Can he come in now? Pavel put the big special in the drawer of his bedside table and nodded. Meade let in the slight Mazarev, whose ascetic's eyes summed up Pavel.

"Pavel," he said, taking the bedside chair.

Pavel nodded. "Speak in English," he said, keeping up his role.

It took some time and many empty words before Mazarev came to the point. "I'm here to ask you to come home, Pavel. We're in a period of détente. Operation *almaz* is off. It was cancelled long ago on orders from the Central Committee."

Pavel's headache had vanished. His eyes took in Mazarev and Meade. It struck him that Mazarev might have gone West.

"It is no fault of yours, Pavel," Mazarev said quietly. "You will be made welcome back home."

Pavel was still on his guard. He began to pour barley water into his glass. Mazarev took over and gave him the full glass. "Tell me—what has Suslov got against you?"

The question shook Pavel. Even with no British security man like Meade within a hundred metres it would have been a tricky thing to ask. He began to wonder if Mazarev had crossed over.

"Suslov used you, Pavel," Mazarev said. "And he was used by others in his turn."

Pavel tried to conceal his shock. He had to lie there and listen while Mazarev spoke openly in front of Meade of a breach of discipline by a group of KGB officers who hated détente and wanted to see Operation Rough Diamond carried through.

"You were used, Pavel," Mazarev said.

Pavel put on an act of being worn out. He was really feeling better than he'd done since before Lenkov shot him. But he let his eyelids fall and studied Mazarev through the slits. He just wasn't sure.

"I will not go back to Russia," he said, no longer sure if he was still playing a part or speaking the truth. He could see Mazarev very clearly through the eye slits. He saw him get up and cross to take in the view of Buckingham Palace.

Meade poured himself a glass of barley water.

Mazarev said, "What do you know about Katerina Suslov?"

All the agony went from Pavel's body, he was so shocked. But he kept up a cool front and took a sip of the drink.

"Pavel," Mazarev said, "we're not in a paternity court."

Pavel could see him through those slits, and Mazarev was as bland as a Hero of the Soviet Union. "Katerina Suslov?" Pavel knew only too well how hollow was the sound of his voice.

"Oh, come," Mazarev said quietly through that sensitive mouth. "We all fall in love, some of us more often than others."

They all heard Big Ben chime nine o'clock. Pavel was rubbing the fingers of each hand against each other. Mazarev sat on the edge of the bed. "She was nineteen, and she had an abortion."

Pavel felt his anger spurt until he saw that Mazarev's face was not gloating or vicious but sympathetic. And the only image he could hold in his mind was of Katerina, dark and muscled like an athlete, her body so alive and her mind so dull.

"You've forgotten her?"

Pavel shook his head slowly.

"Suslov certainly hasn't!"

Memories pinwheeled through Pavel's mind. Katerina was so beautiful and so lacking in intellect.

"Please tell me one thing," Mazarev said quietly. "Did Suslov tell you to swim out second from Helsinki?"

Pavel's mind replayed the Vader scene in the Gulf of Finland, with Vader floating in that bloated skin diver's suit and oozing streaks of blood into the calm sea. He closed his eyes.

He heard Mazarev say, "You'll be welcomed home, Pavel."

He could see Suslov's big, angry face when Pavel had said he could not marry Katerina. And then another face came over Suslov's in his mind. He was seeing Galina.

"Please go away," he said.

Meade knew it was no use for the moment. He winked at Mazarev, and they left. Down in the hospital reception area they saw Galina waiting. They crossed over to her. "Galina," Meade said gallantly, kissing her cheek. Mazarev knew Galina. He bowed. "Galina."

Her green eyes flashed. "Unless you can help me to see

251

Pavel, I would prefer you to go." They could see that she meant it, so they went away.

It was midafternoon the next day when Meade came back with Mazarev. Pavel had told the hospital consultant that he wished to complete his treatment in Moscow. The consultant felt it was an insult. But Meade was told.

Galina's roses were still fresh and the mixed flowers were crisp and upright, all reds and yellows, and a large basket of fruit stood on the coffee table with a ripe peach as its centerpiece. Meade glanced at the card on it. "Love," it read. "Jack and Liz."

"Who are Jack and Liz?" Meade smiled.

Pavel held him with a look. "Diamond millionaires," he said calmly.

"You've made the right decision, Pavel," Mazarev said with an eye on the fruit.

"Have an apple," Pavel said. He was a lot better now. The pain had gone from his head and arm, and even his leg was less stiff as the bruise subsided.

One of the conditions Pavel had made was that he should be given some clothes in place of those ruined by Lenkov's blood. Mazarev laid a plastic clothes container on the bed and said, "I believe they're all about right."

Pavel had a choice from two grey jackets and two pair of slacks, one grey and the other blue, and several light weight shirts. "What time is it?" he asked them.

Meade shot a glance at his watch. "Ten past four."

Pavel took his time dressing.

It was around five o'clock when they went out by the supplies exit of St. George's Hospital to evade any medi men who might still be around. Mazarev had come in the Ford again, avoiding the Zises. He ushered Pavel into the back seat and joined him while Meade took the only spare seat in a Special Branch Triumph. Nobody noticed.

Pavel hoped he had gauged the rush-hour right. The

raffic was snarling up in Knightsbridge. It was very thick
s they took the left fork leading past Harrod's to the mo-
orway and Heathrow Airport. It was crawling along
hen Pavel, having tested the door handle three times,
1ade his bid. He dived out of the Ford and ran into the
ush-hour crowds near Knightsbridge underground sta-
on.

It was the driver who took off after him. He was over-
eight and had no chance to catch up with Pavel even
1ough Pavel's leg was still a painful handicap. Two
pecial Branch men leapt from the Triumph. But they
vere too late. Pavel was lost in the rush-hour crowd.

Amid an angry chorus of motor horns Mazarev moved
ut from the back of the Ford into the driver's seat and
lrove off. "Keep going," Meade told the Special Branch
river. He didn't want another major public incident. And
t as he was, he was past the age to go chasing young
Russians in London, even one with a limp.

Pavel slipped into the cavern of Knightsbridge under-
round station. He then stood stock-still as the overweight
Russian driver trundled past him among a press of rush-
our commuters. Pavel slipped out the way he had gone
1. He had Galina on his mind. All he wanted to do now
vas to find a phone.

Galina picked up the phone.

"Galina?" Pavel sounded distraught.

"Pavel," she said anxiously. She had phoned the hospi-
al a dozen times and had waited twice in the reception
rea. She had been given the most formal bulletins about
is condition and no more.

"Galina," he said. "I want to see you!"

"They won't let me in!"

He told her he was now out of the hospital. He was
bout to say where she could find him when she cut in

253

and said, "Pavel! Don't say where you are! I will see yo
in the usual place!"

And she said it in Russian, knowing that the phon
tappers would have to send the tape to the linguists.

"Galina," he said, "I love you."

"Never mind how long it takes, Pavel," she said. "I w
come to you." And she knew what she was up against.

SEVENTEEN

Sir Sefton Dykes was euphoric. Krueger's share price had closed well up at 208, a big recovery on the day. The media were not on to any link between Pavel and diamonds, and their interest showed signs of being on the wane. And now Nobel had just come in with the breathless news just given him by Saunders that Pavel had asked to return to Moscow. Dykes gazed down at the rush-hour crowds and car jams below and felt a glow of delight at such a wonderful world.

"Well, pour us all a sherry, Charlton," he said through a tight smile.

He crossed to the PR executive Ogilvy and put an affectionate hand on his shoulder. "We should have you on the company's roll of honour, Ogilvy," he said. "Splendid job." He was on about the way Ogilvy had diverted the media with ruse and rumour through these days of crisis. He wasn't sure that Ogilvy should not be put forward as a candidate for the Queen's Birthday Honours List for such brilliant lying.

Nobel Bray felt put out. Much of the praise being doled out by the chairman should really have been his, not the smooth-tongued Ogilvy's. But Bray still had an ace to play. It was a matter of timing. He found Ogilvy detestable, an immaculate yes-man with all Charlton's faults, such as that capacity never to sweat or get his shirt cuffs dirty.

As Dykes paced the vast arena of the office like some

elfin skeleton, Bray thought he saw tears of joy in the o[l]
man's eyes. Charlton gave out the sherries. Bray neve[r]
normally drank the stuff, but Ogilvy was a notoriou[s]
sherry man, and this made Bray feel all the worse.

"And you did vastly well too, Nobel," Dykes said, tak[-]
ing Bray's left bicep in a frail grip.

It was too condescending for Bray's taste. As Dyke[s]
raised his glass to the odious Ogilvy, Bray said, "There'[s]
just one other thing, sir."

They all paused, sherry unsavoured.

"I now know why Lady Naphill and our America[n]
friend Bradley J. Sagar sold their collections."

He paused too long.

"Out with it then!" Dykes snapped.

"They *were* tipped off." He threw quick looks at Ogilv[y]
and Charlton to imply that what he knew was too big [a]
secret for them to share. Dykes nodded to them. "Tak[e]
your sherries with you and wait in the outer office for [a]
moment."

It did Bray's morale no end of good to see Ogilvy g[o]
out with Charlton. Dykes had eyes only for Bray now. H[e]
said, "The tip-off came from an undersecretary in th[e]
Cabinet Office called Humphrey Girton."

Dykes's euphoria had gone. "And who else will he b[e]
tipping off?"

"He won't," Bray said evenly. "He's killed himself."

"Poor chap," Dykes muttered, overcome with relief.

He brought back Ogilvy and Charlton to finish thei[r]
sherries. Charlton was pouring their seconds when th[e]
phone rang. Ogilvy took it and looked puzzled.

"It's for you," he said, giving it to Bray.

It was Saunders, and he was using a public call box[.]
Bray's face fell as he listened while Dykes was again a[t]
his fulsome best with Ogilvy on the other side of the desk[.]
It was some moments after he put the phone down befor[e]

Bray could bring himself to break the news that Pavel had got away and was on the loose again in London.

It was too much for Sir Sefton Dykes. His mouth sagged, and he put a hand to his heart. He fell into his chair and tugged open a desk drawer and swallowed two pills. He looked good for a coronary. But Nobel Bray felt sure the old hypochondriac had a few years yet.

Galina knew she was being followed the moment she set off in the Mini. Two men in an Austin drove off after her.

Knowing her phone would be tapped, she had let an hour pass before she went out, long enough to induce any Special Branch watchers to lose their sharpness. It took all her willpower to hold back, for she very much wanted to see Pavel. But now she knew the delay was a mistake. It would have been much more easy to lose followers in the rush hour. And the rush hour was over now and the traffic light.

She was passing a garage with a car wash when the idea came. The Austin was still behind her as she crossed the line of traffic, and she saw it pull in to the kerb. In the dimly lit garage she saw there was only one other car on the car-wash line. About a dozen other cars were parked, and in the darkest part stood two breakdown trucks. She saw the Toilets sign over an exit that led into the yard behind the garage. As the big Chevrolet went into the car wash, Galina drew up the Mini. She paid the fee to the young attendant and said, "It frightens me in there. Would you take it through for me?"

What does she think's in there? Ghosts? Rapists? he thought, grinning. It might be that bloody great wheel spinning nearer and nearer in that inferno that put the wind up nervous women. He'd known a few who got sex fantasies out of the orgy of high-pressure sprays and that cleaning wheel. Others he knew just wouldn't go through.

He whistled up a pimply youth to look after the control

box while he took the Mini through. As the car was tracked into the machine, Galina said as if shyly to the youth, "You have a ladies, please?" The youth blushed and pointed to the exit labelled "Toilets."

Out in the street the two Special Branch men saw the Mini come out from the car wash into the forecourt like some ingenue. A Pakistani ran a wash leather over the wet spots that had survived the drying process. They saw the young attendant get out. The Special Branch men were out of the Austin and across the road in seconds. One of them ran over to question the attendant and the youth. The other saw the Toilets exit and raced straight for it. He found Galina's pale-blue silk scarf on the cracked concrete path near the ladies' lavatory. He went and stood near the lavatory door, frowning and awkward. The other Special Branch man ran out to him now. He was round forty, probably more than ten years older, and he did not hold back. He went in. There were two cubicles, and the door of one was closed. He put out a tentative hand, and it opened to his touch. It was unoccupied.

Back on the path the two Special Branch men saw the vandals' gaps in the back fence of the garage. They went to check the private gardens beyond. But there was no trace of Galina. They went back through the garage to their Austin to report over the radio that they had lost contact.

Galina let ten minutes go by before she got down from the high cab of one of the breakdown trucks.

Calder had no idea when he met Meade and Caine that Galina had given her Special Branch followers the slip. They were in Meade's office. And Meade had just told him of the phone-tap report that Galina had agreed to rendezvous with Pavel.

Caine was making the most of it. It was to be expected. He resented having to meet Meade and Calder so soon after Girton's suicide just because Calder was still not satisfied that Girton was the only culprit.

Girton had left a note written on a seed packet in that garden shed. It was a pathetic last few lines in which he said he had left a private letter for his wife in his desk drawer and that this seed-packet message was meant for official eyes. "I was tactless and disloyal," he had written in his precise, tiny hand. "I let two dear friends into official secrets to help them protect their assets." It did not take long for Meade's men to get from Girton's widow a list of his "dear friends."

Meade had got Calder to check the list with Nobel Bray. Bray identified only two names on the list. But the sight of them made his blood rise. They were a bit emotive. They were the names of Bradley J. Sagar and Lady Naphill.

Back in Meade's office Calder had bluntly told Meade that Girton's suicide note was not the end of it. It did not account for the heavy selling of Krueger's shares by some people with major holdings. There had to be someone else. Meade agreed and asked Caine to join them.

Caine could not hide his fury. He shifted in his chair now and fixed Calder with a suspicious look. "I take it you *are* still fond of this Russian wife of yours?"

Calder wanted to break his jaw. He had an awful job to keep his self-control. "Galina's not my wife," he said as if casually. "We shack up, that's all."

Caine tut-tutted. "Shack up?"

"And how's *your* wife?" Calder's eyes were livid.

"I think that will do," Meade said firmly.

It rushed through Caine's mind that Calder should be sent to the Tower. But he said, "She's still an alien, and don't you and she forget it. We could deport her tonight!"

Calder darted from his chair like a fresh middleweight. He took Caine by the lapels and shook him about with such violence that Caine's earlobes were flapping like a pig's. He could have killed him there and then.

But even as Meade came round the desk to put an end to Calder's second assault there in a few days, there was a knock on the door and Saunders came in. He knew what was going on. He said in a loud voice, "Galina has given the Special Branch chaps the slip."

The words hit Calder like a poleaxe. He let go of the pop-eyed Caine, with his white face and shaking jowls. He could see only one thing now. He could see images only of Galina with Pavel. He kept his head low as he went out. None of those bastards was going to see him crying.

The concourse of a London main line station is hardly the place to let the emotions rip. Pavel felt she was the most beautiful woman he had ever set eyes on, but he kissed her formally on both cheeks as she came out of the underground.

She took in the battered face with its bruises and stitches and her eyes were moist. "You shouldn't be here, Pavel."

The rush hour was long past, but a lot of commuters were still running for trains.

"I would like to take you to an English pub," he said.

She nodded.

They began to walk out of Euston, and she saw he had a limp.

"Pavel," she said, concerned.

He wanted to tell her right now about the suite he had booked when she had not shown up, but all he said was, "I want to tell you about many things." He took her hand now, and his grip was strong.

They found a pub behind Euston. They could not keep their eyes off each other. The place was a bit seedy with velvet red seating worn smooth and black in places. It was packed with railway porters and shunters. Pavel and Galina found a corner when a couple of railwaymen moved out to make room for them.

"I thought when you didn't come last time, you had made up your mind not to meet again."

She took in the sad eyes and leaned over to kiss him on the cheek.

"I thought perhaps they had frightened you off."

Her green eyes sparkled in the glare from the bar lights. It was still daylight, but the bar's scarlet lights were all on.

"I'm not afraid over here, Pavel," she said simply. "They watch you from time to time. But they don't try to frighten you." She studied him over her gin and tonic.

His mind was made up about his plans, but he thought now he wanted her more than ever. "Galina," he said, "I'm going back."

Her eyes never wavered.

"I'm not what I seem," he said.

"None of us are," she said. He could sense her excitement. There was a fleeting moment when he thought she might be a KGB sleeper planted in Britain. But the moment was overtaken when he took in her eyes and touched her hand on that worn velvet seat cover.

He began to tell her why he had crossed over. "The idea was to—"

She held out her glass. "I'd like one more, Pavel," she said.

He came back with another gin and tonic. He waited for a few people to move out of earshot and said, "I came over with a job to do," he began.

"And you failed?"

There was a long pause. "I love you, Galina."

Their hands were clenched tight between them on the velvet seat.

"I would like to tell you why I came," he said, unsure that Calder had not already done so.

"Are you married, Pavel?"

The question stunned him. Her eyes shone in the lights from the bar. "Are you married?"

Pavel nodded. Galina began to shake her head.

"I haven't seen her for years," Pavel said.

He wriggled uncomfortably and changed his grip on her hand. She did not pull away or try to take her hand from his as she said, "When I came out as an interpreter, they made it clear that I had parents living in Moscow."

"And what happened to them?"

"Not much," she said. "It was difficult for a time, but the spite has died a bit from what I hear."

His grip on her hand became so tight it hurt.

"You have parents?" She was still digging.

He shook his head and paused. "I have two children," he said, "a boy of fifteen and a girl of twelve."

"And their mother?"

"They have different mothers," Pavel said. "And neither was ever my wife."

The way he looked at her now made her feel that he thought more of her than he had ever done of the others. But images of Calder kept imposing themselves on Pavel's battered face.

"I think you're wise to go back," she said, though she found it hard to get the words out.

"I love you," he murmured. He let go of her hand and put his fingers on her knee. "I'd like to tell you all about why I came."

"I don't want to know, Pavel," she said.

He said, "When you didn't come the other night, I had a suite booked in a Mayfair hotel with flowers and everything."

Galina watched his eyes over her glass. For a while neither said a word. It was Galina who broke the silence amid the raucous Cockney voices now filling the pub. "Are you definitely going back?" she asked.

"I have to." Pavel nodded.

The way she was looking at him now, he thought there was a chance they would be together soon. Pavel wanted to book them into the same suite in Mayfair which had been so wasted before.

"No," Galina said. "We don't need that."

Even though it was a room and not a suite, Pavel made sure they had a civilised place with a shower. He still had the best part of a thousand pounds in cash and the big special Meade had retrieved. At the reception desk he put in an order for a big bouquet of flowers. When they arrived, Galina was in the bathroom. She came out wrapped tight in a white bath towel and saw the extravagant bouquet with its centrepiece of orchids.

Pavel was lying on the bed in his underpants with an evening paper. It went through his mind that he should check the Krueger's share price. But he never found it. And it didn't bother him at all.

"Pavel, they're beautiful!"

He put on a show of being deep in the evening paper.

"Pavel!"

He looked up now. Her auburn hair was soaked, and her bare shoulders made her look more slight and vulnerable.

"I hope mine were as good," she said, opening the bouquet.

He wondered what she was on about. Then he saw those roses in his hospital room. He got off the bed and went to her and put his hands over her as she released the bouquet from its cellophane. She made a play of admiring the mixed flowers as his hand undid the bath towel. The towel fell away and he had her neat damp breasts in his hands, and still she was holding the flowers at arm's length in admiration.

He bit her neck. The thick towel had been trapped in its fall between them. He drew back slightly to let it go down to the floor. She felt him hard against her.

"I must put them in water," she said, with the flowers close to her face.

"They really are beautiful!" she said, as his hand came off her left breast. She felt him taking off his underpants.

She put the flowers on the dressing table and felt him hard behind her. They went over to the bed. It was still daylight, and she said, "Close the curtains, Pavel."

"Why?"

"Please."

He went over and drew the gold-toned curtains. In the half-light he could feel her on the bed. He ran his hands all over her and felt the shivers run through her body. He kissed her till they were both gasping for breath. He gave no thought to diamonds or his job, let alone his first idea to use her.

As he went into her, the sound of her gasp was all that meant anything at all.

And it meant everything.

They had lost count of the number of times they had merged with each other. Breakfast had been brought up to them, and a snack lunch, and afternoon tea with a supply of scotch and vodka.

Lying naked on the bed, Pavel said, "Will you come back with me?" It was the fourth time he had asked.

Galina shook her head, her eyes glazed. She could not get Calder out of her mind in spite of the way Pavel had performed. But it was her parents she mentioned, not Calder.

"They've suffered enough."

"What do you mean by that?" He put out a hand to hold her breast, and she pulled it away.

"Galina," he said softly.

264

"Don't drag them back into it," she said. "Not after all this time."

He put his hand back between her thighs and bit into her neck.

"It's no use, Pavel," she said suddenly. "My parents have gone through enough." And again she was thinking not only of them, but also of Calder. He must know she was with Pavel, and the hurt in him had begun to sting her. Pavel tried to make love to her again, but she could not respond.

"I'm sorry, Pavel."

They just gazed at each other for what seemed hours.

Half an hour later they took a taxi to the garage where Galina had left her Mini. She drove out with Pavel. A green Austin with two Special Branch men moved off behind them. It had been a long and patient wait for them. Pavel and Galina seemed to cover the whole of London's West End before Galina headed the Mini round Hyde Park Corner and along the Bayswater Road. It was nearly ten and the streetlights were on, and Galina felt choked as they got near the Soviet embassy. Pavel looked grim.

They parked in Kensington Palace Gardens near the embassy and Galina saw the Special Branch Austin in her mirror. The faces behind the windshield meant nothing in the shadows. Galina switched off the engine, and her eyes met Pavel's. He put out his hand to find hers and his grip was fierce. "Pavel!" She shook her head and closed her eyes.

He glanced over at the Soviet embassy and said, "You're sure?"

She was on the verge of tears. More cars were moving into the gardens now. They were vague and sinister, and the men inside them no more than the flares from cigarette lighters. Galina felt the pressure of Pavel's grip on her knee. His eyes were closed, and she just gazed at him in the half-light. She knew he was still in pain from his wounds. He had winced in agony many times during their intimacy of the past twenty-four hours.

"You *must* go back?"

He nodded.

"Pavel!" Her eyes were more full of warmth than he had ever seen in a woman's face.

The gardens were becoming congested with cars. Among them was Meade's Mercedes. Meade found a spot with a view of Galina's Mini. He turned to his passenger and said, "I realise this must be painful to you, Calder." Calder sat tight-lipped, his nostrils dilated.

In the Mini Pavel felt Galina's thigh muscles tighten on his hand between her legs. Beyond her, through the side windows, he saw Mazarev come out of the embassy towards them. He took his hand away from Galina as Mazarev came up to his door. Galina held back the tears as Mazarev greeted them with a patient smile.

"If you'd both like to come into the embassy to talk it over—"

Galina shook her head firmly.

"I just wanted to help," Mazarev said easily. "You seem to have no privacy out here."

"Please let us be awhile," Pavel said.

Mazarev smiled. "Don't leave it too late, Pavel. Some of us would like to get to bed at a reasonable hour." They watched Mazarev go back, and Galina shuddered. "What will they do to you?"

Pavel shrugged. "Nothing, I should think." He told her about the plan and how he had been the victim of a section of the KGB and Suslov. He was frank about Katerina Suslov. He said it was always intended that he should go back to Moscow once the aims of the plan had been achieved. The damage done to the West's diamond industry and capitalism would be assessed, and Russia would then denounce the operation with the promise not to release undue numbers of stones. The market would pick up, and Yukatulmaz would share in the rewards of the world monopoly. Pavel would be found a privileged job within the KGB.

He was suddenly aware that she had hardly heard a word. He felt her fingers running gently through the hairs on the back of his hand. She was holding back the tears.

"If I stay," Pavel said, "they might not only take it out of my children but your parents."

"I thought détente was about human rights?" she said bitterly, tears flooding her eyes.

"If you were to come with me—"

She was shaking her head. Pavel made up his mind now. He dipped into his pocket and brought out the diamond. He put it into her hand, and as she began to shake her head, he pressed her fingers tight round it as if it were part of himself. When he let her hand free, she released the diamond and put her hand across to feel his flesh under the cotton sweater. He stroked her face and ran his hand over her breast.

In the darkness beyond he could make out someone coming across the gardens against the blur of parked cars. It was Calder. And Calder hated the moment.

He had been waiting with Meade for nearly an hour in the Mercedes, refusing even to cast a quick look at the Mini. He saw the cars with their waiting crews, and it went through his mind that Amberley was not the only bloody voyeur in the business. Maybe it bred voyeurs.

"I'm surprised you don't go over there and speed things up a bit." Meade yawned.

"It's up to her," Calder snapped. He had a seven-edged fifty-pence piece between his fingers. "It's a free bloody world."

"You *are* joking of course?" Meade said.

Calder was turning the coin slowly, feeling each edge. "One potato, two potato, three potato, four. . . ."

Meade felt sorry for him but told himself that Calder

was not a man given to pity for those like Amberley and the late Humphrey Girton.

No more was said for a while.

"If you think I'm going over there to knock the hell out of him, you can think again," Calder said. "It's up to her what she does."

"Very liberal of you," Meade said. "I wish you'd been as civilised when you broke Amberley's jaw and shook the stuffing out of old Caine."

Calder was suddenly out of the Mercedes and on the way over to the Mini. It was an impetuous response. It was so dark he was only a yard or two away from the Mini before he could make out Pavel and Galina. He had an urge to fling open the nearside door and provoke a punch-up with Pavel. But he curbed himself. He went round to the driver's door.

Galina wound down the window and could not look Calder in the face.

"So what are you waiting for?" Calder's voice was biting. "TV cameras? A priest? The marriage registrar?"

"I'm sorry, Calder."

And still she would not look at him.

"It's your life, Galina. Nobody else's."

She was trembling as he walked away, her hands so tight on the steering wheel that they shook. She was looking straight ahead into the darkness, neither at Calder nor at Pavel. Pavel leaned over and kissed her on the cheek. He wanted to have her tight against him, but he put another kiss on her temple and got out of the Mini.

She was in a kind of trance. She heard the door close and then saw Pavel cross in front of the Mini and head for the embassy. Twice he paused to turn. He wanted to come back. Galina wanted to run after him. But Pavel went on and she stayed glued to the driver's seat of the Mini. Mistily she saw the glow of the embassy hall light as the door opened and Pavel went through.

Cigarette lighters flared in the cars parked nearby as if to signal the end of a siege. Calder went over to the Mini. He found Galina sobbing. He thought he had never seen such enormous tears. He had certainly never seen anyone weep so copiously. "Come on, love," he said, pulling the door open. "I'll drive. You'll never see through that waterfall."

EIGHTEEN

Calder felt a surge of relief as he watched the TV monitor in Jayston's office at Heathrow and saw Pavel cross the concourse of Terminal 2 to the departure gate.

"Come on," Meade said, reading Calder's thoughts. "Let's see he gets a decent sendoff."

Calder rose but could not take his eyes off the monitor. Pavel went to the gate between two Russians, one of whom was Galkin, the KGB resident in Britain. It was a diplomatic exit. There would be no formalities, and Pavel would be cleared right through to the waiting Ilyushin 92. It was a fully booked midmorning flight, but seats had been found for Pavel and his escort, and the flight had been held up twenty minutes for them. Jayston saw Pavel and the two other Russians through immigration without check.

It was in the long corridor air side where Calder and Meade saw Pavel in the flesh. Pavel threw them a bleak smile. Just for a brief moment there was a chance he might pause to speak to Calder. But Calder was stony-faced with not even the trace of a cynical smile at his mouth. The bitterness had died, but neither could he summon up any concern for Pavel. He just wanted to see the back of him.

The rest would be up to Galina. She was clearly distressed and mixed up and had not said a word to him since he had driven her away from the Soviet embassy.

It was a new experience for Calder to bottle up his

270

feelings. Several times during the drive he had wanted to explode and ask why the hell she hadn't gone back where she belonged. He didn't know whether it was her tears or his fears that she might promptly agree to go back, but something held him in check. He had poured drinks for both of them. But Galina had gone straight to bed—alone in the spare room.

She had made his breakfast without a word. He tried three or four times to start a dialogue, only to be met with tight-lipped silence. She seemed to be waiting for the phone to ring. All the gaiety had gone out of her. Her eyes were leaden, and even her hair had lost its sparkle. When the phone rang, she started and her instinct was to answer it and hear Pavel's voice. But she felt Calder's eyes on her and held back to let him take the call. It was Meade asking Calder to join him at Heathrow to see Pavel off. Though he was breaking every rule in the book, Calder told Galina what was on and even asked her if she would like to join them. She just shook her head, biting her lip.

Calder shrugged and went out. His old Triumph wouldn't start, and he had to go back and ask Galina for the use of her Mini. She nodded, near to tears.

On the way to the airport he saw the big diamond on the floor near the front passenger seat. He leaned over and put it in his pocket.

Now at Heathrow it went through his mind to give it back to Pavel with his compliments. But that was the kind of cheap move he would expect of the mean little men he knew in high positions.

He saw Pavel turn round twice as they went along the pier to the Ilyushin. Calder and Meade kept a discreet twenty yards behind. At the head of the ramp Pavel stopped to throw back a long and perplexed look at Calder. Neither Galkin nor the other escort did anything to hasten him off. They stood patiently on either side of Pavel as he weighed up Calder.

Then Pavel put up his left hand in a halfhearted gesture of farewell. Calder spared him a nod.

A few minutes later Calder stood with Meade to watch the Ilyushin taxi away. They went to Jayston's office for confirmation of the takeoff. Meade was looking at Calder as he took the phone. "I bet you're the most relieved man in the country just now."

Calder's look was sheer ice. "I reckon a few rich bastards will soon have the same kind of feeling." He was thinking of those who had made or were about to make killings in the diamond market or in Krueger's shares.

"You're a relentless chap, Calder," Meade said as his call rang out.

It was Saunders who answered in the office in St. James's. Meade asked him to inform Sir Harwood Caine that Pavel was now airborne on his way back to Moscow. And he reminded himself to see that Pavel's pouch of diamonds and the cash in the case were sent to the Soviet embassy.

Calder was all for going back home to find some way of breaking Galina's depression. But Meade said he would prefer Calder to return with him to the office.

It was there, just one hour after Pavel's flight had left Heathrow, that he phoned the Stock Exchange prices service. He listened for a few moments and then gave the phone to Calder. Calder heard out the metal prices and the exchange rates and then listened closely as the Stock Exchange news came over. In the first two hours' trading Krueger's shares had shot up forty-five points to 256 and were clearly on their way to a complete recovery from the recent collapse. Calder put the phone down, and Meade said, "I'm with you now, Calder. Girton wasn't the only one."

It was odd, but Calder felt no self-glory. All he wanted was to be back with Galina.

Five rows back in the Ilyushin, Pavel screwed up his eyes against the vivid sunlight pouring in through the port to his right. They must be somewhere over the Baltic now, he reckoned. He felt a tingle of fear and turned to look at Galkin, who was in the middle seat, with the mindless gorilla on the aisle. On the way to Heathrow and for the first few minutes of the flight Pavel had found Galkin full of chat about London and Washington and even Soviet athletes. Then the lull had set in, and Galkin buried himself in *Pravda*.

It had not been lost on Pavel that Galkin's mood had changed from that of matey comrade to that of one who was not so much hard as remote. KGB residents were a weird lot, but more often than not they knew more about what was really going on than the head office people in Dzerzhinsky Square. Pavel felt compelled to say something.

"Will you be going back to London?" he asked.

Galkin threw him a scornful look. *"I follow orders,"* he said bitingly.

In that split second Pavel made up his mind. He spoke with relief about going home. And he played on his theory that Galkin knew quite a lot about him by boasting that three girls in their early twenties would be pleased to know he was back.

Galkin took him for a boastful ram.

Pavel let another few minutes pass before he said, "I must have a piss."

The two Russians pressed themselves back in their seats, and Pavel climbed over their thick legs, holding the seat tops of the row in front. He went forward to the lavatory. He ran cold water into the washbowl. He was shaking with fear.

273

Closing his eyes he put his face into the water. He knew for sure now that his welcome in Moscow would not be what Mazarev had made out back in London or what Suslov had promised at the briefings for Operation Rough Diamond. In the last hour he had begun to feel more like a prisoner than a returning agent.

He kept seeing Galina, not only seeing her, but sensing her body against his hands. He had images of the two kids, Yuri and Anna, but none of their mothers or of the wife he had not seen for years. He even saw in his mind's eye the faces of Galina's mother and father. He saw them vividly, though he had not even set eyes on so much as a photograph of them. Surely they would not be made to suffer? Not these days when some hope was filtering through the clouds of oppression? Yuri was only fourteen and Anna twelve. Soon he would be able to play games in the park with them and see Yuri's vitality and hear Anna's laughter.

Or would he? Galina's face superimposed itself on the faces of Yuri and Anna as Pavel dried his own face. He put the towel down and studied himself in the mirror, but he was seeing Galina.

He moved so quickly the dozing gorilla in the aisle seat never even saw him leave the lavatory. Pavel knew that every Ilyushin carried three pistols for the crew. He also knew where they were kept. He burst on to the flight section, slid aside the panel low to his right, and grabbed the pistol. He knew it was loaded. He cocked it and was making across the cabin to stick it into the captain's neck when the navigator swung an arm and sent him sprawling against the first officer, who was flying the Ilyushin.

The big four-engine machine lurched to starboard thirty-five thousand feet over the Baltic and began to slip from the sky with its engines screaming and its wings almost vertical to the clouds below. Pavel was hurled against the fuselage. He was dazed for a second but kept the pistol in his hand. The flight engineer threw himself across the tilted flight deck at Pavel, who hit him on the temple with the pistol butt. The engineer, a KGB man, fell stunned against Pavel's legs. Pavel could hear screams and the captain shouting that he was taking over. It seemed like a lifetime as the big jet fell ten thousand feet down the sky in thirty seconds in a stall that would have turned into a spin which would have meant the end with a less experienced captain.

The captain fought the jet. The engines howled, and Pavel could hear the creaks and squeals of the fuselage under stress as the Ilyushin was forced out of its stall. As the captain got control and the jet began to level out, he checked on Pavel's position behind him on the flight deck. He reached for a switch near his left hand.

"Touch that and we're all gone," Pavel said, ramming the pistol in the captain's neck. He was familiar with Aeroflot's antihijack devices. He knew the switch would trigger a lethal gas gun which the captain could line up on him. One touch, and Pavel would be dead.

The captain felt the pistol trembling just behind his left ear, trembling because Pavel was shaking with fear. His face was white, and he wanted to vomit.

"Back to Heathrow," he said, holding the pistol with its muzzle deep in the captain's greying hair. "And radio nothing except that you are going back!"

Recovering fast, the young first officer showed an urge to take on Pavel. The captain shook his head.

The big jet banked in the harsh glare of the sun.

"And remember I know Heathrow," Pavel said.

There was no need for such a warning. The captain was almost on course back to London already. He knew the rules, and he knew they were based on psychology and common sense. It wasn't a pilot's job to fight hijackers six miles high in the sky. It was up to the police on the ground.

Galkin had other ideas. He burst into the cockpit with the gorilla. Both flaunted pistols. Pavel's gaze drew their eyes on to the pistol stuck into the captain's neck. "Tell this pair to drop their pistols," he ordered the captain in Russian.

"Do just as he says," the captain said slowly. His voice was strong and gave no sign of the ordeal they had all just gone through.

With his pistol still pressed against the captain's neck, Pavel ordered Galkin off the flight deck. "And close the door behind you."

Galkin went out. The captain had Pavel lined up in his mirror, and his left hand again sought the gas switch.

"Leave it," Pavel rasped. He indicated that Galkin's comrade should now stand against the gas gun nozzle slot. "And now," Pavel ordered the captain, "tell air traffic control you're on course for Heathrow—and then total radio silence."

Galkin's comrade stood petrified against the gas gun nozzle, his eyes wild with fright.

It was to be the longest ninety minutes of Pavel's life.

It was almost too much even for the phlegmatic Meade. "The bugger's on his way back," he said, putting the phone down.

Calder screwed up his face.

"It can only be Pavel," Meade said. "Who else would want to hijack that Ilyushin and turn it round for London?"

It was Jayston who had phoned from Heathrow with the news that the Ilyushin was on its way back with a passenger asking for political asylum in Britain.

"Who else knows about this?" Meade asked sharply.

"Only air traffic control," Jayston replied. "And other aircraft on the same wavelength."

"What was the actual message?" Meade persisted.

Jayston said there had been only one message to say he Ilyushin was now bound for London with its asylum-seeking passenger. There was no mention of hijacking or f Pavel or any other name.

"So nobody else knows a thing about it?" Meade sked.

"The police will have been advised to stand by for an mergency."

"But they have no details yet?"

"Not yet."

"See they get none yet," Meade snapped. It was then e put the phone down and gave Calder the news. His ace, Calder thought, was like a squirrel's, sharp, alert, right-eyed. "We'll have to get back there fast," he told Calder now. "But there's a couple of things I have to do irst."

He called Saunders on the intercom and asked if the heck was on.

"Yes, sir," Saunders said. "All under control."

Then Meade phoned Caine and told him flatly that avel, far from being out of the way, had hijacked the lyushin and was now due back in London soon. When Meade hung up, he kept his hand on the phone and his yes on Calder. He wondered if Calder had caught on. But Calder was in another world. He was thinking what night happen if Pavel were to be allowed to stay in Britin. He had always seen himself as something of a fighter. He was beginning to feel like a loser. And all he had to ose here was Galina.

"Come on," Meade said, a touch dismayed that Calder ad not seen what he was up to. On the way to the airort he switched on the radio news. There was an item about Krueger's share price. It had climbed another ten oints to 266—fifty-five points up on the morning. "Did ou hear that?"

"I heard it," Calder said blankly. His mind was churning.

Calder and Meade saw the Ilyushin land at Heathrow. There were no obvious signs of an emergency.

But the police had drawn their own conclusions from the Ilyushin captain's radio call and had assumed that the man seeking asylum had hijacked the jet. Aeroflot's captains were not in the habit of turning back over the Baltic with some odd character wanting asylum. Special police marksmen were in position as the jet came off the main runway. And the first of the media men were showing up to ask for facilities to film, photograph, and interview. "You can't keep a good secret down," Meade said, chuckling, as he saw a couple of familiar Fleet Street faces and an Independent Television News camera van.

For security reasons air traffic control ordered the Ilyushin to stop several hundred yards out on the tarmac from the terminal building. The Ilyushin pulled up like some lost giant bird in the sunshine. Two minutes went by. Then the captain's voice came over to air traffic control to say that the man seeking asylum was Pavel and that he wanted a guarantee of asylum and a British escort before he would leave the jet.

Calder went out with Meade and two police marksmen in civilian clothes in a yellow car with an amber flasher on its roof. Pavel saw them coming through the cockpit windows. He still had the pistol at the captain's neck. His hand was getting stiff, and when he switched the pistol to his right hand, he did not relax the pressure of the muzzle on the captain's neck. As the yellow car raced to the Ilyushin, Calder and Meade decided it would be good tactics for Meade to go in first.

He found Pavel guarded and suspicious.

"You can guarantee my asylum?" Pavel asked, with the pistol pressed hard into the captain's neck.

"I can guarantee nothing," Meade said coolly. "We can see that your application will be considered."

"But you will guarantee that I will be taken off this aircraft and protected?"

"You have my word," Meade said. He had visions of all kinds of comebacks from on high. Pavel was not welcome, and he knew it. But whatever Pavel was up to, and however convenient it would be to the politicians of détente to have him back in Moscow, Meade could no more yield a prisoner to the *mokrie dela* killers than to the Nazi SS during the war.

Pavel hesitated. Beyond Meade he could see Galkin and the gorilla and two men he didn't know. They were the quick-draw experts from Scotland Yard.

In a passenger seat on the other side of the curtain sat Calder. He could hear the dialogue. He felt a growing regard for the way Pavel fought and defied. He also resented his own respect for Pavel's courage. But Calder was still on the rack with images in his mind of what had gone on when Pavel had disappeared for so long with Galina. Where had they been? How close had they been to each other?

"Calder!"

It was Meade's voice coming from the cockpit. Calder pushed past the two Yard men and Galkin and the gorilla.

His eyes met Pavel's. As calmly as he could, Meade said that Pavel would not accept his word that if the pistol were handed over, they would take him off the jet and guarantee his safety until his application for asylum had been considered.

"I thought he might accept your word," Meade said.

"It's not much to ask," Calder said, moving to Pavel. "You have my word."

The moment was an hour. Calder and Pavel stared into

each other. Then Pavel, his pale-blue eyes alight, slowly offered the pistol to him. In that moment the KGB gorilla drew his own pistol. He was about to fire when one of the Yard's quick-draw experts clubbed him with the butt of a Smith and Wesson. The gorilla groaned and fell, stunned. Calder lazily took the pistol from Pavel. There was a second's hesitation on Pavel's part. Then Calder had the pistol.

He promptly handed it to the captain and said, "Now fly him back." He turned and went out, leaving Meade and Galkin and the captain to sort out the politics.

Pavel tried to run out after him, but Galkin barred his way. The two Scotland Yard quick-draw experts were about to intervene when Meade called, "Don't!"

It was against the grain of his instincts, but he followed Calder out, avoiding Pavel's accusing eyes. He went down the Ilyushin's steps, wondering what the hell he'd ever seen in Calder. He'd seen some filthy tricks in his time, but this one qualified for the finals. The two quick-draw experts joined them in the yellow car and not a word passed all the way to the terminal building.

On Meade's reluctant order, the media were told that the Russian who was seeking asylum had changed his mind when British officials had gone aboard the Ilyushin. It took off at twenty past two, elegant as a rare bird in the afternoon sun. Calder watched the takeoff with Meade.

Pavel gazed down through the porthole as the Ilyushin banked to set course for Moscow. He heard Galkin say as it from a thousand miles away that Suslov had been sent to the Serbsky Institute for psychiatric treatment. He wasn't really listening anymore. He was wondering if somewhere in that panorama of part of London framed by the porthole was Galina. His eyes filled with tears, and he raised his hands against them, using both lots of knuckles because he was handcuffed.

n his office in St. James's Meade glanced at the note given him by Saunders. Calder looked on. Again Meade ad insisted that Calder should drive back to the office. And that was all he had said since they walked off the Ilyushin. His disgust over Calder's behaviour was only too apparent. It showed in his eyes and on his firmly set mouth and the way he drove at very high speed into London, leaving Calder well behind in the Mini. He gave the note to Calder, saying, "I hope you're bloody well satisfied."

The note was very much to the point. Using the information Calder had drawn out of Bray, Meade had given an order for phones to be tapped. The lines of the investment consultant Lintas and the stockbroker Drew had both been tapped. And both men had been tipped off that Pavel was on his way back to Britain, having hijacked the Ilyushin. The times of the calls were precise and only minutes after Meade had first been given the news himself. The caller was Sir Harwood Caine.

"Why should he bother?" said Calder. "An undersecretary of state so near his pension?" He could understand Girton's motives, for it was now known that Bradley J. Sagar was a very close friend and that Lady Naphill had let him sleep with her at least once, though he was one of many. Caine was not the sort to get into any such emotional trap.

"*Why* is for others to decide," Meade said briefly. "Services rendered or promised."

Calder put the note on the desk.

"Now for Christ's sake, get out of my sight!" Meade gasped.

Calder held his ground. "And what about Amberley?"

It seemed for a long moment that Meade would come round and throttle him. "Colin Amberley has been suspended until his case is reviewed."

"Full pay and pension rights intact?"

Meade said nothing, but Calder knew the answer could only be yes.

"I'm glad he's being looked after," Calder said. "We'd better take care of old Harwood Caine as well. Did you know he shoots a lot? He's got a bloody armoury back home. We should see he doesn't do anything daft."

Meade's fists were bunched on the edge of the desk. "If you don't go now, I'll personally remove you!"

Calder gazed at him for a moment or two before he went out.

Galina was on the phone to her boss at Bush House when Calder came home. He heard her say that she would like to change from part-time to full-time work. Ladybird Johnson sat on the hall table listening to her but jumped down to follow Calder into the living room. Calder went to the french windows and looked out on the meagre patch of garden. He heard Galina behind him and saw her go through to the kitchen as if he weren't there. He followed.

"I'm making myself something to eat," she said without so much as a glance. "Have you eaten?"

Her voice was flat.

"I'm not hungry," Calder said, leaning against the open door.

She began to make an omelette. Pavel was haunting her. She had switched on the radio news in case there might be some item about him. The bulletin led with the story of a mysterious Russian who had held an Ilyushin at Heathrow and had asked for asylum only to change his mind in the presence of British officials. It could be only Pavel. And one of those British officials must have been Calder. It was up to him to tell her about it, she thought whipping the eggs in a bowl.

She would never ask. And she was not even sure she would like to know more. Calder came over and stood be-

ind her and put his hands on her hips. She slid away
rom him on the pretext of moving to the cooker. He
vould not be put off. He went over and put his hands on
ier. She didn't move this time, but she was cold as a
tatue. He dipped into his pocket and then put his arm
round her and opened his hand just in front of her face.

She saw the big special, and her mind was full of Pavel
as he let her see the diamonds on her scarf on the grass at
he warren. "It was in your car," Calder said gently. "I
lon't know if he lost it or gave it to you?"

"He gave it to me," she whispered.

"Take it then."

Her head was shaking, but still she did not turn to face
him.

"You know what it's worth?" Calder said, his voice still
quiet.

"I have some idea," she said, making no move to take
he stone.

"An expert told me it would be worth around two
hundred thousand pounds when cut." Calder could almost
eel her emotions. He sensed that she wanted to cry or to
un away or take sleeping pills. "Take it," he said, and
hardly knew himself, he was so tender.

"It was never his to give," Galina murmured.

"He had more right to it than a lot of people have to
heir bloody hoards," he said, and she was suddenly
ware of his warm mood.

She turned now, biting the inside of her mouth. He
issed her on the cheek, and he felt some of the tenseness
o out of her. "Go on. Take it," he said.

Galina took the diamond and studied it in her open
and, seeing images of Pavel in its grey opaqueness. She
ould not hold back the question anymore. "Did you see
im leave?" she asked, her eyes still on the diamond.

"Twice," Calder said. "He came back once."

"Yes," she nodded, her eyes brimming. "I heard it on the news."

He took her by the shoulders now and began to turn her so that their eyes could meet. She made no effort to resist. When they were face to face, she kept her eyes down.

"Galina," he said softly, "I love you too much." His lips touched her forehead. "Did you hear that?"

She looked at him now, her eyes like emeralds in water.

"I said I love you too much," he repeated. He told her now what had gone on in the Ilyushin cockpit. "I could never have done what I did for any other reason."

Her eyes never came off him now. They were wide with confusion and distaste. She backed away from Calder.

"I couldn't lose you," he said.

She put a hand to her mouth, and her head was shaking. Calder made a move towards her, but she ran out of the kitchen. He followed her into the living room only to see her race upstairs.

Ten minutes later she came down, and Calder could hear her on the hall phone asking Olga if she could go over for a day or two. Her voice kept breaking down. Calder went into the hall and saw that she had packed a suitcase. The open cat basket was at her feet and Lady bird Johnson sat on the hall table, his immense blue eyes fixed on Galina. She put the receiver down.

"I'm going to Olga's," she said, lifting Ladybird Johnson into the basket. "Until I find a place of my own."

Calder wanted to raise his arms and scream to God but his voice was measured as he said, "Let me help you with that lot." He made a move to pick up the case.

But it was already in Galina's left hand and the cat basket in her right. Calder fought back an immense urge to go after her and talk her out of it. He went back to the

284

tchen and saw the half-prepared omelette and that big
amond on the stove by the hot plate. His eyes smarted,
t he was determined that not a single tear would roll.
e made the omelette.

Octahedra House Sir Sefton Dykes was strutting about
s office in a fit of sheer joy. He kept thumbing his left
nd into the palm of his right and shaking his head in
light. He was uttering noises that neither Nobel Bray
r any of the others present could make out as real
rds and beaming on everyone. It was a bit eerie, like a
ull coming to life.

Nobel tried to think what the spectacle reminded him
. Suddenly it came to him. It was that classic bit of
wsreel of Hitler's manic prance at the time of the
ench surrender.

Dykes' elation was due to two things: Pavel's return to
e Soviet Union and the performance of Krueger's shares
the two hours that followed. The shares had shot up in
avy trading.

Nobel felt nauseated as he watched Dykes striding to
d fro in ecstasy. Not many hours ago, when news came
that Pavel had hijacked the jet and was on his way
ck, Dykes had ranted and stormed and hurled a paper-
eight at the south-facing window. It would have gone
rough and very likely smashed someone's skull in St.
aul's Churchyard but for the venetian blinds which had
en drawn against the strong sun. Then Dykes had de-
ded his coronary had begun. He slumped into his chair,
vallowing pills, and telling Charlton to fetch the doctor
ickly. In that moment even Nobel had thought it was
al. Suppose the old bastard collapses? he'd thought.
ould I have to try the kiss of life? The thought was so
volting he knew there was a limit to what he would do
en to save life. Nobel had decided he could never put
is mouth to Dykes'.

Dykes was back in full health and vigour now. Ever time he went past the TV monitor he threw it a craze glance of triumph as if it were showing him walking c the sea, and he would extend one arm or the other point exuberantly to it. The monitor was showin Krueger's closing price. It was up more than sixty poin on the day at 272, within six points of the pre-Pav price. He paused now and then to grip the biceps of O ilvy and Maybon and Nobel Bray in a gesture of gra tude. There was not much they could say or do about it.

Sir Sefton had not known such elation since that m ment many years ago when his accountant phoned to sa he had become a millionaire for the first time. He pause now to admire St. Paul's and the churchyard in the brig sunshine. He thought God had given the world a qui beautiful day.

At that moment Galina was driving across London in h Mini and Pavel sat between two KGB officers in the bac of a black Zis car on its way from Moscow Airport to Dzerzhinsky Square. There were moments when Pav would look at their stern, rocklike faces and feel real fea

But most of the time he was seeing only Galina, ar her voice was filling his head with comforting sound. F might have wept if he had been alone.

They were approaching Dzerzhinsky Square. F glanced right and left at those KGB faces. They could their worst now.

BESTSELLERS

] ALWAYS IS NOT FOREVER—Van Slyke	04271-0	$2.25
] KISS—R. Duncan	04112-9	$1.75
] TIM—C. McCullough	08545-2	$1.75
] MIDNIGHT EXPRESS—B. Hayes with W. Hoffer	04302-4	$2.25
] A BRIDGE TOO FAR—Cornelius Ryan	08373-5	$2.50
] CHILD OF THE MORNING—Paulene Gedge	04227-3	$2.25
] A CORONARY EVENT —Michael Halberstam, M.D. & Stephan Lesher	04213-3	$1.95
] DO BLACK PATENT LEATHER SHOES REALLY REFLECT UP?—John R. Powers	08490-1	$1.75
] EARTHLY POSSESSIONS—Anne Tyler	04214-1	$1.95
] THE FURY—John Farris	08620-3	$2.50
] THE HEART LISTENS—Helen Van Slyke	08520-7	$1.95
] TO KILL A MOCKINGBIRD—Harper Lee	08376-X	$1.95
] THE LAST BATTLE—Cornelius Ryan	08381-6	$2.25
] THE LAST CATHOLIC IN AMERICA —J. R. Powers	08528-2	$1.75
] THE LONGEST DAY—Cornelius Ryan	08380-8	$1.95
] MARINA TOWER—Charles Beardsley	04198-6	$1.95
] THE MIXED BLESSING—Helen Van Slyke	08491-X	$1.95
] MY HEART TURNS BACK—Oliver B. Patton	04241-9	$2.25
] SKIN DEEP—Susan Hufford	04258-3	$1.95
] SWEET GOLDEN SUN—Parris Afton Bonds	04226-5	$1.95

Buy them at your local bookstore or use this handy coupon for ordering:

POPULAR LIBRARY
P.O. Box C730, 524 Myrtle Ave., Pratt Station, Brooklyn, N.Y. 11205

Please send me the books I have checked above. Orders for less than 5 books must include 75¢ for the first book and 25¢ for each additional book to cover mailing and handling. I enclose $_____ in check or money order.

Name_____

Address_____

City_____ State/Zip_____

Please allow 4 to 5 weeks for delivery.

HISTORY • BIOGRAPHY
• POPULAR CULTURE

Outstanding Non-Fiction Titles

THE THIRTEENTH TRIBE   0-445-04242-7 $2.2
by Arthur Koestler

This book by a world-famous author proves that the tru
ancestors of Western Jewry were not Semites but Khaza
warriors. "Clear and convincing."—*Newsweek*

KISS   0-445-04112-9 $1.7
by Robert Duncan

They wear seven-inch platform heels and lurid, Hallowee
makeup. They are the rock group that America loves to hat
They are KISS. And this is their incredible story. Illustrate
with photographs.

WHERE ARE THEY NOW?   0-445-04264-8 $1.7
Yesterday's Sports Heroes Today
by Phil Berger

They were the champs, and the sluggers. They made and brok
the records, drew and held the crowds, earned and lost th
money. Here are 50 sports greats and what happened to the
after the applause died down. Illustrated with photograph

ROBERT ALTMAN   0-445-04262-1 $2.2
American Innovator
by Judith M. Kass

Some love him, some hate him. But no one ignores the contr
bution of director Robert Altman to the art of American filr
From *Mash* to *Nashville* and *Three Women*, Altman's filn
are technically outrageous, artistically stunning. Here is th
first book to take an in-depth look at this provocative an
ambitious filmmaker. Illustrated with photographs.